ZANE PRESENTS

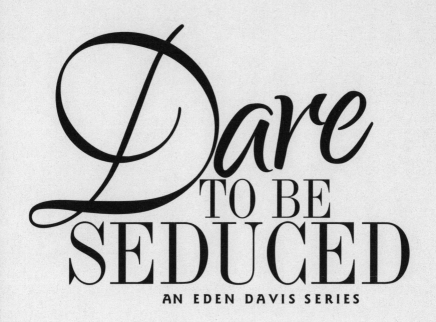

Dare
TO BE
SEDUCED

AN EDEN DAVIS SERIES

T0154579

Dear Reader:

Fire! That is the best way to describe the new "mature erotica" by Eden Davis. *Dare to be Seduced* is a spellbinding account of two people who carry on a salacious relationship after originally meeting during a chance lustful encounter. They use their common love of sports to enhance their sexual escapades. Lena and Jason decide to finally take their "commuter relationship" further and, like all good things, their connection takes a turn for the worse.

Jason is the typical man who wants a woman that turns him out in the bedroom. However, he doesn't want the entire world to be in on the festivities. Once Lena is exposed as the sexpot that she really is, he begins to place unfair judgments on her. Again, the typical man.

Dare to be Seduced is a great discussion piece that couples should read together; not only to reignite their own passion but to take a peek into the intricate lives of strangers. Then they will have to ask themselves how they would react, would they remain together and weather the storm, or would it be time to move on to the proverbial greener pastures.

Eden Davis the pen name of a critically acclaimed author, takes sensuality to the next level in this, the second of a three-book series. Make sure that you keep an eye out for *Dare to be Tempted* and *Dare to be Wild.*

Thank you for supporting Eden Davis' efforts and thank you for supporting one of the dozens of authors published under my imprint, Strebor Books. I try my best to bring you cutting-edge works of literature that will keep your attention and make you think long after you turn the last page.

Now sit back in your favorite chair or, better yet, chill in the bed, and be prepared to be tantalized by yet another great read.

Peace and Many Blessings,

Zane

Publisher
Strebor Books
www.simonandschuster.com

ALSO BY EDEN DAVIS
Dare to be Tempted

ZANE PRESENTS

Dare
TO BE
SEDUCED

AN EDEN DAVIS SERIES

EDEN DAVIS

SBI

STREBOR BOOKS

NEW YORK LONDON TORONTO SYDNEY

Strebor Books
P.O. Box 6505
Largo, MD 20792
http://www.streborbooks.com

© 2013 by Eden Davis

ISBN 978-1-59309-517-8
ISBN 978-1-4767-3112-4 (ebook)
LCCN 2013933644

First Strebor Books trade paperback edition September 2013

Cover design: www.mariondesigns.com
Cover photograph: © Keith Saunders/Marion Designs

10 9 8 7 6 5 4 3 2 1

Manufactured in the United States of America

For information regarding special discounts for bulk purchases, please contact Simon & Schuster Special Sales at 1-866-506-1949 or business@simonandschuster.com

The Simon & Schuster Speakers Bureau can bring authors to your live event. For more information or to book an event, contact the Simon & Schuster Speakers Bureau at 1-866-248-3049 or visit our website at www.simonspeakers.com.

This book is dedicated to grown and sexy women everywhere.

Acknowledgments

Welcome to the Eden Davis Series, hot and beautifully erotic stories written for grown and sexy women. *In Dare to be Tempted*, you met Aleesa Davis, a happily married woman who is tempted to blur the line between fantasy and fidelity when she hits a rough patch in her marriage. In this story it's Aleesa's best friend, Lena Macy's, turn to shine.

At work, Lena is bold, ambitious and always in control, but her private life is the victim of her professional ambitions. In *Dare to be Seduced*, the workaholic goes wantonly delinquent when she loses a bet to a hot stranger who turns her on, and out, in all the right ways. As the wagers continue, she can't get enough, but as the stakes get higher, Lena has to determine how far is too far.

What about you? Have you ever been left wondering if "that's all there is" after a round of lukewarm sex? Looking to get your sexy on or even back? Maybe you'll find some tricks and treats within these pages to pump up your sex life. Be sure to check out my Ticket to Paradise at the end of this book. It will give you step-by-step instructions on how to add Lena's "Pearl Jam" trick to your own repertoire.

Thank you to Sara Camilli, for her endless attention and support; Zane for her creative foresight, and Charmaine at Strebor Books for her gentle handling, and my friends who are the best supporters and focus groups around. And I extend my gratitude to you for your continued love and support. Do reach out to me on Twitter @EdenStories, and on Facebook at Eden's Stories with any comments.

Now sit back and enjoy this story in good health and great sex!

—*Eden*

P.S. Look out for Livia's return in *Dare to Wild*. She's the shyer, more conservative of the three ladies, but with her fu*k-it list in hand, you'll see how she blossoms, romantically and sexually, in her story, due out soon. Stay tuned!

Chapter One

Lena Macy rummaged through her Super Bowl party swag bag in search of the only thing she could think of that would satisfy her urge for sex—chocolate. On any given day, Miami was a hotbed of testosterone, estrogen, alcohol, drugs and hot and horny beautiful people, there to party and have sex. But on a Super Bowl weekend, the place was like an orgy on steroids. The Miami heat was definitely getting to her, in more ways, and in more body parts, than one.

She'd been down in Magic City for two days, losing much needed sleep and reluctantly partaking in the pre-game festivities— all in an attempt to land her man—Rickie Ross. Lena wanted Rickie. She needed him. And she wasn't leaving town without him knowing how much.

She'd been damn near stalking him for months—calling, emailing, showing up wherever and whenever, trying to make a good impression. But getting next to a famous and hugely popular football hero, a man surrounded by groupies and hangers-on, all trying to get him or give him some, was no simple task. It would be a lot easier if she merely wanted to fuck him, but she didn't. Lena wanted to hire him.

Since being put in charge of Sports Fan Network a year ago, her job was to turn the struggling SFN around and make it a must-see experience for sports-loving viewers. Lena's plan was to shake up the programming by moving away from the traditional talking head analysis, making the network more user-friendly and inviting to women as well as men. Fine-ass, charismatic Rickie Ross was central to that task, but until he finally decided on a new agent, talking business with a man whose main mission in life was to fuck, fraternize and play football, was a non-starter.

Lena bit into a Godiva hazelnut truffle, let the sweet creamy goodness settle on her tongue, closed her eyes and savored the moment. She heard several wordless moans, the kind let loose when THE spot gets hit, escape her lips and settle into the air. She'd read somewhere about a study where fifty-two percent of the women surveyed said they preferred eating chocolate to having sex. Lena couldn't rightly say where she stood in that poll, but at this moment she understood it. Between her demanding work schedule, her last break-up nearly a year ago, and her crazy family issues, the only thing rushing her endorphins these days was chocolate. Usually all she had the energy and desire for was Godiva and Big, her trusty, always on the ready, never argumentative vibrator. But at this moment, after two days spent immersed in the closest thing to a modern-day Sodom and Gomorrah, she wanted more than chocolate. More than Big. She wanted dick. Real. Live. Hard as a rod. All up in her fuzzy stuff, penetrating dick.

Lena moaned again, this time out of frustration, and popped another truffle into her mouth. It was halftime and being upstairs in her suite watching this gridiron face-off alone was depressing. She decided to head down to the bar, grab a bite, down a drink or three, and watch the rest of the game in the company of strangers. Changing into a slim, white, shirt dress with a long string of gray, gold, and white pearls, Lena slipped on her strappy Jimmy Choos, added a spritz of Bellissima by Blumarine, and headed downstairs.

"ONE GRAN PATRON PLATINUM COMING UP," THE BARTENDER SAID, removing her empty glass and smiling over the anticipated size of his tip. This pretty lady not only had looks, but class, and a wallet to match. He removed the sterling silver stopper from the lead crystal decanter and poured the thirty-dollar-a-shot, premium tequila into a shaker, gently chilling the liquor before pouring it into a shot glass with a twist of orange.

Lena sat, sipped her drink and people watched, uninterested, like most in the room, in the half-time show currently in progress. His cologne, a heady shot of Creed, hit her nostrils and commanded her attention seconds before his words. He smelled delicious. Downright edible.

"Well, it ain't nipplegate, that's for sure," a low voice painted with wit and audacity, spoke to her as the celebratory crowd milled around them.

"Where's Janet when you need her?" Lena responded, making friendly bar talk but keeping her eyes purposely glued to the row of flat-screen televisions lining the lounge walls. "But in the big picture, does it really matter who plays during halftime?"

"Absolutely! Everyone knows that if you wanna hold someone's attention, a little sex, or even the idea of a little sex, will always do the job." He finished his statement and let a devilish grin loose on her.

She heard his tongue-in-cheek delivery, and it made her laugh. *Do I have* horny bitch *flashing across my forehead*, she wondered. Usually, such an obnoxious opening would have been ignored, but the shot of tequila that preceded his arrival was too smooth, and she was too bored to brush his comment aside.

"So you're saying that a two-second glimpse of a naked breast— fake at that—trumps a world-renowned, internationally revered rock band?"

"Fake but with a pierced nipple. There is a difference," he schooled her, the flirtatious smile in his tone enticing Lena to turn his way.

Not sure if it was the talk of erotic piercings or the chocolate brown face sporting a dazzling combination of pleading brown eyes and a can't-say-no smile that made her nipples stiffen, but he'd proven his theory. He definitely had her attention.

STOP IT, her brain shouted, demanding that the girls ignore his Djimon Hounsou look-alike qualities and simmer down.

"So you're saying all men like body piercings on a woman?" his prize questioned, surprised to find herself willing and wanting to engage in the conversation.

"Nooo. Not all men. And not all body piercings. Take belly button or nipple rings. What men are drawn to is *the idea* that a woman who would do such a thing is sexually free and adventurous. The piercings suggest that she's daring and willing to experiment."

"And down there?" Lena inquired, too polite to say the word *clit*, even though hers was warming up, without permission mind you, to the conversation.

"A clit ring? That's like crazy sexy, and not in a good way. Little too hard-core S & M for my tastes."

"And tongue piercings?"

"Nah. That just screams slut. Too visible. Too obvious. Unless, you know, you're simply looking to get your knob slobbed."

Witnessing the widening smile of this bodacious charmer, one who had the nerve to be talking blowjobs to a perfect stranger, for some odd reason, only made the girls tingle all the more.

"But I thought the idea of you know…getting worked over by a studded tongue…really turned men on."

"Well, yeah, but no man wants *other* people thinking that his woman is a blowjob machine. That just ain't right."

"I don't know…why else would all these young girls be doing it?"

"Cuz they're stupid little girls and not thinking about how ridiculous they're going to look when they're real women," he said, adding a silent but complimentary, *like you* with an appreciative eye caress of her glistening bare legs. "Look, if you don't believe me, let's ask him," he suggested, calling over the bartender. "I'll bet you the next round, that if given the choice, he'd pick nipple ring over tongue ring."

"You're on."

"Dude, could you settle a bet for us?"

"Sure."

"Tongue ring or nipple ring?"

"Depends. Girlfriend or one-nighter?"

The face with the uninhibited grin, sitting below a perfectly bald, domed head, erupted into a deep and rolling laugh that shook the cobwebs from her vagina. Lena joined in, her sing-song chuckle blending nicely with his.

"Bartender, another round please, on me," she requested, taking her loss with grace.

"Sir, what can I bring you?" the bartender asked over the hubbub of fans cheering the second half kick-off and the New York Jets' bullet train return to the New Orleans Saints' forty-yard line.

"Grey Goose, straight, on the rocks with a twist."

"You got it."

The cheers following the Jets' touchdown turned to boos as the snap was bobbled and the extra point drifted wide. Still, New York moved ahead of their rivals 20-7.

Lena raised her glass to his before tipping it to her lips.

No wedding ring. His eyes grabbed hers, electric interest flying between them, before lowering to check out her luscious, peach-stained lips wrapped around the rim of her drink. He exhaled the decidedly devious request for those same lips to be wrapped around his wakening dick, replacing them with a more apropos, stranger-friendly query.

"Jets or Saints?"

"Well, I'm definitely no sinner," she cooed, raising her eyes to meet his, while fingering the edge of her glass. Her looks, actions and words didn't match, leaving him wondering how much of an angel she could possibly be.

"I'll take that to mean that you're rooting for the Saints."

"You are correct."

"So you're a big Kim Kardashian fan?"

"What?" The out-of-left field quality of his question threw her. "Oh please, do explain," she requested with an amused chuckle.

"After she put Reggie Bush on her show, every woman in America became a Saints fan. They love her, so, by association, they love him, too."

"Women love her?"

"Yeah, they relate to her combination of innocent, but smoking hot, sex appeal. It's like she's saying, 'I'm a good girl, but I can be bad when I want to.' Beyoncé is the same way."

It's like he's reading me, Lena thought as she felt the good girl inside of her smile in agreement. Even at 42 years of age, she understood all too well the concept of being good while her bad girl was screaming to get out. But like most women she knew, she'd been taught from birth to be refined, respectful and mindful of her reputation, so she ignored the screams and carried that good girl mind-set in and out of the bedroom.

"No, I'm a Saints fan because I appreciate the skill and drive of Drew Brees. Given his foot agility, his release, his accuracy and the fact that he is smart as hell, he's got a skill set that makes him an amazing athlete and great quarterback.

"And, yeah, Reggie is a cutie, but he also can haul ass," Lena continued. "In just four seasons, he's rushed for nearly four thousand yards and scored twenty-four touchdowns. And let's not forget Garret Hartley. The boy has a leg on him. Deadly accurate inside of forty-five yards. He would have never missed that field goal like Feely did in the first half."

"Hey, it happens. But you're selling the Jets short. Mark Sanchez is just now coming into his own. He's got a strong arm, makes good decisions and is a leader on the field. His first year in the league, he led his team to the playoffs. How many rookie quarterbacks have done that and actually even won the first game?"

"Four," Lena offered, happily showing off her knowledge of sports.

"Really?" he asked, biting his lip and turning up the twinkle in his eye. "Damn, I think I'm looking at the perfect woman—a hottie who knows football."

And basketball, and baseball, and even a little hockey and NASCAR, she wanted to tell him, but didn't. You can't sit at the helm of one of cable broadcasting's first sports networks and not pick up a thing or two.

Lena gave him a wink and a tilted smile before turning her attention back to the Super Bowl. It was an exciting game; one that looked like it might go all the way down to the wire. The two watched as possession of the ball changed hands several times, neither team giving up enough yards for a score. On occasion, Lena could feel the stranger's eyes drifting away from the television and over to her. They never seemed to settle on one spot for long. Instead, his gaze roamed like a player in the backfield, weighing the options in front of him.

They jumped up with the rest of the crowd, brought to their feet by the running prowess of the Saints' Rickie Ross. His dodging and weaving brought New Orleans three yards shy of the Jet's thirty-seven-yard line and a first down.

"What do they say? Poetry in motion."

"Oh, so you're a Rickie Rosster?" he asked, referring to the player's legion of fans while trying to determine if she was just another groupie in town to get laid by a baller.

"He has skills." Lena downed the rest of her tequila, allowing the silky smooth liquid to coat her throat and loosen her tongue. "So skilled that he's about to take the lead. I will bet you another round that the Saints will *penetrate* the Jets' defenses and *score*."

He took in the body language that accompanied her offer—one heavily punctuated with sexual innuendo. She crossed her shimmering bronze legs and drew them closer to her body, all the while allowing one high-heeled sandal to dangle from her well-pedicured foot like a fishing lure. Was she fishing? He certainly hoped so, because between the foot, the flirting, and that woodsy floral scent that kept wafting over to his side of the bar, he was already hooked.

"You're on." He smiled, happily taking the bait.

"Bartender, another round on me," Lena requested with good-humored exasperation after the Jets stopped the Saints at the line of scrimmage with no gain.

"Here comes your boy," he teased. "Care to sweeten the pot?"

Her competitive nature, like the rest of her, was now aroused. Lena threw back her shot of tequila and smiled in response, secretly wondering if his chest was as smooth as his head. "Name your wager."

"If Hartly hits this field goal, dinner is on me. If he misses, it's on you."

There's that smirk again. Goddamn, this boy is good looking, she thought, while quickly visualizing the literal interpretation of his suggestion.

"That makes the assumption that we are having dinner together," she replied, adding a little cat to her mouse.

"But aren't we?" he asked. There was no challenge, just matter-of-factness in his eyes.

"It's on." *Who am I trying to kid?*

"Excellent."

"YES!!" Tequila and competitiveness combined caused Lena to stand up and cheer, and add a corny Cabbage Patch dance to her celebration. Thanks to Hartley's sure foot, Lena had dinner plans and the Jets lead was narrowed to seven points.

"Looks like I owe you. So I assume eating here at the Setai will work for you?" he asked, while in his head running down his room service menu, one that included everything *but* food. "I mean, I'd love to take you anywhere you'd like to go, but considering the fact that this town is crawling with Super Bowl fans, I don't think we're going to have much luck."

"Are you staying here?" Lena asked, not revealing that she was already a guest in one of the suites.

"Yes. I'm here on business. And you?"

"Same." *Though mixing in a little pleasure seems like a real possibility,* she thought, but didn't add. "And, yes, dinner here is fine."

Another round later, the two-minute warning sounded, leaving the Saints with possession of the ball. Lena and her mystery man watched as their quarterback led his team up the field and into scoring position. On the next play, with only twenty-six seconds left on the clock, the New Orleans fullback rushed past the New York defense and into the end zone, making the score 21-20.

"He's got to go for it. They need two points to win," he declared.

Tipsy and feeling flush, Lena leaned in close enough to breathe in his smell and with it, watered the seeds of arousal sprouting like wildflowers in her. "I'll bet you *anything* that they make this conversion."

"Anything?"

"Yep. Winner takes *all*."

"That's a hefty wager to make with a perfect stranger."

"I'm Pocahontas," she said, raising her empty glass to his. "Nice to meet you."

"Pocahontas?" he asked with a chuckle. "No last name?"

"Why be so formal?"

"True, and Disney characters don't tend to have last names anyway."

"Exactly." Lena smiled at him. When she upped the ante, she'd already decided to have sex with this stranger, but she had no intention of being herself while doing it.

"Well, in that case, Pocahontas, I'm Mr. Johnson." He smirked.

Lena giggled to herself, amused by not only his willingness to play her game, but his choice of moniker. She leaned in close to his ear. "As in Mr. *Big* Johnson?" she whispered coyly.

"Oh, I see you've heard of me," he said, shivering slightly from her warm breath tickling his ear.

"I have a *very good* friend with the same name," she continued while lightly brushing his earlobe with the tip of her tongue. Johnson turned his face to meet hers, leaning in, wanting to touch her lips with his own.

Lena gently backed away. "You haven't won yet, Mr. Johnson."

"It appears that I have," he said before devouring her mouth as the room exploded into joyous bedlam. The New York Jets held firm, denying the Saints their two-point conversion, and winning the championship game by one point.

The room melted away under the heat of Johnson's kiss. It was the perfect kiss for the occasion. It was not fueled by quiet discovery or the sweet pretense of sensuous coupling between lovers. This kiss was powered by an overwhelming need to get to know each other on the basest of levels—a lust demanding to be satisfied. This kiss was the prelude to a fuck.

His tongue crossed her lips, at first like a wandering vagabond looking for a place to land, but as Lena greeted it with her own, it stiffened and began to rhythmically move in and out between her lips as a preview of things to come. Lena felt every erogenous zone on her body come to full attention. Through a series of well-choreographed tingles, pulses and throbs, they informed her that the bad girl was making a break and the bitch wanted a full-out, one-night-only, fuck-fest. A sexual romp designed to clear her mind and body from the want and need that had been distracting her for months—hell, years, if she owned up to the truth. Forget her reputation, her mother, her peers and colleagues. Even forget Douglas. Tonight, she wanted hot, heavy, uninhibited, one-night stand, never see your ass again, *stranger* sex.

The party atmosphere reappeared as Lena pulled away and opened her eyes.

"So, you won. Name your prize," she said, her voice rough with desire.

"Do you have to ask?" he said, gently running his finger across her lips. "I want you."

"Looks like everyone's a winner tonight," Lena declared as she gathered her things to follow him upstairs.

Chapter Two

It took all the restraint Lena could muster not to jump Johnson right there in the lobby. By the time the elevator arrived, his deep kisses and naughty whispers had pumped her imagination into overdrive and were unmercifully teasing her body. She was tipsy and horny and didn't want anything at this moment but him.

As the doors closed, creating a private den of exploration, she leaned into him, their lips and bodies melting into each other. In that tiny space, Johnson and Lena explored each other for as long as the ride to the twenty-third floor would allow. At six-two, he towered over her, and even under his linen shirt and slacks, Lena was impressed by the athletic body that rivaled those professionals who had invaded the city for this party weekend. Her hands slipped through the crack of his unbuttoned collar to answer for themselves the question posed earlier: yes, his chest was as smooth as his head. The quick vision of her tongue hungrily tasting the ridges and dips of his torso excited her, causing a seductive moan to slip from her lips.

She was a moaner. He liked that.

"Oh, Baby," was Johnson's response as he quickly unbuttoned the several more buttons down the front of her dress and reached inside. His hand met a stiff nipple dressed in lace, an implied invitation for his mouth to drop down and investigate further. He licked and sucked her nip through the lace, feeling it grow longer and harder.

In a move surprising to herself, Lena reached for his other hand and guided it under her dress, wanting him to feel her clit, which was as taunt and hard as the nipple in his mouth. His hand lingered first on top of the matching lace, feeling the dampness on his fingers, before reaching inside. Once there, he delved into the pudding, swirling it around the opening of her hole before dipping in and moisturizing her pearl.

"I want you to taste my pussy," she directed in a voice she didn't recognize as her own. There was no way that Lena would consent, let alone demand, a strange man to lick her in a public elevator, but apparently Pocahontas had no problem issuing such a decree.

"I will, Baby, I promise," he told her, passion seizing the air in his lungs and forcing him to breathe in gulps. "We're almost to the room. Hold that thought."

The elevator slowed and then stopped, a discreet bell announcing their arrival. Between the bell and the doors sliding open, Johnson quickly buttoned his shirt and adjusted his pants, trying to hide the big boner that had erupted during their ascent. The doors opened and he stepped out into the empty hallway, turning to wait for Lena. His eyes grew wide with "oh fuck yeah wonder" as Pocahontas stepped out from the lift, dress and purse in hand, wearing nothing but a flesh-colored, lace balcony bra trimmed in white, a matching thong, her string of pearls, and strappy sandals.

His eyes drank in her body in its near naked entirety. He started from the bottom, wanting to savor each hot spot on this wickedly sexy stranger's copper-colored body. Her feet were perfect. No hammer toes, no corns, just pretty feet sporting toenails adorned with a French pedicure. "Suckable" was the word that came to mind. His eyes followed the shapely lines of her Tina Turner legs—small ankles, well-formed calves, and thighs worth begging for a hug from. Her belly was flat but for a tiny little pooch that housed a bellybutton his tongue was dying to delve into. Her arms and shoulders were toned and strong and held up a very kissable neck and heart-shaped face that was the perfect backdrop for her tempting, doe-shaped eyes and succulent mouth.

"Girl, I like how you think," he said, throwing his head back in lustful laughter as his dick sprang front and center from its hiding place.

Lena walked several feet past him, allowing him to take in the seductive swing of her moving tail. Her ass was not outrageously bootylicious in the way say JLo's or Beyoncé's was, but it was round and perky and just as enticing.

She stopped midway down the hall, aroused further by her own brazen behavior, turned and asked, "Are you coming?"

"Damn near!" he said, giving his cock a Michael Jackson grab for emphasis. Johnson collected his wits and room key and followed this intriguing and unpredictable stranger down the hallway to his room.

Once inside, lust and the sweet element of surprise allowed Lena to push Johnson up against the back of the door. She pounced on him like a baby on ice cream, her lips devouring his warm and welcoming mouth, tasting mint on her tongue.

"How about we get way more comfortable," Johnson suggested, gently breaking away to turn on a light. Lena replied with a low murmur, keeping her eyes closed as she savored the sensations running though her body. She listened to the voices popping up in her head, which with temptation out of sight, had suddenly come down to dueling opposites. The ethically upright, "reputation trumps spontaneity" Girl Scout in her was tussling with her newly discovered, adventurous, decadent twin sister.

You do realize you're in a strange man's hotel room and nobody knows you are here, threw out the Girl Scout. *You don't even know his name.*

But I don't want to know his name or him to know mine, Pocahontas countered.

Compromise, Lena suggested. *Call Aleesa and let her know where you are. And use a condom.*

"Bathroom?"

"First door on the left."

Once in the bathroom, Lena quickly dialed Aleesa's cell phone number and waited for an answer. "For someone who says they have no life, you never pick up your phone," she scream-whispered a message. "Omigod. I just walked down the hallway in my underwear! Now I'm in his bathroom…this guy…I met in the bar…we made a bet on the game…I lost…and well, now I think I'm about to fuck the black off this sexy motherfucker…he's a bald and beautiful piece of chocolate thunder…seriously…his name is… get this…Mr. Big Johnson…well, that's not his *real* name, but we're not sharing that information…I told him I was Pocahontas…. okay, I gotta go but I wanted to tell you where and who I was with…you know…just to be safe. Girl, I'll fill you in tomor…" The machine beeped and cut off her rambling.

"Everything okay?" Johnson's voice called through the door.

"Be right out." Lena shut down her mind, tossed her phone in her purse and took a moment to fluff her hair. She stood, avoiding the mirror as best she could. She didn't want to see herself, preferring to let Pocahontas's spirit move her in mysteriously sexy ways.

Lena opened the door and tiptoed into the room and over to the bed where Johnson lay waiting for her. Before joining him, Lena stood at the foot and took a mental snapshot of the moment. It looked like a scene from a Hollywood movie. Crisp white sheets provided the perfect canvas for this gorgeous chocolate specimen of a man. His muscled chest and arms were laid back against the cool cotton sheets, his face full of anticipation, eyes full of lustful approval. Lena had read about, watched movies, and even day-dreamed about a moment like this. And here she was, about to actually live the scenario of a one-night stand with the sexy stranger.

"You look beautiful," he told her, feeling like he'd never before said those words with such conviction. She did look like a vision, standing there in her matching bra and panties, wearing heels and pearls. Jason nodded his head in obvious approval. Amazing what you could learn about a woman from her underwear. Stripped down to her lingerie, this was a sensual and elegant woman. A woman who lived her sexy whether she was alone or in the company of others.

"Thank you. You know, Mr. Johnson," she began, Girl Scout wanting to let him know that this was an unusual situation for her and that she was not your typical "pick men up at the bar and fuck them" kind of girl. *Shut up*, Pocahontas interrupted. *What are you—sixteen? Act like a grown woman. If you want this man, have him without excuse or pretense. Follow your own damn rules.*

"I know what?"

"I know you won't mind if I join you and get to know you a little better," she said with a tone in her voice that was less asking for permission and more declaring her intentions.

Johnson pulled the covers back in response, revealing a dick already hard and ready for action.

Lena sat on the edge of the bed to take off her shoes. Johnson, deciding she was way too close in proximity not to touch, leaned over and kissed the small of her back before running his tongue up the length of her spine, stopping to nibble at her neck and do some serious damage to any lingering resolve. Lena let out a soft sigh of delight and crooked her head to the left, giving him full access to the most potent erogenous zone residing above her breasts. As Johnson moved on to making a savory appetizer of her earlobe, the last smidgen of reserve she'd been holding on to vanished. She felt sexually overwhelmed, but strangely at peace being in this hotel room with this nameless man.

Lena reached up and palmed Johnson's bald head, gently caressing his smooth dome with her fingertips while turning his face to meet hers. Lena looked him straight in the eyes, engaging in a moment of ocular conversation. Her look revealed her intent—she was about to let loose and tear his ass up. Johnson's expressive brown eyes responded in kind, letting her know that anything she wanted, he wanted, too.

"Girl, you have a *scandalous* spark in your eyes right now. It is sexy as hell," he told her.

She concluded their discussion with a wink and then gave him the kiss of a lifetime. It was a kiss that declared, "game on," and sent them both into sexual overdrive. Lena climbed onto the bed, pressing her chest to his as her nose breathed in the bracing, herbaceous notes of his cologne. Her lips immediately found his eyes, kissing each one of them shut, before nibbling on his nose and licking his lips like a kid with a Tootsie Pop. Lena captured his bottom lip between hers, pulling and sucking on it before inserting her tongue into his mouth in search of the chocolate nugget within.

Johnson's hands got busy, reaching around Lena's back and undoing the hooks on her bra. She sat up to release her breasts from their lacy constraint, causing her long, double-wrapped string of pearls to swing, hitting him in the face. She grabbed the string, reaching up to remove them only to be stopped by Johnson.

"No, don't. I like you wearing nothing but pearls."

Lena smiled, dropped the necklace and kissed him again. "I believe you promised me something back at the elevator."

"I'm not sure what you mean."

"Yes, you do," Lena insisted.

"I know, but I want to hear you say it."

Lena chuckled briefly before turning dead serious again. "You know."

"I like a woman who asks for what she wants."

"Well, what I want right now is for you to lick my pussy until I come on your face. Clear enough for you?"

"Crystal. Just so you know, talking shit turns me on."

The couple switched positions so Lena was lying on her back while Johnson began a seductive trek across the trail of freckles sprinkled across her nose, down her neck and shoulders until his lips came to rest on Lena's large nipples. His talented tongue traveled round and round her toffee areolas, soaking them with his sweet, minty saliva and blowing on them like the wind. His cool breath turned her nipples hard and sent a zinging jolt straight to her clitoris, turning her into a woman possessed. She was enjoying what he was doing, but wanted oral sex and wished he'd move it along. Nothing mattered to Lena more at that moment than to have that cool mouth buried in her snatch.

He said he liked a woman who asked for what she wanted. If you want it, tell him, Pocahontas coached her.

"I need you to eat my twat, NOW!" she demanded, using her hands to push his head toward her crotch, while still not quite believing what she'd said. *Twat,* like *cunt,* were considered filthy words in her personal vocabulary. Words she usually found degrading and disgusting. Words that were now coming out of her mouth, not only with reckless disregard, but specifically for the sexual shock value.

"Baby, I got you. Now feed it to me."

Lena's legs reached for the far corners of the bed as she slipped her hands down to her vagina and gently pulled open the petals of her feminine flower. Johnson took a minute to inspect it, marveling at its beauty and wafting in the musky scent of her arousal, before lightly running his fingertips down the length of her inner thigh and muff-diving between her legs. His tongue ticked away the seconds, moving around her swelling bud in an achingly sensual, clockwise motion. Two or three times around the clock and time stopped as Johnson began a maddening pattern of sucking, pulling and then stopping to give it a series of soothing licks. Lena's hips pushed forward as her hands simultaneously pulled his face deeper into her pelvis.

"Wider," Johnson demanded, lifting his head, his chin glazed with her natural lubrication. She complied, opening both her legs and her pussy lips. He swiped the wet and juicy middle with his tongue, savoring the sweet taste of Lena's pussy juices.

"Baby, you taste so fucking good," he told her, his dick growing harder and wider with each lick.

"Oh shiiiiiit," Lena let loose a loud moan of satisfaction—finally a man who knew how to properly dine at Ms. Vaginny's table! She took a quiet moment to thank whatever woman in his past had trained Johnson for this moment and then relaxed into the multitude of sensations that were invading her body.

Johnson teased her nib with a gentle but concentrated stream of warm breath before giving it a tickle first with the tip and then the whole of his tongue. The floating sensation that followed pulled her hands from between her legs and sent them to the edge of the bed, which she grabbed to steady herself. With a corkscrew motion, he pushed two fingers deep inside her, causing Lena to instinctively begin pumping his face. Grunting, she clenched her inner muscles around his fingers, wanting to catch and hold them inside her.

"Oh, oh, oh…" slipped from Lena's lips. The sexy sounds encouraged Johnson to finger her harder as he treated her clitoris to a performance of oral acrobatics. "Oh fuck, this feels so fucking delicious," she said, reaching the point of no return. "Make me cum. OH, Baby, make me cum. Oh, OH," she moaned before exploding in his mouth and climaxing in waves of powerful spasms.

Lena lay back and broke into joyous giggles, thrilled by not only the pleasurable release, but by her newfound sense of wanton lust. She felt powerful. "You are amazing," she complimented him. "Just amazing."

"Thank you. And you have one of the prettiest pussies I have ever seen."

"Well, pretty pussy wants to get fucked," she told him, his compliments ignored by her need to feel him inside her.

Johnson's face broke out in a slash of white teeth followed by a deep and lusty chuckle. "Fuck, you are one sexy girl, Pocahontas."

"Do you have a condom?"

"Always prepared." Johnson reached over to the nightstand for his wallet and pulled out a Trojan. As he sheathed his member, Lena smiled and waited, pacifying her desire to have that beautiful, brown, rock-hard shaft inside her by pulling the string of pearls between her lips.

"Baby, you look helluva good in those pearls," he said, shifting his weight to mount her.

"Well, I think they'd look really good on you," she said, stopping his movements as she unwound the necklace from around her neck. As she reached up to put them around his head, another idea occurred to her. Instead of draping them over Johnson's neck, Lena reached down and starting at the beautiful plum head of his cock, wrapped the strand around his dick from front to back, leaving a trail of pearls between his legs.

Johnson looked down at her with amazed delight. His dick grew harder and felt deliciously squeezed in its bejeweled encasement. *Sensual, elegant and freaky! The perfect combination in a woman*, he mused. *Lucky fucking me!*

He climbed on top of her and slowly entered her pussy. Their gasps were simultaneous as each surrendered to the new and luscious feeling of his adorned cockhead entering her. He parted her slowly, his already large penis made even larger by his sheath of pearls. Johnson's dick stretched the walls of Lena's pussy as he gently eased deeper and deeper, taking her breath away, and causing her to moan again.

She felt every inch of him. The sensation of hard and smooth pearls sliding back and forth, grinding against all of the erogenous nerve endings of her coochie was mind blowing. Lena felt her arousal elevate to a higher level, turning the faucets of her pussy on high. Johnson shifted position, adjusting the intensity of this unique friction with a series of circular thrusts followed by hard, unrelenting strokes. She spread her legs wider and lifted her butt higher to receive him, causing the tail of pearls to rub delightfully back and forth against her slick anus, made slippery by the pussy juices dripping between her ass cheeks. Ooh, it tickled so good.

"Omigod. OMIGOD!" she called out getting lost in the intensity of their coupling. "This feels so fucking GREAT!"

Johnson answered her exclamations with a series grunts and moans and the look on his face that told her he was chasing heaven. His rhythm became uneven and Lena could tell that Johnson was fighting with himself not to surrender into orgasm. She couldn't blame him. She wanted to ride this studded horse as long as she possibly could. Lena drew her legs up so he could penetrate her even deeper, and at the same time squeezed her vagina around his shaft while moving her hips in a circle. But rather than prolong their intercourse, her actions set him off.

"Shit, Baby, I'm gonna cum. You want this cum, Baby? You want it now?" Johnson asked as he let go and stopped fighting the rush of climax. Lena felt his cock go into one long, incredible-feeling spasm, and then begin pulsing as he poured himself into her.

She felt his dick go limp and the pearls unwind and fall away as he disengaged his body from hers. The two lay back on the bed to recover.

"Wow," was all Johnson could manage from his exhausted lips. Words gave way to silent wonder as he slipped into a post-coitus snooze.

Lena felt wide awake and more alive than she'd ever felt before. She smiled into the darkness, amazed by what had just taken place. It wasn't that the sex was so unusual or freaky—though that pearl thing had proven to be a novelty for both of them. It was the way she felt about herself at this moment—free, uninhibited, joyful, curious, and spontaneous—that made this experience so fucking fantastic. Pocahontas may have lost a bet, but Lena had gained a scrumptiously scandalous memory she'd relish for the rest of her life.

Chapter Three

"So you bet him sex?" Lena's best friend and main confidante, Aleesa Davis, asked with stunned disbelief. "You nasty ho!"

"Well, not exactly," Lena said, smiling at the memory. "It was his choice."

"And then you fucked him and left his fine ass in bed?"

"Yep."

"Now, let me get this straight, after strutting around the hotel damn near naked and then screwing his brains out, you walked out without leaving anything, not even your email address, behind."

"I can pretty much guarantee you that I left plenty of good memories to keep him going for months—hell, years!"

"Damn, girl. You actually sound proud of yourself. Okay, where is she? Where's my workaholic, no time for a life let alone men, conservative, what will people think, boss and friend?"

"You know what?" Lena asked rhetorically, totally amused and understanding of Aleesa's bewilderment. "I finally get the joke about stranger sex. In the most basic way it's the greatest sex around. You can really let yourself go and not worry about your partner thinking that you're slutty or easy, and you can just ask—no *demand*—what you want. If you want to scream, talk dirty, bite him, whatever, you CAN without worrying about a thing."

"Except disease or getting stuck with some crazy stalker…the list goes on."

"We used condoms, and that's exactly why he knows me only as Pocahontas, and why I called you to tell you where I was and with whom."

"Yeah, I'd have lots of luck hunting down a Mr. Big Johnson a.k.a. Chocolate Thunder."

Lena winced. "Ohh, did I really call him that?"

"It sounds like it was a mutual turn-out. If the sex was that good, you don't want to see him again?"

"The sex was AMAZING, and so was he—funny, sexy, a gentleman despite his freaky ways. I liked him. And maybe another time or place, well, maybe…but you know that I have no time for a relationship. I have one year left to turn this company around and to quote Renee Russo in the *Thomas Crown Affair*, 'Men make women messy.'"

"So you wouldn't consider keeping him, not even as a boy toy?"

"Damn, Lees, he's not a puppy. But hell, after some of the shit I pulled, I think I'd be too embarrassed to hook up with him again! Nah, it is as it should be—a memorable night of never going to see you again sex—sweet and simple."

"I have to say, that's one of the things I wished I'd done when I was free and single—that one-night stand thing. Ah, but it's too late; I've been married way too long."

"Your husband has been in Afghanistan for damn near a year, even the military has that 'don't ask, don't tell' policy. Doesn't that extend to those left at home, too?"

"You're not suggesting that I cheat on Walter, are you?"

"No girl, that was Pocahontas talking. My bad. You've got a great and heroic husband. You just add that fantasy to your slutty little journal you're keeping for him while he's away."

"You joke, but can I tell you, if it wasn't for that outlet, I would have to follow in your whorish footsteps, cuz I am horny as a motherfucker."

"What about Buzz Lightyear?"

"Only so much a plastic dick can do for you. I really miss being touched and kissed…"

"And getting that ass tapped, I know. Here, this will help," Lena said, smiling as she opened her desk drawer and handed Aleesa a box of Lindt chocolates.

"You keep it. I've got my own supply—Costco size! All right, girl, I have to get back to work. The boss is a bitch, you know. And slutty one at that!"

"True that. And speaking of work, I need to see the promo storyboards for the new show this afternoon. I know the all-network meeting isn't for two months, but I want time to make any changes," Lena requested, seamlessly switching from girlfriend to boss mode.

"Lena, you know I got your back. The new season presentation is going to be fabulous. Relax."

"I know you do, that's why I had to have you, that and because you're the best in the business. I don't think ABC is ever going to forgive me for stealing you away."

"Lena, sorry to interrupt but…" Her secretary, Rolanda, a holdover from her predecessor, opened the door and stepped inside.

"Just a second, my meeting is almost up," Lena said. She watched as Rolanda backed out the door. "Damn, that girl pops out of nowhere all the time."

"Well, be careful because you don't want Douglas to find out what ho you are. He will not be happy."

"And who's going to tell him? Girl, I will fire your ass quick as you can say, 'please, big daddy, may I have another," Lena joked, confident in the knowledge that her secrets were safe with Aleesa. In the twenty years they'd known each other, Aleesa had never betrayed her confidence. "But seriously, Lees, he can't hold on to me forever. Our relationship, as it is now, has to change at some point. I have to be my own woman. He and I both know that."

"Another one of your dramas to work out another day."

"True that."

Aleesa left the room with a wave, leaving Lena to crack open another Coke Zero and count her blessings. She and Aleesa had met while working together in their twenties at the local CBS affiliate station in New York. Since those early days in their careers, Lena had moved up in the production and programming ranks, spending the last four years as an independent producer before signing a contract with PBC; while Aleesa had scurried up the promotion and marketing ladder, leaving her job at the ABC network to answer Lena's plea to become the sports network's VP of marketing and promotion. It was a strategic move, as Aleesa was a wizard at creating not-to-miss spots to promote their programming, and also had a real knack for recognizing hit shows when she saw them. With everything riding on the outcome of this one season, Lena needed a friend among the foes.

"Lena, you have messages," her secretary reappeared, trying not to smile. She'd pegged her boss as the sexy enough, "look but don't touch" kind of sister, but who knew that Miss All Work and No Play was a closet freak!

Lena waved her in and then sat back to see the show. Rolanda, bless her heart, was a study in simultaneously wearing your heart, bust and butt on your sleeve for the world to see. A cute and curvy chocolate drop, in any other corporate environment her every day, up-down-and-all-around uniform (skirt up to there, cleavage down to there, and hair weave all around) would not be tolerated. But here at the SFN, where Lena's office was a revolving door of athletes, salesmen, and advertisers, Rolanda's out-there, come-fuck-me wardrobe often proved to be an asset with said gentlemen—that plus her insider knowledge of the network.

"What's up?"

"Jason Armstrong…"

"Who?"

"Rickie Ross' agent."

"Finally, he got himself a new agent!" Lena cheered. "Maybe now we can get this thing wrapped up."

"Yeah, well, they are available to meet with you on March eighteenth."

"That's two weeks from now."

"I know, but that's the earliest he can do. Ohh, can you all meet here? I am dying to meet Rickie," Rolanda requested.

Again, Lena had to chuckle to herself. Rolanda's career intentions were so transparent that they damn near glowed. Despite being college educated and quite intelligent, the girl had absolutely no desire to move up the corporate ladder or improve her job title. She was there for the perks—the free tickets to major sporting events, her celebrity by association status with friends and family, and most importantly, the ability to rub shoulders (and whatever else if the consensual mood hit) with some big-time sports stars. This was the most important perk because what she wanted most in this world was to get a rich man and live a life of blinged-out excess. She aspired to be one of those housewives of Atlanta— shopping 'til she dropped, lunching with her girls and hatin' on those who were not. And what better way to get that life than to snag a million-dollar athlete, especially when one had access to said athletes on the daily by working in the president's office of a cable sports network? So she worked hard and kept herself indispensable by knowing not only the fine inner workings of the company but where all of the skeletons were hidden as well. The girl's goals may have been simple but she was no dummy.

"Rolanda, I'm sure at some point you'll have the opportunity to meet Rickie, but not at this meeting. So make one o'clock reservations at Nobu 57 for three, okay? What else?" Lena moved on quickly as she was not about to entertain any discussion on the topic. Rickie Ross was too instrumental to her future success to let a gold digging assistant get in the way.

Ro sucked her teeth, turning down the excitement in her voice several decibels and replacing it with the low drone of a bored and irritated underling. "T.J. Reynolds confirmed for Friday at two p.m., and Mr. Paskin wants to see you."

"Damn, I really don't have time to get down to corporate today. Can you please call and try to reschedule for later in the week?"

"He's already on his way here."

Lena tried to drown the sudden tension that had engulfed her body with a long chug of soda. She hated when he simply showed up at her office or sent for her at his whim. It wasn't fair and it put her in an uncomfortable position. But what choice did she have? No matter what their relationship, like it or not, Douglas Paskin was her boss.

"It's only a meeting. Why do you let that old white man get all up inside your head?"

"I don't think that's the appropriate way to speak about the man who signs *your* check and mine," Lena lit into her, feeling her protective nature rise. "And I don't want to hear such blatant disrespect again, understood?"

"Yes, *ma'am*," Rolanda replied, miffed that the high-and-mighty Lena Macy would dress her down over some white dude who even she thought was a pain in the ass.

Lena waited until Rolanda had firmly shut the door before plopping down in her seat and exhaling a gust of frustration. So much about that short exchange with her secretary had irritated her. First of all, she had no right to be so disrespectful. Douglas Paskin had never done anything intentional to raise any racial ill will among the employees of his company. In fact, most people didn't realize the extent to which he bent over backward to make sure that PBC was fully represented by people of color at all levels. Rolanda's attitude simply had no basis in reality.

Secondly, and most importantly, this wasn't *just* a meeting. No meeting with Douglas ever was. He owned not only the Paskin Broadcasting Corporation, but her future as well. With his nod, Lena could become the head of her own broadcasting empire. He had the power to put her in the same league with the Oprahs and Bob Johnsons of the world, or not, making every conversation they had feel like a summit. Their personal interaction only muddied the waters. But she had no intention of letting their relationship neither help nor hurt her pursuit.

Douglas was notorious about keeping his personal life personal, but Lena had heard the scuttlebutt that the only Paskin heir was either unable or uninterested in following in their father's footsteps, leaving Douglas to shop for his own replacement. Everybody throughout the company knew that T.J. had had his sights set on the chairman's job for years, and that Douglas seemed to have a genuine respect for T.J.'s business skill and ability to get things done. And despite her stellar performance these past few years, Lena also knew that some people around the network had recognized the extra attention he paid her, but she refused to give any one cause to question her business prowess. Lena was either going to earn this gig on her own merit or walk away knowing the best man won. Well, if you considered T.J. Reynolds the better man.

Lena had met him exactly four times, each occasion being the annual all-network meeting, and frankly the jury was still out. At thirty-nine he remained single, most believing his story that he was too focused on his career and unwilling to subject a wife and family to such a rolling stone existence, but there was something about his personality that kept Lena from wanting to know him any better. She couldn't be the only female who felt the same way.

On paper, Travis James Reynolds, a Princeton graduate with an MBA from Stanford, appeared pitch perfect. With athletic good looks and a brilliant head for business, he carried himself with a cocky swagger and a charismatic personality that translated well both with the ladies and the powers that be he'd bumped into on his way up the corporate ladder. After a summer internship at the local ABC affiliate in New York, he was bitten by the broadcasting bug and following his graduation from Princeton, secured as a sales associate at a local radio station in Washington, D.C. T.J. quickly worked his way into television sales, earned his MBA, and landed the general manager spot at a local station in Lexington, Kentucky. He moved around the country for several years, landing in one local market higher than the next until the networks came calling. He worked as a broadcast executive first at PBS, then CBS and finally NBC when T.J. met Douglas Paskin at a Princeton alumni dinner where Douglas was being honored. The two formed a mutual admiration pact and when the opportunity presented itself, Douglas hired T.J.

After bringing her into the company six months later, Douglas had pitted Lena and T.J. against each other. For the past four years he had given them each one-year rotations through nearly all of the PBC subsidiaries around the country, forcing them to learn and understand the broadcasting empire they'd potentially be running. Both had worked, at different times, at the flagship network, PBC; the News Headlines Network; the Paskin Satellite Radio Network; and Paskin Media, a publishing group of small trade publications. With this last rotation, Douglas was giving them both ultimate responsibility for the companies they headed. Currently, they both sat at the helm of the two least profitable

PBC acquisitions. While Lena was charged with turning around the sagging ratings of SFN, a dinosaur sports network located in New York, T.J. was responsible for branding the newest addition of the Paskin broadcast family, LiveYou, television for women, housed in Secaucus, New Jersey. Douglas' thinking: If you're going to be successful running the entire corporation, you've got to be successful running the parts that are most foreign to you.

The rap on her door abruptly ended Lena's emotional prep time. She stood up, smoothed the nonexistent wrinkles from her perfectly fitted black Michael Kors dress, and walked over to greet the boss. She opened the door to find the tall and illustrious gentleman smiling broadly at her. For a man of sixty-nine, Douglas was fit and, yes her biased opinion, fine—kind of Richard Branson meets Sean Connery fine. He had the distinguished look of a buttoned-down, wealthy tycoon who fed his rebellious streak in the shadowy edges of his life. The scar above his left eye, rumored to have been received during a skydiving landing gone bad, gave credence to the common belief that the man was an adventurer—in and out of the boardroom. Lena's smile grew wider as he entered her domain. Their relationship could be difficult—downright contentious at times—but she couldn't help but love him.

"Lena," he called her name as if he was witness to sweetness personified and opened his arms, moving in close for a welcoming hug.

"Not here," she insisted, backing away. "You know how I feel about that." Suddenly a surge of guilt overwhelmed her. Douglas would be so hurt and disappointed by her Miami indiscretions. And yet, the residual glow from that chance encounter felt not only deliciously risqué, but right.

"Yes, no public displays of affection," he replied, reciting her golden rule. His green eyes took in her appearance, approving what they saw. "Well, you look beautiful today."

"Thank you. You're looking quite yummy yourself," she said, returning his smile. Lena moved to close her office door so they could speak in private. Her eye caught Rolanda's and for just a moment, she thought she saw a glimmer of amused disbelief.

"Come in, Douglas. Tell me what brings you by."

As soon as the door shut, separating the powerful from the peons, Rolanda pulled out her cell phone and dialed Monique, her friend in accounting. "Girl, you won't even believe who has a big ole case of jungle fever."

Chapter Four

"Love it, love it, love it!" Lena gushed as the sales presentation for next season faded to black. "Aleesa, this is wonderful. It's like the perfect invitation to a coveted party. It gets you all excited about the event weeks before it happens. I don't know how the advertisers are going to be able to resist the SFN line-up next season."

"My team did a great job. And just so you know, I am personally editing a thirty-second spot for *Sports Watchin' Women*, so if we do get Rickie signed on, we can insert it into the presentation. I've also got the mock press kit ready to go for your meeting with him."

"You are a genius! Thank you. I don't know how he could not love the concept, and with Rickie's Q rating, the show will be a monster hit."

"Especially if you make him do every show shirtless. Damn those abs! And speaking of women, what about the cross promotion with LiveYou TV?" Aleesa asked.

"Meeting with T.J. tomorrow about it. It's damn near six o'clock, but do you have time to go over my pitch?"

"Sure, what else do I have to do but go home to an empty house."

"Thanks. I'm more stressed out about that than the all-network meeting."

"Don't worry about him."

"But I have to. T.J. is good and he's hungry. Very hungry. He wants to be king."

"And you don't?"

"Are you serious?"

Well, you said that Douglas damn near offered it to you straight out when he brought you into the company, but you turned it down. If you really wanted it, why didn't you say yes then?"

"It's complicated," Lena said, succinctly wrapping her explanation in Facebook brevity. She had no intention of explaining, even to her best friend, how complicated her relationship with Douglas was. "You know, being a woman, and a Black woman at that, I don't want people to think that I got the gig because of some affirmative action thing. I have to earn people's respect and if they think I was handed the job, they won't give it to me."

"But T.J. could say the same thing—white man doing the brother a solid."

"Different. Black men running major companies, while still rarer than it should be, is not such a novelty anymore. Hell, we have a brother running the entire world! But for Black women it's still a different version of the same old story."

"Point taken. Like I said, don't worry. Look what you've already done since you've been here. You sifted out the dead weight and now the shows look and feel modern and energized, and ratings are on the uptick. Advertisers are happier, even in this economy and the staff is pumped. Morale is off the charts; my crew is very happy with the changes. And with the new shows coming next season, SFN is going to catch fire. So do what you do."

"Like I said, it's complicated," Lena replied, still feeling unsure.

"Let's continue this discussion over drinks. You need to talk and I need to feel like I have some semblance of a social life."

"Done. I'll meet you down in the lobby in fifteen."

Lena walked her friend out of the office, continuing across the hall to the small conference room where Rolanda was putting together two gift bags to send prior to the meeting with Rickie and his agent. When it came to getting what she wanted, Lena was not too proud to butter.

"All the good stuff, right?" Rolanda reconfirmed with her boss.

"Yep, and remind me to include the private jet gift card."

"Damn! You are going all out."

"I'll give up whatever it takes to get him here." If she was pulling out all the stops, she might as well include a roundtrip ride on the corporate jet. She saw Ro's eyes go bright at the thought of zipping around on a private plane with Rickie Ross. "I'm leaving now for a meeting. I'll see you in the morning."

"Okay. I'm going to finish these and then send those emails to the West Coast before I bounce."

"Thanks, Ro. And don't forget to lock those up in my office before you go." Lena left her assistant working. She might have been crass, and had more "around the way" than corporate flair, but at her core, Rolanda Hammon was a hard worker.

It was nearly ten after six when Rolanda finished sending out the emails. She still had over an hour to kill before meeting Monique at the 40/40 sports bar. The plan was to flash their bootleg SFN press passes, and make their way into the VIP area, hook up with some big spenders, and to toast Thursday night in style. If none of them were in the house, there was always her SFN expense account to wine and dine them both. Technically it was her boss' account, but what's a little forged signature here and there. Especially when she handled all of the paperwork. And if everything worked out, maybe she'd find some interesting mischief to bring in Friday morning.

Rolanda picked up the gift bags and carried them into Lena's office. She locked them securely in the credenza behind her desk, while deciding to wait out her time in the comfort of the boss' office. She grabbed one of the chilled splits of champagne designated for executive suite celebrations, kicked off her heels, threw her feet up on the desk and made herself comfortable in Lena's chair. After six o'clock it was absolutely dead on the twenty-sixth floor. One of the things she loved most about working for the network head was that the executive offices were tucked away on a separate floor. With the distance and intimidation factor working together, people tended to leave her the fuck alone.

Rolanda popped the champagne and took a healthy sip through the straw, her mouth and throat enjoying its effervescence. Another long sip and she could feel the bubbles going to her head. Savoring the buzz, she reached over and picked up the file of resumes and photos of pro athletes being considered as on-air talent for the last show to be cast.

She studied Vikings' running back, Adrian Peterson, with his hard body all covered in tats. "Wonder what he's packin'?" she speculated aloud as she flipped to the next photo. She was greeted by linebacker Jason Taylor, shirtless and sitting legs spread in a hammock. She remembered his tight ass and molded thighs displayed during his *Dancing With the Stars* stint. "Shit, I'll swing on you," she offered, wanting to experience the salty taste of his skin in her mouth.

Rolanda swigged hard on the split, while focused on NBA hottie, Dwight Howard. "Slam dunk me, motherfucker."

Saving the best for last, Rolanda rubbed her finger over the bad boy good looks of Rickie Ross. Her eyes feasted on his shredded abs, hard nipples standing tall and calling her name. She allowed her finger to follow the girdle of his pelvis leading her eyes to his crotch. Ro felt her clit jump. It was no wonder that even Miss Pole Stuck Up Her Ass, priss of a boss of hers wanted Rickie Ross so bad. The boy was tasty, tasty. She'd met, and even fucked enough ballers to know that this boy was special. There was a hot and horny charisma about him that made him irresistible to damn near anyone with a vagina, and plenty of those sporting dicks as well.

Rolanda lifted the picture to her face, lapping the sports icon's privates with her tongue. She closed her eyes, letting the champagne buzz and her imagination bring to life the object of her lustful desire. Just the idea of fucking this famous player turned the valve on her cooch on high. She'd just had sex two days ago but Rolanda's cravings were insatiable, especially when it came to the rock hard, rich and famous. Moreover, Rolanda loved sex. Adored it. Couldn't get enough of it. Mainly, she loved the power it provided her. The thing that set her off toward orgasm, even better than a big, thick pole, was that helpless look in some lover's eye that announced that he had crossed to the other side and she now was in pussy control.

Craving to feel his touch, Rolanda propped Rickie's picture up against the desk lamp and put her hands to much more pleasurable use. Swiveling the chair until it was parallel to the desk, she lifted one leg onto Lena's desk, top spreading the other, opening herself wide.

Rolanda parted her pubic hair with her middle finger and pulled her pussy lips open. She dipped inside, pulling out her finger, now drenched in coochie juice, rubbing it on her engorged clit. She let herself imagine her finger to be Rickie Ross's tongue playing with her little girl dick and making it grow long and hard.

Thinking he was operating under the element of surprise, it was T.J. who was shocked when he reached Lena Macy's door. He had traveled into New York from LiveYou's New Jersey headquarters to see if he could get an informal heads-up from Lena about her agenda. Instead he got a peep show.

The moist scent of pink drew him farther into the room. Lost in her sexual fantasy and obviously on a mission, he stood quietly, not wanting to disturb and stop the show. T.J. bit the inside of his cheek to silence his groans, as he watched this freaky girl pleasure herself, his dick growing hard and dripping with pre-cum.

Rolanda raised her hips to her hand, thrusting two fingers in and out of herself, her face translating the letdown feelings of her greedy pussy. This was not satisfying her. She needed girth and hardness, and with no boys or toys around to do her bidding, the always enterprising Rolanda reached for the champagne bottle, guiding it toward her crotch. The sight of the split's mouth kissing hers nearly made T.J. wad all over himself. Being a silent voyeur was no longer an option.

"Might I be of assistance?" he asked, pulling his suit jacket aside to reveal his hard cock straining against his pants zipper.

Rolanda opened her eyes to find T.J. Reynolds standing in the doorway. She recognized him from the photos she'd seen in the Paskin Broadcasting Company's annual report. Rather than be embarrassed, she felt her arousal kick into fifth gear as her mind quickly assessed the situation. Tall and lithe with skin the color of peanut butter and a sexy goatee framing a pair of succulent lips, he proved the circulating rumors that the brother was extra yummy. His reputation as a first-class cocks-man was prime conversation throughout the Secaucus headquarters. Why not finally see if it held up on this side of the Hudson? Though it was her policy to not swap body fluids with anybody who carried a key to the executive washroom, T.J. Reynolds technically worked for an entirely different company. Plus, if he were the ultimate winner of the chairman's lottery, it couldn't hurt to have a friend in high places. Based on her relationship with Douglas Paskin, Lena apparently thought so.

The exhibitionist in her responded to his offer with a sly curl of her lower lip and the widening of her legs, giving him an inside view of her jewel box. Her action was also accompanied by a look daring him to turn down this fine specimen. As he watched, his mouth opening wide with amazement, Ro thrust the bottle head into her dripping pussy, while fingering herself into a mini orgasm.

"Ah, AH, AHH. Hmm. Bring that dick over here."

T.J. understood immediately and crossed the room in three steps. His hand reached for the bottle, taking it from her hands before lifting Rolanda from the chair and onto the desk. In response, she quickly reached for his buckle, unfastening his belt and pants, hearing the cry of his grateful dick, which was begging for not only air but the moist heat of this girl's horny hole. Within seconds his pants were pooled around his ankles.

Not a word was uttered between them. None were necessary. T.J. reached behind her, grabbing her hips and sliding her to the edge of the table. With a forceful grunt he pushed his stiff rod into her, groaning loudly as the 4,000 nerves on his penis got acquainted with the deliciously unfamiliar nooks and crannies of her pussy.

There was no pretense to their coupling. It was straight, go-for-the-gusto fucking. T.J. wrapped his hands around her hips, his thumbs positioned on each side of her pelvis. With this grip he was easily able to control the timing and rhythm of her move-ment. He pulled her coochie toward him, the tip of his dick intent on finding the right spot and angle to position itself relative to her g-spot, clit or both. Its aim was perfect as indicated by the loud screech coming from Rolanda's mouth.

"You like this big dick, don't you, girl?"

"Yeah, just as much as you like this juicy pussy," Ro countered. T.J. stroked her hard and fast, both enjoying the heat the friction of their bodies were producing. He fucked her hard; the sound of his balls slapping her wet crotch filled the air. The tip of his dick teased her spot; the one that sent spasms throughout the cave putting the climax gods on high alert.

"Harder!" Ro screamed, digging her nail tips into his tight ass.

T.J. responded with a growl, too intent on the task at hand to bother his brain with finding appropriate words.

"Shit. I'm gonna cum. I'm gonna cum. I'm gonna shoot this wad all up in you. Ah, ah, ah," he grunted. Ro could feel his balls contract and his dick pulse as he shot spurt after spurt of cum into her hole.

T.J. pulled his rod from her and collapsed onto the chair. The briny scent of sex lingered in the air. Their breath was still rapid and shallow, both fighting to regain their composure and sort out their silent but very similar thoughts. T.J.'s mind was convinced that judging from this quick sampling, he may have stumbled on the fuck of the century. This chick was a temptation to be reckoned with. Given more time and space, he couldn't help but wonder what tricks this uninhibited wild child would treat him to.

Rolanda, too, was impressed by his sexual ability. He didn't fuck like a corny suit and tie. Oh, on the contrary. The boy could wield a dick, and knew just how and when to find her spot and set her off. She still had to wonder about his mouth skills, both kissing and pussy eating, as this encounter had been strictly dickly. They hadn't taken the time to get into anything oral. But based on this little quickie, it was worth finding out.

"So, I'm assuming that this isn't actually your office," he said after removing the condom and pulling on his pants. He took a quick survey of Lena's office, surprised by its earthy colors and contemporary décor. The clean dark lines of her furniture intersected with the soothing tones of sand, sea blues and rust that took you in and urged you to relax. Despite being head of SFN, he'd expected a much more feminine fiefdom. Instead, this was the domain of a cool, calm, sophisticated corporate leader. A savvy force to be reckoned with.

"No, my desk is outside."

"You're Lena Macy's assistant?"

"Yes."

T.J. smiled. He had just banged the very juicy secretary of his rival. This was a most fortuitous fuck.

"I'm assuming your boss has no idea of your afterhours use of her office."

"And I'm assuming she won't ever find out." Ro looked him directly in his brown eyes, daring him to think otherwise.

"That would be a mutual assumption, Ms. ...?"

"Rolanda Hammon."

"Well, Ms. Rolanda Hammon, I don't see the point in anyone knowing about this."

"Neither do I."

"Particularly if we were to both agree to..."

"Mr. Reynolds..."

"T.J."

"T.J., know this about me. I am no office fuck. *If* I want to see you again, it won't be here screwing on a desktop."

He laughed, his dick twitching in response to her bravado. Her spunk turned him on, but he was no punk.

"And Ms. Hammon, know this about me," he replied in a voice smooth as sixty-five-year-old Scotch, "*when* I want to see you again, it might be for dinner or a weekend in Paris or yes, right here fucking on a desktop."

Their eyes met in mutual understanding. She may have had the power of the pussy, but he had the power. Period.

Chapter Five

Lena sat alone in the LiveYou TV conference room waiting for her colleague. T.J. was twenty minutes late. According to the call from his secretary, he was tending to a personnel emergency and would be with her as soon as possible. The meeting had been originally scheduled at SFN, but T.J.'s office had called to change the venue, pleading a packed schedule and the need to stay close to the office. Lena found his excuse suspect, feeling it to be a power play by a competitive rival. And now he was keeping her waiting. Another five minutes ticked by and just as she was about to reschedule, T.J. barreled into the room.

"Lena, I am so sorry to hold you up like this," he said, rushing to her side and taking his hand in hers. "You know how it is, best intentions waylaid by the unexpected."

"Of course," she replied, her body standing to greet him, her smile not quite reaching her eyes.

T.J. took a moment to size up his guest. They'd met several times over the past few years and as he had been then, he was impressed that, unlike most businesswomen, she didn't feel the need to don the masculine armor of some corporate hard ass in order to be taken seriously. Lena apparently understood the inherent power of a woman's femininity. Her simple and fitted combination of crisp, white blouse and black pencil skirt was unable to hide the combination of well-placed, straight lines and curves that spoke of a woman who exercised regularly. Her jewelry, a Chopard watch and diamond hoop earrings, was simple and tasteful. In other circumstances, he'd have found this woman, with her sun-kissed bronzed skin and long, wavy honey brown hair, a definite head-turner. But appealing as she may have been, Lena Macy was the last obstacle standing in his way to the chairman's office. So yeah, she was beautiful, but she was still a pain in his ass.

"So how can *I* help *you*?" he asked, a veneer of sincerity coating his question. His demeanor and body language were not lost on Lena. His query was an attempt to put himself in the power position.

"Well, actually, I'm here to talk about how we might be able to help our two respective networks and the corporation as a whole." The sunshine of her smile hid the steely revolve in her eyes. She was no pushover.

"And what magic have you got up your sleeve to accomplish that?"

"A cross-channel promotion that would expose your viewers to some of our new programming directed toward women, and our female viewers familiar with some of your programming jewels."

Poker face were the words that came to mind, as Lena's eyes met his. It was clear that T.J. was processing her proposal, but she had no clue as to his initial reaction.

"Hmmm. Interesting. And how do you see this working?"

Lena took a deep breath, exhaling the nerves gently through a smile. "SFN is planning to add additional programming this upcoming season that speaks more directly to the women sports fans who are basically ignored by the other sports networks; hell, if you think about it, all networks—cable or otherwise.

"We're not addressing a large segment of our audience. A segment that can bring in new and different advertisers to both of our networks. Look, according to a SIMM study by BIGresearch, women are more likely to be regularly or occasionally watching sports than soap operas."

Lena saw T.J.'s eyebrow lift in surprise. Perhaps there was hope after all.

"In that survey sixty-two percent of women said that they watch sports regularly or occasionally on TV, while forty-two percent say they watch soap operas with the same frequency, yet we're only programming to the soap watchers. SFN has plans to change that, and we think it would be a great cross promotion opportunity for LiveYou TV as well."

"Yes, I've seen the same study," T.J. lied, his interest piqued. "And what is this programming that you are suggesting we co-promote?"

"I'm afraid I can't talk about the specific program. We are very close to putting the final pieces together, but it is not yet a done deal. Until then, while extremely hopeful, I am reluctant to declare it a go."

"Hopeful?"

"Confident," Lena revised, smiling broadly to hide the cringe she felt. She knew that this was the main weakness in her pitch. Until they had secured a host for *Sports Watchin' Women*, she was reluctant to talk about her pet project for fear of the concept being stolen. She realized that she must have sounded unprepared but she had no other choice. "But I will tell you that it is a novel concept that is meant to involve women in the sports they, and their men, love; thus making it a more shared experience by all."

"Hmm. But you have no actual show. Might your inquiry be a bit premature?" T.J. asked with a 'why are you wasting my time?' tone to his voice. "I'm sure such an agreement would require shifting the programming schedule so as not to diminish the ratings on the very shows you propose we promote, not to mention on-air promotion schedules and media buys. The list goes on. How can we even begin to discuss any of this without knowing what we are actually working with?"

"Fair point, and yes, I recognize that no real decisions can be made today. My goal was simply to plant the seed and get the talks going."

"Hmm. And why would I want to steer our viewers to a rival network?"

"That's just the mindset I am suggesting that we abandon. Are we separate channels? Yes. Two entirely autonomous companies? Yes. But rivals? Why must that be the way we approach this? The fact is that we are both part of the same broadcasting family. Sibling rivalry has no place when trying to improve PBC's ultimate bottom line. And I am truly *confident* that this plan will help do just that."

"Please don't take this the wrong way, Lena, but aren't you being a tad naïve?" T.J.'s mouth betrayed his poker face with a split-second smirk. He was goading her and his attitude was beginning to irritate her.

"On the contrary. This idea is not without precedent. Other broadcasting companies have promoted their shows on their cable subsidiaries for years."

As previously scheduled, T.J.'s BlackBerry began to chime. Lena knew her time was up. He'd orchestrated everything to put her on the defensive—changing the venue, arriving late, bombarding her with negative questions while giving absolutely no positive feedback, and then ending the meeting abruptly. T.J. had treated her not as an equal but as an underling.

"I'm sorry but I have to get to my next meeting. If I may be candid with you, Lena, we already have a sports show in development. Like you, I can't really reveal much about it. Your idea is not without merit, though I am unclear how we all would benefit. Perhaps when we both have all of our ducks in a row, we can sit down again."

"Of course. I expect to have contracts signed by next week. And will announce the show with the lineup presentation at the all-network meeting. I hope to be able to announce our partnership then as well," she replied, feeling much less confident than she sounded.

"And you think this show is a game-changer for SFN?" he fished.

"Without a doubt. The new additions to the line-up are going to do for sports entertainment what wedding shows did for WE tv. And it will create a new advertising stream."

"Hmm." With his standard, noncommittal reply, T.J. accompanied Lena to the elevator. "A pleasure. I'll be in touch."

Lena shook his hand, thinking it had been anything put pleasurable. Fine, if T.J. Reynolds wanted to play this game with her, she was up for the challenge.

T.J. strut back to his office, a thousand thoughts racing through his head. Lena's idea not only had merit, it was fucking fantastic if—and it was a big if—the programming was strong enough. The thorniest issue he'd had to face in his attempt to turn this den of estrogen around was how to create programming for women that was not more of the same old slop being slung on the competition's airways. How many more wedding, make-over, and cooking shows could the market withstand. And please, if one more producer darkened his doorstep hawking another bitch-fest reality show, he'd put a fucking foot up their ass. Douglas had put him in charge of the "vagina network," as he likened it, to test his skill and creativity. And thus far, he'd come up with zilch that proved his innovative capability to foreman the entire broadcasting empire.

A show centered around men's sports for women. What genius! Damn, Lena was good, but he'd be damned if *any* bitch, whether company or colleague, would keep him from what he'd worked so hard to achieve.

"Sally, get Linda in here, pronto," he barked through the intercom.

Could it be that Lena Macy had handed him the opportunity he'd been searching for? Just the kernel of description she'd supplied had whet his appetite. A sports program that catered to women but welcomed men was just the novel idea that could be the centerpiece of SFN's revival. It could also be the birth of LiveYou's branding as a hip resource for modern-day women. He had to find out more and he had to find out quick. Any move that may be advantageous to his cause had to be accomplished before Lena Macy could unveil her ideas at the all-network meeting.

"You wanted to see me," Linda Barr, LiveYou's vice president of programming, stuck her head in the door to ask.

T.J. looked up from his desk. "Yes, have you seen the BIGresearch study on the number of women who watch sports shows regularly versus those who watch soap operas?"

"No, I haven't."

"Why not? It's your job to follow the research and develop new programming accordingly. Why are we only programming to the soap watchers?" T.J. queried, parroting Lena Macy's words. "Aren't we missing a huge chunk of the audience?"

"Uh, it appears so," Linda said, nervously shifting her weight from foot to foot.

"I'd say absolutely so. One hour, programming meeting here in my office. Bring your senior producers and be ready to present some ideas on how we can capture this audience," T.J. commanded before dismissing his employee and sitting back in his chair to think. Time for Plan B. He buzzed his secretary. "Sally, get me two tickets to Jay-Z's concert and VIP seating at Clementine for tomorrow night."

"Any messages?" Lena asked, walking into her office.

"Where have you been?" Rolanda inquired. "Your phone's been blowing up."

Angered at both herself and T.J. Reynolds, Lena had taken a walk in an effort to shake the negativity and put her head back into the challenges that stood before her. First and foremost, signing Rickie Ross to a contract and starting pre-production on *Sports Watchin' Women*. With or without T.J. Reynolds and LiveYou TV, she was bound and determined to get this pivotal show on the air and make it a hit.

"What's up?"

"Rickie's agent called..."

"Please tell me they didn't cancel."

"No. He wanted to say thanks for the gift bags, that they both appreciated the goodies and that they would both see you on Friday."

"At Nobu 57? I don't want them headed downtown by mistake."

"Yes. At Nobu 57," Ro replied, still miffed that Lena was denying her a private meeting with Rickie. *All in due time*, she thought, remembering the little something extra she'd slipped in Rickie's gift bag.

"Anything else?"

"Aleesa called and needs to discuss the sales presentation with you. Franti Clifton from the NBA called, and I printed out all of your emails since you've been gone and put them on your desk. Oh, and your mom is in your office. She's been here waiting for about twenty minutes."

Lena smiled, thrilled that her best friend, who just happened to be the woman who'd given birth to her, had dropped in. "What brings you by?" she asked, walking through the door and immediately into her mother's arms. Until this very moment, she hadn't realized how much she needed this maternal hug. Building empires, fighting foes and keeping secrets could take a toll on a girl. Nothing soothed one's jagged nerves like a little mama love—*unless it's some fan-fuckingtastic stranger love*—her thoughts interrupted and begged to differ.

"I am not ashamed to admit that I come hat in hand," Tina DuPree informed, wiping a stray lock of hair from her daughter's face. "I'm on my way to my fund-raising meeting for the ballet company and I need you to part with some fabulous prizes for the auction." Tina punctuated her words by wrinkling her nose and turning the high beams on that fabulous, "dare to defy me" grin of hers.

"Of course, what did you have in mind?" she asked, knowing her socialite mother always knew exactly what she wanted before asking. Lena liked to think that much of the boldness she showed in business, along with her high cheekbones, lyrical laugh and perfect hands and feet, was delivered through her maternal DNA. Tina's charm and get-it-done abilities were legendary in the New York social circles that she inhabited.

"Darling, you know it's for a great cause and that with the economy's downturn, this silent auction is the key to our very survival in the coming year.

"I want to put together an entire package...did I tell you that Dior is giving me tickets plus backstage passes to the fall show in Paris AND I've managed to get a private plane and five-star hotel included. Now I need something just as delicious for the gentlemen."

"Something tells me you brought a really big hat."

"Now what I need, darling, are two VIP Super Bowl tickets for next year, in the PBC private box…of course…"

"Of course," Lena parroted with amusement.

"…sideline passes and round trip on the corporate jet."

"No rooms in the players' hotel?"

"I was working on a hotel and limo separately, but can you pull that off?" Tina asked in wide-eyed excitement.

"No ma'am, I don't think I can. In fact, I don't know if I'm even going to be able to meet all of your other requests. Rather pricey, Ma."

"I know, but I hear you have connections." Tina grinned. "I have total faith."

"Let's not even go there."

"Okay. If you don't want to talk about Douglas, tell me what's got you upset?"

Grateful to have the ear of her loyal and trustworthy ally, Lena shared with her mother the status of her ideas meant to turn SFN around. She also revealed her frustrations over her stalled show project and how the competitiveness between her and T.J. Reynolds was coming into play. "I should have never gone to him in the first place. I mean I realize that I wasn't able to give him the total picture, but there was enough detail there to begin to brainstorm the possibilities. But he wouldn't even entertain the idea. He just sat there like a smug, condescending asshole."

"Not a word? No inkling of interest?"

"No, though he did say that they already had a sports program in development themselves."

"And you believe him?"

"It's not like the research was top secret or anything. It's plausible."

"Watch him, Lena. I've come to learn that a totally negative reaction only means one thing—he likes it. A lot."

"You know, I always thought that I was pretty good at reading folks and playing the corporate game, but this time, I'm constantly questioning myself."

"Darling, that's because of this inane competition Douglas set up between you and this T.J. Though, I have to say it's your own fault. You could have avoided all of this by taking what he was willing to give."

"Mom, you know how I feel about that. Let's table it or you can go elsewhere for your auction prizes," Lena said, knowing her threat held no truth.

"Fine. Discussion closed. So how is your father?"

"Don't act like you don't talk to him on the regular, especially about me."

"And you don't act like it's some kind of crime that we do. You are our only child, after all. How's the birthday party coming?"

"Fine, though it's really kind of an afterthought. He and Akira are going hiking in the Himalayas to celebrate his official birthday. Apparently it's going to be small—just family. Are you and Kenneth coming?"

"Yes, darling. I wouldn't miss the old man's seventieth, though I'm sure his Mrs. would love it if I did."

"Daddy and Akira have been married nearly twelve years now, and you and Kenneth for eight. Surely you don't think she still views you as a threat?"

Tina's wide grin filled the room. "Oh, darling, certainly not a threat to her marriage, but maybe her health. It gets chilly standing in the shadows once the sun comes out!"

"Ma, get over yourself." Lena laughed.

"Oh Darling, and what fun would that be?"

Chapter Six

Lena sat in an upstairs booth in the dining room of Nobu 57, waiting for Rickie and his agent. She nervously looked around, trying to soothe her jangled nerves by taking in the trendy, understated décor. The fluid imagery, reminiscent of an Asian river with its flowing curves, carried her eyes to the narrow, wavelike chandeliers made of silvery abalone shells, and the planes of old-style fishing nets draping the ceilings and windows.

Burnished woods, rich hues and soft lighting created an ambiance of hip elegance and serenity.

She'd chosen this celebrity owned and frequented New York eatery with Rickie Ross in mind. Not only had Rolanda's very thorough research revealed his love of sushi, Lena wanted him to know that she recognized his status by choosing to dine where his peers did. She couldn't believe how many stops she'd pulled out for this one man, but hopefully her efforts would be rewarded.

Lena glanced at her watch; eight minutes until their scheduled time of arrival. She wanted to order a glass of wine to take the edge off, but was reluctant to do so, wanting to stay clearheaded for the task that lay ahead. So much was riding on this meal of miso and fish. Lena started going over her pitch again, but her brain locked up, refusing to rehash this information another time until it was for real.

Calm down. Relax. Think of something entirely unrelated, it commanded her.

Immediately, with nary a prod nor push, her Super Bowl sexathon flooded her head, causing her to gush over the month-old memory. Funny how the luscious remembrance of that night had quickly become her safe and sexy haven—the place she escaped to when she needed a mental vacation or sexual satisfaction. She may not have time for two-party sex, but masturbating to her memories was something that had become a regular activity. Each time she made a conscious effort to relive the deliciously scandalous feeling of that encounter. It never felt quite the same, but Lena was still amazed by the fact that she wasn't drawing upon fantasy to escape, but instead real life. Her life. It may be something that she'd never experience again, but the liberation that came with giving into her desire without judgment or justification that one time would stay with her forever.

A montage of scenes from that seduction flashed through her head. Her brazen stroll down the hallway in her underwear. The surprised delight on his face turning her on even more. The way he licked her pussy like it was a bowl of yummy, creamy Häagen Dazs. Spontaneously wrapping those pearls around his dick and feeling them slide against the inner grooves of her pussy. The way she stayed in the moment with every thrust and kiss, not needing to turn herself on by leaving what she was doing and fantasizing about what she might like to do.

"Mmmm…mmmm…good." She breathed into her water glass. She felt the lingering lust from that night gush through her body.

"Ms. Macy?" The deep, rich baritone brushed the back of her neck and caused a shiver to run down her spine. She knew that voice. That very voice had whispered naughty and yet very nice suggestions in her ear; had caused her pheromones to fire and her inhibitions to burn away. That voice had brought out the nasty girl in her; had teased and tempted her to do things to its owner and have things done to her, that she'd never even considered before.

Lena felt a cocktail of nervous excitement and erotic embarrassment shake and stir her stomach. Yeah, she definitely knew that voice.

"Mr. Big Johnson?" She smiled both at the coincidence and the luck.

"Pocahontas?" He laughed. "Wow, the universe is really fucking with us today, isn't it?" There was an awkward moment while he decided the correct protocol. The lover in him wanted to kiss this fabulous freak he'd thought lost to him, but the agent in him was expected to do some serious negotiating. He had to remain neutral. He opted to land in the middle and planted a kiss that lingered just long enough to make it an amicable "friends with benefits" kiss, before sliding onto the bench next to her.

"Why didn't you tell me you were Rickie Ross' agent?"

"Why didn't you tell me you were SFN's Lena Macy?"

The absurdity of the situation struck them both, causing the two to break out into uproarious laughter.

"Jason Armstrong," he revealed, reaching his hand out to hers. "Out of all the gin joints in the world…"

"Yeah. This is a little awkward," Lena admitted.

"Why, cuz we already got all up close and personal without knowing each other's real names? I, for one, loved it and truthfully, can't stop thinking about those pearls or you, Pocahontas." So much for remaining neutral.

Lena took in his words but it wasn't until he licked his lips to punctuate his revelation that she felt herself blush. When he leaned over and put his hand on hers, she thought she was going to melt from the skin-on-skin contact.

"You can't tell me that you don't think about it, too," he challenged.

She crossed her legs in an attempt to cut off the burst of blood to her awakening nib. "I have," she admitted, donning a Cheshire Cat grin.

"Why are you smiling like that?"

Lena couldn't admit that she'd not only been daydreaming about their time together nearly every day since they'd left Miami, but only minutes ago as well. "Like what?" she countered.

"Like you're reading my mind that we should ditch Rickie here while we run cross the street and tear up some hotel room with wild butt-naked sex."

Her nervous giggle gave her away. Right now that's all she ever wanted to do for the rest of her life was climb in bed with this man to fuck and be fucked.

"Actually I was thinking maybe we could go buy you some pearls. Now where's your client?" Lena asked, flirting back while at the same time deflecting his comment.

"He's on his way."

"Great. I'll be right back. Just ah, give me ah, a minute," she said, standing and quickly heading to the ladies room. She had to get herself together before Rickie's arrival. Finding out that Jason was actually her Miami heat was truly mind blowing, but hot stud or not, she still had work to do.

In the bathroom, she let the cool water run through her fingers as she gazed at herself in the mirror. She bit her lip and searched. There it was. That bad girl spark of scandal was back in her eyes and there could be no confusion as to its source.

The ring of her BlackBerry alerted her that she had a message. Lena quickly dried her hands and punched in her password. She clicked open the first message, leaning back on the counter as she read:

Rickie has arrived. Take off your panties. If you return to the dining room with them on, the deal is off. And, Pocahontas, I will be checking. ;-)

As it had in Miami, Jason's bodacious personality turned Lena on. Every sexual challenge he issued, was one she felt compelled and eager to meet. Turning back to the mirror, she searched for the spark in her eyes; the spark that informed her that she was a spontaneous, grown and sexy woman—and a touch slutty one at that. Lena winked at her image before reaching down to pull off her sheer black thong. And with a cool breeze on her ass, she exited the restroom, walking taller and feeling sexier than she'd ever felt in her life.

The two men rose as she approached the table. Lena avoided Jason's inquiring glance but the mischievous purse of her lips gave her actions away. From the corner of her eyes, she could see a victorious smirk scamper across his face.

"Rickie, I am so glad we finally have this opportunity to meet for some serious negotiations. I'm sure you know by now how eager we are to have you join the SFN family of anchors and show hosts."

Rickie's eyes gave Lena a good going over. Other than the fact that she was older than most of the babes he dealt with, with her bangin' body and a face pretty enough to put on one of his kids, she was just his type. He dug these coppertone chicks with their golden brown coifs. They were exotic but still sisterly looking.

"Well, I'd say you already pulled out the stops with this," Rickie said, handing her a small business card. "I've received a lot of gifts and a lot of offers from a lot of media companies, but this was by far the ballsiest."

Lena took it, immediately recognizing Rolanda's business card. Scrawled in her spirally handwriting were the words: 'Rickie, *whatever* it takes, I am more than capable and willing to handle. Ro Hammon.'

Lena felt her jaw drop in total embarrassment. How dare Rolanda do this? The girl was literally resorting to offering sexual favors just to meet this jock. And to make it worse, she did it under the auspices of the network. That weaved head of hers was going to roll this time.

"I am mortified and embarrassed," she apologized. "All I can say is this was definitely not sanctioned and by no means is it an official…uh…offer from SFN. I'm afraid my assistant, who is obviously a huge fan with an even bigger crush, has crossed the line, and I will deal with her as soon as I get back to the office."

"Hey, she ain't the first. Now lay out this show and tell me how and why it's gonna make me a star."

Once the waiter took their lunch order, Lena launched into her pitch. She repeated the viewing patterns she'd discussed with T.J. Reynolds, emphasizing that with Rickie's popularity among women, the show was bound to be a huge hit. It was heartfelt and enthusiastic and she could tell that the player's interest was real.

"The reality is that people are staying home more and experiencing things like sports events together as a couple or family. Women want to be able to fully share this experience and we want you to teach them about the sports that matter to their men and why."

"So you're sayin' that I would host a show for women about sports but it's not just a sports show?"

"Exactly, *Sports Watchin' Women* is a show that not only teaches women the rules and fundamentals of several popular sports, like football, baseball, basketball and NASCAR. But at the same time, we'll give them up close and personal interviews with their favorite players and their families, recipes and tailgate party ideas, stadium fashion shows, and playoff parties with celebrity fans. In and outside of the locker room you'll be the man these women are watching.

"For example, it's March Madness now. This time next year, you'll be helping women pick their brackets…"

"Maybe suggesting some sexy wagers they can bet with their man," Jason threw in with a grin. "By the way, Ms. Macy, as a Hoya fan, I have to ask who you have in the Syracuse vs. Georgetown game?"

"That's a tough one. Both have won the whole thing once. Georgetown has been to the Final Four five times but hasn't won since 1984. Syracuse has been four times and beat Kansas in 2003, so I'm going with Syracuse," Lena answered, though puzzled why Jason would interrupt her pitch to Rickie with inside jokes.

"Wow, woman, you know your stats," Rickie marveled. "That's sexy as hell." He gave her his trademark grin and wink, clearly flirting with her.

Jason felt his stomach tighten, uncomfortable by the jealousy he was feeling.

"Thanks, and with you on the show, just think, you'll be making the world a sexier place one game, one woman at a time. It's sports for women with the Rickie touch," Lena chimed in, taking advantage of the interested look on his face while ignoring the salacious smirk on Jason's.

"I don't know. I can't really see myself cookin' and doing all that chick stuff."

"Tiki Barber sure could," Lena threw out, speaking of the former *Today Show* correspondent.

"Hold up," Jason interrupted. "You're going with Syracuse because they're the most recent champion?"

"No, I'm going with the Orangemen because they have better-looking uniforms," Lena replied, not totally successful in keeping the irritation out of her voice.

Both Jason and his client stopped what they were doing to look at Lena, disbelief scrawled all over their faces. Her face was expressionless, giving the men no clue to if she was joking or not.

"It's a girl thing." She smiled. "One of the quirky things you'll be covering when you're hosting *SWW*. And as host, you'll be able to show off how well rounded you are, which will serve you well down the line as you pursue that television career."

"Still, I wasn't thinkin' about starting off my television career with a chick show," Rickie said, shaking his head.

Lena looked over at Jason to see if he and his client were on the same wavelength. He was on his BlackBerry, and gave Lena a disturbing wink. She looked away, not wanting to let desire derail her deal.

"Okay, I've crunched some numbers and here's what it would take for us to entertain your offer. I've emailed it to you," Jason said. While his agent negotiated, Rickie took the opportunity to send some texts.

Her BlackBerry buzzed. Lena opened the message expecting to see a number containing several zeros. She was shocked to find only words:

I can smell your delicious pussy. How do I order it for lunch? I'm desperate to taste it again.

Lena coughed, trying to hide her surprise and wonder. She wanted to be mad at him for not taking her meeting seriously, but her sexy itch triumphed ire at the moment. "Is this per episode?"

"Yes, unless you have a counter-offer in mind." Jason paused while Lena typed.

Only after you suck my nipples until they are stiff and my clit is throbbing so hard I can't stand it anymore.

She pressed send, and waited for it to run through cyberspace and hit his phone. Lena was amazed by her message, not believing that she'd said nothing about his pleasure, nothing about how she'd service him. To those who didn't know her, her response might have sounded hugely selfish, but in all the years she'd been having sex, Lena had never put her pleasure first. Had never been concerned about getting satisfied, only giving satisfaction. After all, wasn't that a woman's role?

His phone buzzed as Lena felt his hand slip under her skirt and creep toward her unfettered nookie. Light as a feather, he dusted her inner thighs, coming close enough to whisper across her pussy lips but stopping just short. The public setting, Rickie sitting so close, and Jason's teasing touch was driving her crazy and she fucking loved it.

Lena slightly spread her legs in invitation. Jason's fingers RSVP'd by slipping inside her wet and warm box. With a gentle flick of his thumb, he caressed her clitoris, feeling it jump and causing Lena to camouflage her moan with a cough. Her hand drifted across his thigh into his lap, feeling his dick rise to the occasion as she rubbed his balls.

"We appreciate your offer," Jason said, feeling her legs twitch. "Rickie and I will discuss it and get back to you."

Lena was confused. Why was Jason shutting down the meeting like this, particularly when it was clear that Rickie was not yet convinced that this was the gig for him? Still, she followed his lead and played along. "Great. How long will you be in New York?"

"We're on the next plane back to Chicago."

"That's too bad," Lena said, pushing her pelvis closer to his hand while fighting with her face to remain still and expressionless.

"Okay, so like Jason said," Rickie piped in, closing his phone and getting back in the conversation. The snap of his phone forced Lena's hand back onto the table. "We'll rap when we get back to Chicago, and then get back to you with an answer."

Jason gave her pussy lips a gentle squeeze before pulling his hand from under her skirt. "Yeah, this entire meeting had a *great* feel to it."

"I agree, and I will expect to hear from you soon," Lena said, replying to both with a message meant for Jason's ears. "Oh, and just so we're clear, I'm pulling on Syracuse because they have averaged a show in the Final Four every nine-and-a-half years, while Georgetown averages every thirteen. And, of course, because their uniforms are cuter."

Chapter Seven

In the cab back to the office, Lena's business brain crept back into her head. She'd gone to Nobu 57 on a mission and other than getting her twat tweaked, she was going back to the office with nothing. What was it about that man—still a stranger in so many ways—that hijacked her good sense and turned her into a sex fanatic? Her BlackBerry started buzzing with a multitude of messages. She managed to respond to four before deciding to send one of her own. The man may be sexy as hell but apparently, he was no professional.

Why did you shut the meeting down like that? Rickie was far from being convinced about this position. But instead of helping him see the merits of this offer, you were too busy with your hand between my legs. Highly unprofessional.

Before she'd traveled a New York block, a reply from Jason, marked urgent, came through.

Lena, I realize that most of my behavior this afternoon was totally unprofessional, but you must know that being close to Pocahontas again, and so unexpectedly, made me so fucking hot that I couldn't help myself. That said, know that contrary to what you think, I actually was acting on your benefit.

"Who are you trying to kid, Jason Armstrong?" her mouth shot back while her fingers typed.

Besides trying to make me cum right there in public, how were you possibly acting on my behalf? Lena looked out of the window and watched New York go by as she awaited his response.

Look, in all seriousness, I never take my eye off the ball, even when I'm holding the most beautiful pussy I have ever seen in my hands. I know my client. Rickie was not feeling that show, at least not with what you were emphasizing in your pitch. I knew that if you kept pushing he was going to turn off and walk away without even considering it. So I changed the subject. I will talk to him and present to him all the pros and cons I see with this deal, and he will make his decision. As his agent, I do think there is a lot of potential in this hosting job, and you were right to cite Tiki as an example. The more versatile Rickie is, the more options he has open in the future. But it is ultimately his decision. So you let me do my job, and I promise we will try to make this thing work.

Lena read Jason's email, her irritation turning into admiration. She'd misjudged him. His explanation made perfect sense and she was grateful that he'd followed his obviously professional instincts and kept the deal alive. But before Lena could respond with her sincere apologies, her BlackBerry buzzed again.

And now that I've done my job, I'd like to get back to you and me. I'd like to officially make a bet on the Georgetown versus Syracuse game. Winner decides on place and pleasure. And if it's anything like last time, win or lose, prepare to win!

Giggling to herself, Lena replied.

No worries. And I apologize. We were both a bit unprofessional today, but hell, why wait to be scandalous until you're old! Re: Hoyas versus Orangemen. You're on. Care for a point spread?

She sent the message and moved on to the next few, grinning and shaking her head. Why wait to be scandalous? What was she saying? Unless you counted stealing a glitter lip gloss from the drugstore when she was twelve, and of course their night at the Setai, Lena Macy hadn't had a scandalous day in her life. When her phone buzzed, she saved her current message as a draft, instinctively knowing the incoming email was from Jason.

I love me a bold woman! Hey, the only spread I am interested in is you out on my bed. That said, knowing that Georgetown will beat Syracuse (despite their apparent lack of fashion sense), I thought I'd send a list to aid you in satisfying your upcoming debt. So behold: A Few of My Favorite Things

Ice cold Vodka, straight up with a twist (sipped preferably in bed)

Calvin Klein briefs not boxers (BTW: Believe it or not, I'm picky about who comes between me and my Calvins :-))

Lump crabmeat with lemon and cocktail sauce with lots of horseradish

The blue, blue waters of the Caribbean

Skinny dipping in those same waters

Toenails painted red (hers, not mine!)

Gucci loafers

Black lacy bras and panties (to ogle not wear!)

A little pain with my pleasure

Eating lipsmackin' good pussy

Secret tattoos

A public angel and secret whore

A woman bold enough to state her desires

Spending at least one Sunday a month in bed making love

Hearing the words "fuck me" and talking dirty

Sucking pretty, toffee-colored nipples

Slapping a beautiful ass

Jelly Belly jelly beans

Now, care to share some of yours?

Lena bit her lip as she leaned back into the taxi seat. This was quite a list—not only for its sexy and suggestive content, but also for what it said about the author. *Spending at least one Sunday a month in bed making love.* Now that was a weekend ritual that she could really wrap her arms around. The last time she'd done anything like that was—well, never. No one had ever engaged her lust in such a profound way that she'd ever wanted to devote an entire day to the pursuit of his orgasmic delight.

A woman bold enough to state her desires. She'd been that woman in Miami. Never had she felt like such a grown and sexual woman. There was something about Mr. Johnson that shut down her inhibitions and brought out her adventurous side. It had been only one time, true, but even today at lunch, she'd acted bold and a bit reckless. So was it the man or the stranger sex? Would she behave the same with Jason as she had with Mr. Johnson? There was only one way to find out.

Lena sat back and pondered. Nearly all the women she knew and had intimate details of their sex lives, were like her. Yes, they got horny sometimes, but for the most part, sex was something they had when their man wanted to. None of her friends spoke candidly of their sexual needs to their lovers, and asked for what they wanted in bed as a truly bold woman would. For them, communicating about sex with their partners was paramount to talking about it with their parents. How sad was it that in her circle of friends nobody measured up to the daring kind of woman that turned on Jason and most men, she would imagine.

Nobody except Rolanda Hammon.

The fusion of sex and work thoughts brought Lena out of her sexual meditations and back into reality. Her fingers angrily punched out the number to her office. Despite that all the sexting with Jason had left her feeling unsettled in a multitude of ways, she had to get her head back into work. She'd achieved her mission with Rickie and now she was headed back to the office to deal with Rolanda.

The phone rang until Ro's away message came on, announcing that she was not at her desk. Lena left a curt message. "I'm on my way back, and when I get there, I want to see you *immediately*."

She disconnected the call thinking that in a strange way Pocahontas could relate to, and even admire, her assistant's sexual bravado. Rolanda's actions gave voice to her inner sexual self without apology or judgment. Ro's motto seemed to be "the pussy wants what the pussy wants," and she allowed her wants to be satiated on the regular.

Lena, the boss, on the other hand, found the girl's actions totally unacceptable. Fuck whoever you want on your own time, but bringing her sex life into the office had totally crossed the line. Rolanda had literally offered a highly regarded and sought-after job candidate sex, and offered it in a manner that appeared tied to the acceptance of the job. Though she thought it a long shot, Lena was not sure of any possible legal ramifications. She was certain that Rickie Ross, if he wanted to, could create a major ruckus over this, not to mention the field day the press would have with such a scandal. And had the football star's ego not been so huge or his agent's interest in her so personal, this deal could have been lost. Most importantly, the Sports Fan Network's reputation could have been seriously damaged due to Rolanda's whorish behavior. And that was an unthinkable outcome.

Lena vacillated between suspending and outright firing her, but there were too many important things coming up that demanded Rolanda's expertise and experience.

While Lena rationalized the upcoming workload as a reason for keeping Rolanda employed, she knew full well that Douglas Paskin would see it as an unacceptable excuse, and hold both Rolanda and Lena responsible. It was common knowledge that when it came to business dealings, Douglas valued his pristine reputation as a tough but fair man. Yes, he was ambitious and hard-working, and could drive a hard bargain, but his integrity was unquestionable. Yes, he could be controlling, and when it came to his personal life—über private, secretive even. Douglas and his family had not, and would never be in the future, fodder for the tabloid media. It was also his decree that neither would PBC nor any of its subsidiaries would be either. Not even a hint of scandal would be tolerated and his wrath unleashed in past episodes had been swift and career deadly. Reputation was everything to this son of a naval officer and his expectations were equally high for his family and his employees. Lena would have to handle this with the utmost discretion and pray that word of the incident never got out.

"PROPOSITIONING A POTENTIAL HIRE WITH SEX?" LENA BORE INTO her. "Just tell me what the hell you were thinking?"

Rolanda stayed calm and held her ground, the slight smirk on her face the only clue of her irritation. "I didn't offer him sex."

"I'm not stupid, Ro. You implied it. You said you'd do 'whatever,' double underlined, it took to get him here that you were more than capable of handling."

"Yeah, so. I said nothing about sex, and anyway, isn't that what you said yourself...that you'd give up whatever you had to to bring him on board?"

Lena stared her down with disbelief. Was she really trying to both refute and excuse her behavior? "I should fire you, but I'm not, at least not today. Rolanda, you're going to finish out the day and then you're suspended for one week without pay. When you return, you will be on probation for the rest of the year."

"That's not fair," Ro argued, already feeling the dent in her bank account. Rent and recreation in this town were not cheap. And she certainly wasn't trying to get fired in this ugly employment environment.

"Well, considering that I'm not bringing human resources into this, *yet*, nor am I firing you, I think it's a pretty good deal. As far as they'll know, you're taking unpaid leave. Now I'm going downstairs to my programming meeting. You need to get back to work, and don't let anything like this happen again. Is that understood?"

"Yeah." Rolanda left the office in a silent huff. Damn Rickie for putting her on blast like that, and damn Lena Macy for making such a big fucking deal about it, particularly since she was cozying up with old Mr. Paskin to get what she wanted.

She plunked herself down in her chair in front of the computer to print out Lena's emails. Before she could log in the phone rang. "Lena Macy's office."

"I'd much rather speak to her hot and sexy assistant," T.J. Reynolds' voice whispered through the phone.

"Speaking."

"What color panties are you wearing?"

"Who says I'm wearing any?"

"I guess I'll find out for myself tonight."

"Really?"

"Yeah, when I take you to dinner and then the Jay-Z concert."

"Better yet," Rolanda purred, her mood doing a 180-degree turn. "Why waste time on food? Let's fuck first and then do the concert."

"Oh hell yeah! Much better idea. Be out front at six."

Rolanda threw her head back and laughed. Men were so fucking easy. Give 'em a little shock and awe and they were literally eating out of your drawers. *I wonder what Ms. Macy would have to say about this?*

She turned back to the computer and logged into Lena's mailbox. Oddly enough, there were several emails from Rickie's agent within minutes of each other, all with Mr. Big Johnson in the subject line. She clicked open the first message.

"Holy shit! 'If you're wearing any panties the deal is off'? What the fuck?"

Rolanda kept clicking and reading, her eyes and mouth growing wider with each word. "'Smell your delicious pussy'? Oh fuck, 'suck my nipples 'til they're stiff'? And who the hell is Pocahontas? Yeah, some of my favorite things, all right."

If she hadn't been so pissed, Rolanda might have felt turned on, but the boss lady had a lot of nerve lambasting her for writing that note to Rickie. Lena knew damn well that yes, she was offering Rickie her sex, but it had nothing to do with getting him to work here. It was a straight-up personal matter. She simply wanted to fuck him and see where it led. But it looked like Lena was all about fucking the roadie to get to the rock star.

"Damn, girl, first old man Paskin and now the agent. Who's fucking herself to the top now, Lena Macy? What a hypocrite." Rolanda finished muttering under her breath long enough for her plan to crystallize. She printed out a copy of the email to put into a file she marked, "insurance," and then deleted them. Clearly, Lena, who had never had any personal emails sent to the office, had forgotten that emails that appeared on her BlackBerry were coming to her office computer as well. She didn't need to remember, at least not until Rolanda was ready to remind her.

The Tonight Show with Jay Leno WAS ON, BUT WITH NO ATTENTION being paid. Lena sat on her bed, computer in her lap and a bowl of plain M & Ms by her side. Chocolate was definitely a necessity, considering the hot and horny email she was attempting to compose.

Confidence in a man is sexy, but so is his ability to lose with grace and humility. I guess we're about to find out just how sexy you are, Mr. Johnson. RE: your list. I appreciate your sharing and I am happy to return the gesture. I totally concur with your thought that knowing the things that turn me on will make your payment all the more pleasurable. So here are a few of mine.

Lena grabbed a handful of M & M's and mindlessly washed them down with a swig of Coke Zero as she gauged her emotions. *Delight* was the first word that popped in her head. This sexual flirtation felt good and right and surprisingly natural as she began her list.

Sipping ice cold Gran Patron tequila straight up with a twist of orange (Preferably sipped nude and in the company of a familiar stranger!)

"Good one, Lena," she praised herself before continuing.

Brazilian tango panties

San Francisco sourdough bread

The Amalfi Coast

Men brave enough to tell me their secrets and sensitive enough to keep mine

A public superman and secret softie

Lump crabmeat with creamy avocado served in a martini glass

Stilettos (preferably sandals)

Black lacy bras and panties (to wear and be ogled!)

A man who doesn't feel it necessary to immediately remove said bra and panty

Chocolate!

Mango, strawberries (dipped in chocolate doesn't hurt either!)

Figs wrapped in prosciutto

Long, hot, luxurious candlelit bubble baths

She stopped and read over her list, thinking that while interesting, she was avoiding the true purpose of the exercise—to reveal some of her sexual preferences. Lena laughed as her bad girl, playing Cyrano, took control of her fingers and typed.

Having my pussy licked by someone who understands that my clit is bashful and doesn't like to be manhandled. Who knows that she has to

*be coaxed out to play, and that if you play too rough, she'll get tired and
go home.*

A gentle tongue on my clit, sucking, licking, swirling...

Getting my nipples sucked or pinched while said activity is going on

Whoa! Coy flirtation had turned to outright cock teasing. Ohh!
Pocahontas was a naughty little ho! Lena was turning herself on
and enjoying the thrill of cyber sexual abandon. She finished up,
amazed by the words that flowed from her fingertips without
consulting her head.

Fucking on top

Fucking between my tits

Feeling like a nasty girl

*There you have it. In no particular order nor is it complete! Gleam
from it what you will and be prepared to serve some of them up when
Georgetown gets its ass waxed!*

Lena sent the sexy communiqué on its way, powered down her
BlackBerry and turned out the light. First, she slipped into bed,
and then she slipped her hand down her pajama bottoms to coax
her little girl out to play.

Chapter Eight

T.J.'s dick grew harder and longer in her mouth as Rolanda took him deeper into her throat. The sound of wet oral fucking drifted throughout the back of the limousine. Rolanda felt his ass clench and heard the grunts of a man about to lose control. She let her mouth widen away from his dick for a moment and then gently ran her teeth up and down his shaft and head.

"Hmm. Hmm. HMMMPH!"

Ro smiled, knowing that she was steps closer to having T.J. Reynolds under her pussy control. Whoever said that the way to a man's heart was through his stomach was one totally lame bitch.

"Ah FUCK YEAH!" he screamed as his crotch gyrated in her face. She returned his grunts with moans of her own, knowing that T.J. thinking that sucking dick was just as much a pleasure for her as it was for him would set him the fuck off. A quick tickle of his balls and T.J. went stiff, shooting his warm, salty cum down her throat. Rolanda took it all in and sat up, looking directly in his eyes and licking her lips for extra emphasis.

"Lena Macy doesn't know what a gem she has in you," T.J. said, planting the seed while wiping the spunk off her chin.

"The bitch is not my type, but you ain't never lied about that."

"Trouble at work?" he fished, while popping a cork on another bottle of Dom. "We will have none of that. Here, drink this," he said, handing her a flute. The vision of her fucking the bottle in Lena's office flashed across his brain, making his dick twitch. "I want your mind to be just on us tonight, not any work woes."

Rolanda sat back bare ass on the seat; the panther tattooed on her left breast peeking out of her disheveled brassiere. The two toasted their great evening together. The concert had rocked and so had the limousine. Not bothering to wait to get to any hotel, they had turned the limo into a fuck palace right there on the curb in front of Madison Square Garden. Another reason to love tinted windows!

Rolanda gave him a champagne kiss, touching his open lips to hers and dribbling the drink from her mouth into his. Her tongue took care of the wayward drops and T.J. felt his dick twitch again. He filled her glass again; this time transferring the golden bubbles to her. Three glasses later, she was ready to talk.

"Baby, you seem down tonight," T.J. probed.

"I got shushpended," Rolanda volunteered, giving a slurred confession.

"Suspended? How long? For what?" He didn't like the sound of that. T.J. needed Rolanda on the inside with full access, at least until he knew what the hell was going on over there.

"For a week over some bullshrit. And bitch haasss brig nerve considering she's fucking everything that…everyone—agents, probably even players. I don't get it though. She ain't all that, but even ole head whitey in charge has jungle fever." Rolanda paused to take another sip of champagne, managing to spill much of it down her chin.

"Paskin?"

"Well, old as he is…"—she stopped to lick the bubbles from her chin—"Bitch gotta be ridin' the big dildo to the top!"

"Are you sure about this?"

"Defin…it…itely. I saw him…try to hug up her…hug her in the office, but she was playin' all coool and frigid. Or so I thought," Rolanda continued swinging her glass and splashing champagne on the window. "…'til I read the emails from Jason—or Mr. Johnson as she calls him. All about titty suckin' and pussy lickin' and dicks."

"Damn!" T.J. swallowed a chuckle. *It's always the quiet ones!*

"I didn't see anything from that fine-ass Rickie 'fuck me' Ross, but I wouldn't not… be surprizzzzed that she fucked him, too, not as bad as she wants him…for that new show. And then she has the…the…nerve to stuspend me."

Rolanda reached over his chest for the champagne bottle but T.J. stopped her with a kiss. Based on the slurring and breakdown in polite discourse, she was already too drunk to risk her drinking more. This little whore had been a goldmine of information tonight. Not only had she revealed that his corporate rival was an old-fashioned freak, willing to go old school and climb the corporate ladder on her back, Ro had just cracked the safe on the information he'd actually been after.

"Oh, yeah, that sports and women show she met with me about," he slipped in after removing his tongue from her mouth.

"Yeah. She's good, I'll give her that. *Sports Washin' Women* is gonna be a big hit, 'specially if she signs up fine-ash Rickie."

"*Sports Washin' Women*?"

"Noooooo. *Watchin'*, silly. *Watchin'*. A show to teach us how to understand…you know rules and stuff…and rules of sports and you stuff like…like…um…" Ro's eyes closed, signaling that between the sex and drink she was about to crash.

"Stuff like what, baby?"

"You know like…um…girl stuff…clothes and parties…some kind of parties…tailgrates…and interviews with the…play…player and what they do after playing. How they play after playing." The nonsensical phrasing made her crack up and flop back into the soft leather seats of the limousine.

"Look, you let Daddy take care of Lena Macy. I'll make sure she can't hurt you."

"K," she said before drifting off with a quiet snore.

"*Sports Watchin' Women*," T.J. said with satisfaction as he leaned back into the seat as well. He felt happy and satiated. Almost like he'd cum again.

"Lena Macy," she said, picking up her line.

"Happy Monday. Why are you slumming and answering your own phone?"

Jason's voice caused a wave of white to ripple across her face. "My secretary is on…a…vacation this week."

"Well, it's nicer to hear your voice anyway. So I got your email. *Very* enlightening to say the least. I particularly liked the instructional bits. I like knowing what pleases you."

"Same."

"I'd have called you this weekend after the game, but I only have your work number."

Lena paused, not really sure that she wanted to move in that direction yet. It seemed crazy, considering that they'd already been totally intimate with each other, but they were still strangers nonetheless. She needed a little more time to be convinced that he should have an all-access pass. "Perhaps you'll win that information in a future bet," she countered, pleased with her coy response.

"Sounds like a worthwhile wager," Jason responded, a bit disappointed that Lena hadn't come through with her home digits. He tried to understand her reluctance, and be encouraged that she hadn't closed the door all the way.

"So are you going to finally get to the real purpose of your call?" Lena taunted him.

"Yeah, yeah, yeah. Congratulations."

Lena could not help smiling into the phone. There was something about hearing Jason's playful voice that made the sun shine within her. "You know what this proves, don't you?" she said, savoring her recent win.

"What? That your theory on style over substance has merit?"

"Hey, when you feel good about your outfit, you can face your opponent with confidence. Every woman knows that. And, how can you even suggest that Syracuse has no substance? My team did open up a big ole can of whup ass on yours."

"Winning by four points does not an ass-whupping make," Jason countered, his grin coming through loud and clear as well.

"You lost, didn't you?"

"Yeah."

"Well, then I say you got your ass whupped!" Lena insisted, enjoying their playful competitiveness.

"And I'd say, not yet but I'm hoping to soon," he said, turning the conversation in an entirely different direction. "Speaking of which, I thought we better lay down some ground rules before the big payout."

"What kind of ground rules? I thought it was winner takes all—place and pleasure at *her* discretion."

"I just hope you'll have my favorite things list posted above the bed, Ms. Pocahontas."

"Dude, you're confused. I'm the winner. My list should be the one pinned up."

"You know, we should give you a new handle—how about 'She Who Sells Wolf Tickets.'"

"Funny, Mr. Johnson. Now what are these rules you are proposing?"

"Just so we're on the same page, I'm suggesting the following set of guidelines…"

"Go on."

"Winner must be paid in full no more than two weeks following an outcome."

"We should add that in the case of a scheduling conflict, the payment can be made at the earliest mutual date possible," Lena suggested.

"Agreed."

"Winner gets to decide place and pleasure."

"Yes, and now Clause No4U. Winner or loser," Jason added, "has the option of backing out anytime if he or she feels threatened or compromised. No questions asked, no trying to change minds."

"No for you? Cute, and a really considerate addition," Lena said softly.

"All jokes aside, Lena, this game between us is freaky, yes, but mostly it's supposed to be fun and pleasurable for both of us. We really just met and I don't know you well, but I do know that if you don't feel safe and secure, you'll never let that nasty girl you like so much out to play."

Lena sat back on her office phone and listened, appreciative of Jason's thoughtfulness. He was mostly right. He hadn't known her long but he seemed to know her as well or better than any man who'd shared her bed in the past.

"Are we in agreement?" Jason asked.

"Yep."

"So then, what's your pleasure?"

Lena felt a tingle creep up her legs and tickle her clit. The thought of being pressed up against Jason's hard body again excited her. "That is yet to be determined, but why don't we pick a date now."

"Cool. As per the rules, two weeks from today?"

"I have to be in Montreal for a meeting then. How about we

move the party to Canada?" Lena suggested, liking the idea of removing herself from the familiar so her freaky could stay fresh.

"Works for me."

"Okay, I have to run. My phone is lit up like a scoreboard," she told him, missing Ro like hell right then, "but I will be in touch with more details."

"Cool. And Pocahontas..."

"Yes?"

"I don't need to pin up your list. I've memorized it," Jason informed her, his voice lowered to a husky whisper, "and look forward to making some of your favorites, mine. Talk later."

Lena hung up the phone, feeling herself blush while reveling in a moment of exquisite anticipation. "Good to know," she whispered back.

Chapter Nine

As Friday's sunlight slipped away, Lena was happy to kick off her pumps and settle back into the huge and comfy pillows adorning Aleesa's family-room floor. It was early April, but Aleesa had lit the fireplace anyway, giving the room a warm, relaxing ambiance. A girls' night in eating Chinese food and simply chilling was just the thing she needed after such a tough week at the office.

Without Rolanda around to take care of the day-to-day operations and put out the hundreds of tiny fires that erupted each day, getting to her own work had been difficult. Lena was forced to stay in the office late into the night playing catch-up. Ro would be back at her desk on Monday, and as much as she hated to admit it, Lena was looking forward to her return.

"I think you can forget T.J. working with us," Aleesa said, dipping into her moo goo gai pan. "He's a dick wad anyway."

"Yeah, he's totally blowing me off. I guess since he has his own sports show to promote he can't be bothered."

"I don't think he has a show at all. I have a friend over there whom I used to work with at ABC. She's heard nothing about any damn show. He was just giving the party line to put you off. I agree with your mother. He likes the idea a lot but doesn't want to give you any kind of leg up by helping it be successful."

"But successful not only for SFN but for his network as well," Lena argued.

"But it's *your* idea, not his. That makes all the difference."

"Well, it would've been nice, but we can do it without him. Getting Rickie on board was all I was really worried about; thank God for Jason."

"Big props on getting your man." Aleesa raised her martini glass and toasted her friend. "Here's to bagging the player and his agent!"

The tinkle of glass filled the silence as the women drank. Aleesa used the opportunity to figure out how far she would delve into Lena's personal life. She was dying to know if Pocahontas and Mr. Big Johnson were planning a repeat performance, but was reluctant to infringe on her friend's privacy. She knew she was living vicariously through Lena's new hot and heavy sex life, but until Walt came back, Lena's sexcapades were all she had. And besides, what were friends for?

"Speaking of which, we made another bet. He lost."

"So now he owes you sex. So much for one little memory," Aleesa replied, glad that Lena had opened the door. "So what's his I.O.U.?"

"I don't know; I still have to decide. But he's going to meet me up in Montreal when I'm there for the Budweiser party."

"Their annual networks shindig? Isn't Douglas going to be there with you? How are you going to pull that off?"

"No, not this year. He and the Mrs. are going to be in Peru. Believe me, I have no intention of the two of them meeting."

"Douglas is not going to like the idea of another man in your life."

"He has no choice. It's time for me to move on. And anyway, technically there isn't a new man in my life."

"Hmm, hmm. So, what are you planning for your date?"

"It's not really a date—more like appointment sex."

"But you like him," Aleesa stated quietly, and waited for Lena's reaction. She knew her friend, and Lena talked about this man like she had no other in a very long time. The question to be answered was: would she admit it?

"I do, but the fact is that it's a 'relationship'—if you can even call it that—centered around sex."

"So test him."

"What are you talking about, Lees?"

"He owes you, right? Well, ask him to do something nice for you that lets you know another side of him."

"Nasty and nice," Lena blurted out with a mouth full of cashew chicken. "Now there's a party theme for you! I do something nasty for him…"

"And he does something nice for you. Hopefully he'll come up with something that gives you a hint to his feelings."

"I love it! So help me with the nasty part. What should I do?"

"What does he like?"

"I don't know. Probably everything. Boy is definitely freaky."

"He sent you a whole damn list! What was on it?" Aleesa got up to refill their drinks. She was enjoying the hell out of their evening, as most of hers were spent alone trying to keep the longing for her soldier husband down to a minimum.

"My favorite thing on his list was spending one Sunday a month in bed making love."

Aleesa looked at her friend through soft and caring eyes. Lena was definitely falling for this guy.

"Well, that sounds like it belongs on the nice side. What's he got going on in the nasty column?"

Two cocktails later, Lena had run through Jason's Favorite Things list and the two had tossed around ideas that, while sounding good in theory, Lena didn't feel confident or capable enough to execute.

"He likes the idea of girl scout on the outside and a porn star on the inside. The whore/Madonna thing, which sounds a bit archaic if you ask me."

"Nobody's perfect."

"And he likes, as he put it, a little pain with his pleasure. But the whole S and M thing doesn't really interest me."

"Okay, well, do something along the same lines that does agree with you."

"Like?"

"Like a little light bondage maybe?"

"Aren't they the same thing?" Lena asked, curious not only about the answer but also by Aleesa's depth of knowledge on the subject.

"Well, technically, sadomasochism is basically sex that involves pain and/or humiliation and a *willing* partner. You know, the master/sex slave scenario."

"Punishing the disobedient servant thing."

"Yeah. That's one scenario," Aleesa said with a giggle. "Now bondage is using stuff like handcuffs or ropes, whatever you want to restrain your partner. It kind of has an S and M flavor to it, but there's no pain involved unless, you know, you both want it. So bottom line is even though they seem to be used together a lot, they really aren't the same thing.

"So tie him up and have your way with him. He gets what he wants and you aren't doing anything that makes you feel uncomfortable."

Lena took a moment to finish her martini and look at her friend with new eyes. *Damn, you think you know someone...*

"What?"

"You know damn well, what. You're over fifty! Where the hell? What...? How do you know about all this shit? And does your husband know you know?"

"First of all, biatch, being over fifty means nothing! You're as sexy as you feel, no matter your age. And shit, if I can't be a slut now, when? Secondly, research. I've been doing a lot of studying up on the subject."

"For Walt's freak book?"

"Yeah."

"Whoa. This thing goes a lot deeper than I ever imagined, though trust me, I'm not trying to picture your and Walt's sex life!"

"Look, Walter's been in Afghanistan nearly eighteen months now. I miss the hell out of him, in and out of the bed. I can't have sex but I can think about it. And do. A lot. I love sex! I crave it! Probably because it's on my mind all the time. When I'm not working I'm fantasizing about all the ways I'd like to pleasure and be pleasured by my man. And it turns out I have quite a vivid imagination. I've been writing my fantasies down as kind of a welcome home gift for him. He's in every one of them and my hope is that we'll try a few out when he returns stateside and before, you know, I become the cane-wielding senior citizen you obviously think I am."

"Don't be so sensitive," Lena teased as she let her eyes wander around the room to check out the many framed photos of their family. Lieutenant Colonel Walter Davis, her second husband, was an oral surgeon and Army reservist, who'd become Aleesa's, and truth be known, Lena's hero when he met and married her and her two now grown kids. He'd rescued them from the aftermath of a nasty fall-out following her divorce from her first, lying, cheating, whore-mongering husband. Walt had brought love, trust and tranquility back into their lives. But it turned out that Aleesa was just as much a heroine, and despite their long separations, Walt and Aleesa were truly happy and fiercely committed to each other.

Not that she could blame Walt for falling for her friend. There were many things that were simply average about Aleesa—her height, the size of her bust, feet and hands. The color of her hair was basic black, her eyes an unremarkable brown. Her lips, ears and nose were regular and serviceable. God knows her interior decorating (a lime green and brown kitchen, really?), bartending (a bit too much vermouth in the martini) and cooking skills (plating microwaveable dinners was not cooking) were absolutely nothing to toot her horn over.

No, what set Aleesa Davis apart from the crowd, and lifted her from the average heap, was her loving and charming spirit. Those regular brown eyes and facial features that gave shape to a smooth face, the exact color of a Hershey's chocolate kiss, became unique and unforgettable in the glow of her welcoming smile. And her curvy body that was neither plump nor overtly shapely while still, became sensuality in motion when she traveled across the room. Lena teased but, Aleesa, with her energetic ways and youthful point of view, was the personification of the saying "fifty was the new forty." She could only hope she held up as well.

"That's really sweet. He's going to love it and you for doing it. So what kind of nasty bondage fantasies have you been writing about that you can share?"

"Well, without going into all of the gory details, I do have this fantasy about taking complete control," Aleesa began, before downing the rest of her drink.

"Walt is in the garage working on something or other, and I come out dressed in his camouflage jacket and heels. He asks me what I want, and I don't answer him in words, but instead open the jacket and flash him. When he sees that I am totally naked underneath the coat, he comes toward me, but I stop him.

"Of course he protests, but I tell him if he wants to see more, he has to

sit down in the lawn chair. He's happy to comply and sits down, his hands still reaching for my body. I slap his hands away and warn him that if he doesn't follow orders, he won't see what else I have in store for him. So, of course, curiosity wins and he sits down, and I tie his hands to the chair.

"Once he's all tied up and secure, I climb onto the hood of his car and lay out, like that famous poster of the girl on the Porsche. I slowly remove the jacket and then start playing with my titties—lifting them up and squeezing them together. I push them up to meet my mouth and tongue down my own nipples. This, of course, gets a big reaction, and I hear him groaning. It's a sound that really turns me on and to mess with him, I yell at him for looking at me and tell him to close his eyes.

"Well, he does, but we both know it's not for long, cuz as soon as I let out a big moan, they pop open and he sees me begin to explore the rest of my body, caressing myself, running my hands over my body while pretending they are his. When I can't stand it anymore, I start masturbating in front of him, rubbing my kit cat, that's what he calls my pussy, and playing with Clitina…"

"Clitina?"

"Shut up! That's his name for my clit. Now do you want to hear this or not?"

"Yes."

"Okay, so again, I yell at him for watching me, but this time, to punish him, I slip off the car and go over and put a sleep mask over his eyes. He protests and begs me to let him watch, but I won't.

"So now I stand there in front of him, rubbing and tugging and finger fucking myself into a 'she's gotta have it' state, all the while moaning and groaning and letting him hear how hot and horny I'm getting. He's going crazy, squirming in his seat and begging me to take off the mask. I tell him to shut up and when I can't take it anymore, I take my wet fingers and smear his lips with my kit cat juice and then give him a real taste by sticking my finger between his lips. He is so *relieved to do something with his mouth that he sucks my finger hard, almost like a dick, and with each pull I feel Clitina getting longer and harder. Teasing him like this is so damn stimulating. I am so hot.*

"Anyway, I pull my finger from his mouth and replace it with my titty. He sucks on that hard, too, and my kit cat is going crazy standing there with nothing petting it. So I pull away, which gets him begging for me to come back, and undo his pants and pull them down to the ground. He thinks he's getting fucked but I'm not ready to give up the coochie yet, so I spread his legs and straddle his thigh so I can grind up against his leg. I grind my clit up against his hard muscles feeling my juices drip down his leg. He moans and I decide to take off the mask so he can see what's going on.

"He has this look on his face that is a mix of wild lust mixed with surprise and love, and I pump harder into his leg to increase the friction. He bends down and consumes my breast again, this time leaving bite and hickey marks all around it. It hurts but in a good way. And all that sucking and biting lights a rocket fire in my crotch and I come all over his legs and collapse against his body.

"As I am recovering, Walt manages to loosen the ties around his arms. He picks me up and tosses me gently back onto the hood of the car and proceeds to pound and lovefuck me like never before."

Aleesa finished, leaving out the part about her neighbor watching and eventually joining them. She didn't feel it necessary to reveal all of her dirty little secrets. The two women sat in silence, each imagining the fantasy scenario and simmering in the lust the story had aroused within them.

"Well alrighty then," Lena proclaimed, sending them both into fits of edgy giggles. "I am scared of you!"

"I need a refill," Aleesa said, fanning herself as she got up to grab the shaker.

"And bring back some of that chocolate cake!"

Chapter Ten

T.J. Reynolds looked out into the audience and smiled. He had charged his publicity department to get the folks out for this all-important announcement, and they had certainly done their job. The room was packed with trade and entertainment press from publications big and small. They were there to spread the word that LiveYou TV was the home of innovative television for the modern woman. Everyone was represented, the TV critics from the *New York Times*, *The Daily News*, *Wall Street Journal* and several women's magazines. A score of bloggers, including those from the *Huffington Post* and *Daily Beast*, were also in the house. He spotted Josh Scotch from the *Hollywood Reporter* and Ted Phillips from *Sports Illustrated*. Joining them were several specially invited guests, all sports market advertisers. T.J. wanted them to have first dibs at what he was sure was going to be a sold-out schedule.

T.J. took in a deep breath and did a quick gut check. Yeah, some might think that what he was about to do—well, had already done—was wrong, but none of those naysayers had the presidency of a multi-billion dollar conglomerate at stake nor did they work in the television business. Stolen ideas, or as he preferred to call them borrowed inspiration, were the price of doing business in the production game. If he had a nickel for every wannabe producer or scriptwriter who'd heard the phrase, "oh, we already have something similar in development," while sitting in a pitch meeting, he and Bill Gates would be neighbors.

Besides, he hadn't really stolen anything. Ideas were not subject to copyright and he was confident that while loosely based on Ro's description of Lena Macy's pet project, LiveYou TV's *SportsMom*, was a bigger, better version of the original concept. He doubted that SFN was focusing specifically on mothers and it certainly was not going to be hosted by a real-life celebrity soccer mom.

If he could be accused of anything remotely underhanded, it was his timing of the announcement. It was purposely staged while Lena was out of the country. By the time she heard about the press conference, the cat would be out of the bag and the damage to SFN's fall lineup already done. All was fair in business and pleasure. And as far as T.J. was concerned, putting Lena out of business was his pleasure.

He stepped closer to the mike, leaning back as feedback squealed into the air, demanding the audience's attention. T.J. took another deep breath and began the unraveling of his rival's career.

"Thank you all for taking time out of your day to join us," he began, laying some of his charm directly at their feet. "We know you're busy and I promise it will be worth the trip. We are so excited about LiveYou TV's new direction in programming that we didn't wait until this summer when we announce our new fall lineup. What we've got planned for next fall is going to revolutionize the way women look at sports, and their husbands look at them.

The media, interest piqued, sat attentively, pens, pads and recorders at the ready.

"When I was brought on board at LiveYou TV, my mission was to give this fledgling network a real identity by creating programming too compelling to let life get in the way of watching. In other words, appointment television for bright and brainy women looking for a little relief from their everyday grind. And if we do our job right, maybe we can teach them an interesting thing or two in the process.

"There's enough programming out there about cooking, decorating, shopping for new wardrobes and weddings. In fact, LiveYou TV offers some of the best. But in addition to those scheduling staples, we want to fill a programming void in an arena that has for far too long ignored its female fans. I'm talking about the sports arena. Our quest this season—and I suspect many seasons to come—will be to entertain and educate women in the sports that they, their men and children love, thus making the usually male bastion of athletic competition, a more enjoyable and shared experience for the entire family."

A positive murmur of curiosity buzzed through the crowd. Their reaction gave T.J. reason to relax and continue in a manner less about convincing the wary and more about communicating to those won over.

"*SportsMom* will go behind the scenes of the favorite sports their kids like to play and their men like to watch. We'll teach them the rules; get up close and personal with the star players and their families, all the while giving our ladies a friendly dose of fashion, food and famous sports celebrity gossip. And who is going to lead viewers on this journey? None other than super sports mom herself, Miyori Jackson, former Olympic track star and wife of the Oakland A's star pitcher, Kevin Jackson.

"Take a look at this short clip and you'll see just what we mean when we say 'A SportsMom is a Happy Mom.'"

The lights dimmed as the clip rolled highlighting the concept of the show. T.J. looked on, proud of what Linda Barr and her department had been able to come up with on such short notice. True they were brainstorming around an already rock-solid concept. Still a yeoman effort had been made by all to get this concept nailed down and Miyori signed on so it could be announced before the PBC all-network meeting next month and then later at the dog and pony show for advertisers. The hard work of getting it into production had yet to begin, but they still had time for that.

The conclusion of the presentation was met with a bounty of curious and complimentary questioning. T.J. and his programming VP fielded the queries from the interested press, fortifying their belief that this was the right program being offered at the right time. As he basked in the spotlight, warmed by the glow of success, a small and admiring voice from within forced T.J. to admit that Lena Macy knew exactly what she was doing. T.J. listened and acknowledged the truth, countering it with his own thought: *by any means necessary, I will stop her from succeeding.*

LENA SAT NEXT TO THE KING-SIZED BED IN THE DESK CHAIR, bathed in candlelight with her legs splayed open for Jason's viewing pleasure. She ran the feathery side of the crop up her thigh, while running the leather fringe on the other side through her fingers. With Aleesa's help, she'd chosen this risqué ensemble consisting of a black lace shelf bra that framed her fully exposed breasts and gave them a "don'tcha want a mouthful" lift, matching g-string and garter skirt with stockings. It was a costume that Lena would never dream of wearing, but one that left Pocahontas properly attired for "Operation Tie Him Up and Make Him Beg," the game they'd concocted for this auspicious occasion. Gotta love those military wives!

Jason sat upright in the bed, his arms spread above his head, his legs spread eagle, across the bed. His appendages were currently untethered, but he had strict instructions that if he made a move toward her, the game would be over and she would retire alone to her suite.

"Please tell me how you like me to play with your clit," Jason begged with a telling squeak of arousal in his voice.

"You'd like that, wouldn't you?" Lena replied as she morphed further and further into her sexy alter ego, Pocahontas. Taking control, calling all the sexual shots as it were, left her feeling forceful and sexy. She liked it. "You want to know how to please me, don't you?"

"Yes."

"Tell me why, Mr. Johnson."

"To make you happy."

"The real reason!" she ordered, reaching over with the crop and spanking the top of Jason's thighs. She felt her eyes close and face cringe as she brought the whip down, still uncomfortable with the idea of bringing pain to an act that was supposed to be about ultimate pleasure. But the look of ecstasy that skidded across Jason's face helped her to stay in character. "You want to know so I'll keep wanting to fuck the shit out of you."

"Yes. Please fuck me," Jason begged, the slight sting on his legs making his cock rise. This new and freaky side to Lena was making him ultra horny. "Please give me that pretty pussy."

"Well, I will tell you as long as you promise to listen and then do exactly as instructed. Do you promise?"

"Yes."

"Say it!" she demanded again, slapping the fringe harder and closer to his balls. This time she managed to keep one eye open.

Jason jumped and let out a slight yelp.

"Oh shit. I'm sorry. Are you okay? Oh, shit. Did I hurt you?" Lena panicked.

"Oh no, baby. It hurt good. Trust me, I will let you know if..."

"Then shut the fuck up and promise," Lena interrupted, jumping right back into demi-dominatix mode. She gave him another spank for emphasis.

"I promise. Please tell me how to please you."

"Well, then, my favorite way is for you to play with my clit with your dick. I love the head. It looks and tastes like a small, juicy delicious plum."

Jason closed his eyes, picturing the images in his head.

"I like sliding it up and down and all around my clit until she's super wet," she said, caressing the head of a neon pink vibrator to make her point. "Look at me!"

Jason opened his eyes and sucked his teeth, informing Lena how much her descriptions were affecting him.

"When she gets good and hard, I like sliding your head up and down 'til my clit feels like it's going to burst." Lena brought action to her words by first dipping the vibrator into her pussy pool, getting it all lubed up, and then rubbing it up and down her bud. She began to moan, enjoying the tingling sensation of her battery-operated dick.

"It feels so good when I grind up against your big dick, making my kitty purr." Lena closed her eyes and let Jason watch as she rubbed and tugged and brought herself to orgasm. "OWW WWWW!" she moaned, letting loose.

She sat back into the chair, recovering while congratulating herself on another first—masturbating in front of an audience.

"Baby, please. Let me join the party. I can smell your pussy from here. I want to drink all that cum juice."

"Ohh. You want my twat all up in your face, don't you?" Lena said, surprised by how much she was enjoying herself.

"Yes. I want to eat you and then tear your ass up. You have me so fucking hot right now."

"Well, you are going to have to wait until I'm ready to give it up. In fact, I don't trust you not to touch me or yourself. I need to fix that." Lena got up and sauntered over to the desk, giving Jason plenty of time to check out her erotic getup. She reached into the drawer and pulled out two silk neckties, essential gear packed for the operation.

Lena's eyes stayed glued to Jason's as she walked over to the bed and leaned over his body. She teased his dick with a nice long lick, watching it grow in her hand before opening the Trojan by the bed and unrolling it on his excited member. Slowly and expertly, she straddled his body. He felt her legs part and the warm moisture from her post-orgasm pussy slide across his belly. She leaned forward, teasing him by putting her luscious tits in his face, her nipples ripe for the picking. As Lena reached forward, taking his right arm and tying it snugly to the headboard, Jason couldn't resist and latched on to her beautiful breast.

For a few ecstatic moments, she forgot the game, allowing him to proceed. Lena leaned her head back so she could watch him suck, enjoying the electric current rushing from her nipple directly to her clit.

"What the fuck are you doing?" she managed to squeak out with a minimum of authority. "Did I tell you could do that?"

"No," Jason replied, playing along, not giving a fuck and knowing that whatever punishment she applied would be pleasure he accepted.

"Then you must be punished." Lena tied his left wrist to the bedpost before sliding down and positioning her mouth over his nipple. She gently took it into her mouth, lavishing it with loving attention. Her tongue alternated between lapping it like a cat drinking milk and twirling it round and round until she felt it rise in her mouth and then shw changed her technique to gentle sucking. Jason's dick jumped expectantly between her legs, her cue to increase the suction, pulling harder while biting down until she got the reaction she was waiting for.

At Jason's yelp, she released his nipple and replaced her mouth with her fingers, pinching, rolling and twisting as she watched his face contort in pleasure.

"Scratch me," he suggested.

Lena hesitated, unsure if she could actually do as he had requested. Other than a little slap and nibble, she was more of a nurturer than a punisher.

"Please."

Drawing on her freaky twin persona, Lena gripped Jason's shoulders and raked her nails down the length of his chest.

"Harder," he begged.

She took a breath and repeated her actions, this time going deeper. Immediately red welts where she had broken his skin appeared. She winced at her actions, until Jason's look of excitement coaxed her to relax. Lena allowed herself to leave the moment and become an observer. This idea of pain actually being pleasurable was fascinating to her. She'd always thought of herself as a sensual lover, putting sexual activities like spanking, bondage, biting, scratching and rough sex in the kinky corner, left untouched by the refined and dignified. But now Pocahontas was having second thoughts. Perhaps under a controlled and playful situation, and with a partner she trusted, she might be willing to try.

Lena's smile, a direct result of this sexual growth spurt that was urging her to be more open and adventurous, faded away as Jason's latex-sheathed groin began to push up into hers, searching for her hot slit to slip into.

"Not so fast. There will be no fucking this pussy until you can behave yourself," she informed him.

"Please, baby. I want my dick inside you so bad. Please, don't make me wait."

Lena threw her head back and laughed. Operation Tie Him Up and Make Him Beg was successfully underway. "No, and if you ask again, I will take my pretty pussy away and you'll never have it."

She pushed her breasts together, leaning them into Jason's face once again. He hungrily took one in his mouth and then the other—lapping, sucking and nibbling, loving the way her body was responding to his touch. Testing her limits, he bit down on one nipple, releasing a deep and lusty moan from Lena's belly and felt her ass clench against his torso. Apparently, his little nasty girl was coming around to his way of loving.

The pain shot through Lena's nipples straight to her clitoris, like a wakeup call, taking her arousal to an entirely different level. She lifted her ass off of his body and moved forward, opening her pussy lips with her hands and shoving her twat in his face.

"Taste it. NOW!" she commanded. Jason's tongue went to work, concentrating its attention on her lovely clit, wishing his hands were free to jam inside her hole. Lena's wet and juicy snatch pumped his face as he licked and sucked her off. The smells of sex, mixed with the wet and gushy sounds of oral satisfaction, added to the hedonistic ambiance. Her moans became grunts, her grunts obscenities, as she came closer to reaching her peak.

"SUCK MY FUCKING PUSSY, JOHNSON. MAKE ME COME," she shouted out, not giving a damn who else in the Queen's Fairmont Hotel might hear.

Lena bucked up against his head several more times and kneeled perfectly still as he licked and sucked the come from her body. Her own fingers manhandled her breasts until the hurt of pinched nipples mixed with the joy of licked clit, causing her to lose control. Her breaths became shorter and shallower, stopping altogether as she burst into orgasmic delight.

Lena rolled over and collapsed on the bed next to Jason. She closed her eyes, luxuriating in the glow of satisfaction.

"Untie me," the voice beside her commanded. Gone was the dutiful lover begging for his pleasure. He'd been replaced by a hot and horny man demanding to get laid. "Untie me, NOW."

Lena did a quick survey of her feelings. Fear was not among the emotions bubbling inside her. She trusted him. She did as instructed, once again straddling her lover and kissing each wrist before releasing him from his bondage. Quicker than she could react, Jason grabbed her wrists and flipped her onto her back. He held her arms pinned to the bed, restricting her ability to move freely. He gazed into her hazel eyes, searching for a clue to her comfort level. His eyes smiled into hers, asking permission to proceed. Hers sparked, returning his gaze with a nasty knowing. Lena felt herself relax into the soft mattress, allowing Pocahontas to submit to Big Johnson's will.

"Spread your legs," he demanded, once given the green light. Lena submitted to his request, moving her legs to a wide V. Jason's lips came down hard on hers, devouring her mouth as he thrust his dick hard into her vagina. He'd waited so long to have her again—not just tonight during their game, but all during the weeks that had followed their passion-filled Miami encounter. The waiting was over. He ground his pelvis into hers, pushing his thick, hard rod deep inside her pussy, searching for that magic spot that had released the freak in her in Florida. He pumped her hard, letting the ridges of his head connect with the tiny grooves of her pussy before colliding with her G-spot, and taking delight in the starburst of micro orgasms exploding inside her pussy.

"I'm about to cum in you," he announced, his voice getting higher and more frantic. "You want all this cum, don't you?"

"Yes, baby. Give it to me!"

Johnson grunted and trembled before ejaculating his huge load into her. He collapsed on top of Lena, their chests both rising and falling together as they fought to breathe normally. After several minutes of breath-catching bonding, Jason disengaged herself and pressed his belly to Lena's side, laying his head in the niche of her neck and shoulders like lovers do.

Lena closed her eyes, feeling safe and satiated, marveling how their sexing had come full circle tonight. It had started with Jason lying meek and helpless in the bed, and was ending the same way. Damn, being the boss never felt so good!

"No, no, no, baby. No time for sleep. Not yet. You were so incredibly nasty, it's time for me to pay up with my something nice."

"Mmmm," was all Lena could respond.

"No seriously," Jason said, gently slapping her pussy to alert her. "Give me ten minutes and then come down to my room."

Lena's fatigue quickly morphed itself into sexual stimulation as she witnessed her body's response to his sexy assault. Her pussy, still a jangle of simmering nerves, tingled as the stinging sensations caused her hot box to contract with tiny explosions. She couldn't believe it! Orgasm was her body's natural reaction to the application of a little pain to her genitals.

Holy fuck, Pocahontas! What has happened to me?

"Lena, did you hear me?"

"I'm sorry. What did you say?"

"Ten minutes, down in my room. I still have my part of the wager to pay," Jason reminded her of the I.O.U. still due her.

Sexual stimulation immediately turned to romantic anticipation. Lena was so curious to see what he'd come up with, and what if anything it would reveal about his feelings for her.

"What's the attire?"

"What you have on is perfect," he told her, eyeing her luscious nude body as he pulled on his clothes. "But you know how you are; better pull on a robe for the trek down to the next floor."

Dressed in a violet silk slip dress or nightgown—who could tell the difference these days—and barely there stiletto sandals, with not a stitch underneath, Lena tapped lightly on the hotel door. Her nipples, chilled *and* aroused, poked through the thin fabric. Her brazen look excited her.

The door opened to reveal a smiling Jason, bare-chested and wearing drawstring pajama pants, with the twinkling skyline of Montreal behind him. Her nose detected a floral scent before her eyes settled into the dimness and sought out the dozens of roses placed around the room.

"Come in and have a cup of nice with me," he told her, extending his hand and leading her into the room. Her toes giggled, tickled by the soft silky touch of cool freshness at her feet. She looked down to find a path of multi-colored rose petals leading to the bathroom.

Lena followed the trail to the bathroom, welcomed by the sight of the most beautiful, romantic and well, *nicest* set-up she'd ever seen. The lights were off, candlelight providing whatever illumination would be necessary. The large, round soaking tub was filled with steaming water, invisible below a layer of rose petals. The heat released the rose essence, adding a sexy, innocence to the air. A champagne bucket with two glasses sat in one corner of the tub.

"Long, hot, luxurious candlelit baths," she said, softly quoting her list.

"Now, if I may have those sexy, leaving nothing to my freaky imagination, scrap of a dress and shoes, we'll get this party started." Jason did not wait for any indication that Lena had heard him and quickly flicked the thin straps of her chemise off of her shoulders. The light silk fluttered to the ground and puddled around her ankles, leaving Lena wearing nothing but her shoes.

The tip of Jason's talented tongue appeared between his lips as he shook his head in appreciation. He offered his shoulder as support, and bent down, gently picking up her feet, one at time, and removing her shoes. "One last taste," he said before letting his tongue quickly dart between her pussy lips. "You taste like us. Now in the tub."

Lena stepped in and sunk deep into the petals and hot water, liking the heated sting on her ass.

"That was quite a wicked display you put on earlier, Pocahontas. You must be starving."

"I could eat a little something. Let's order room service."

"Oh, I am way ahead of you, Girl. You soak and enjoy the champagne. I'll be back with dinner soon."

Lena leaned back and exhaled. What a heavenly ending to a heavenly day. Lena bit her lip to hold back her excitement. Jason's expression of nice was awfully romantic and she liked the way it felt. He could have simply bought her flowers or some trinket but he hadn't taken the easy way out. Instead, he had shown her a creative sensuality, proof positive that he didn't view her as just a fuck but as something much more. How much more was yet to be determined, but his initial effort was very sexy!

"Room service," Jason said, returning fifteen minutes later with a tray. He put it down on the counter and ran more hot water into her tub before picking up a fork and martini glass full of crab salad. He speared a fat juicy lump and a chunk of avocado and guided it into Lena's mouth. She savored the succulent shellfish on her tongue before washing it down with champagne.

"Yummy."

He placed the next taste on a toast point and fed her again.

"Sourdough? What else is on that tray?"

"Well, in addition to the lump crabmeat and sourdough bread, we've got some shrimp, fresh figs wrapped with prosciutto, mango and of course, chocolates."

"You really did memorize my list. This is so incredibly sweet of you."

"I didn't want you to think that I'm just a big dick and a pretty face."

"I would never think that, though one should always lead with one's strengths, Mr. Big Johnson," she teased. "Seriously, you are also smart, charming, ambitious and a tough negotiator. You managed to land one of the biggest sports stars. Believe me, I know that was no easy feat."

"Yeah, Rickie was a big score but the pressure to bring in big clients is unrelenting. I'm trying to make partner and frankly, it's all about keeping my nose clean and signing stars. Now how about a little juicy chocolate-covered mango?" he asked, not wanting to spoil their moment talking about work.

After Jason paid his debt by feeding and bathing her, he toweled her off and helped her into one of the hotel's fluffy terrycloth robes. He and Lena retreated to the bed with their champagne flutes and for the first time in their young relationship, simply talked. The longer they sat the less they felt like two people enrolled in a highly pleasurable freak game; it was more like a man and a woman determined to shed the faux cloak of intimacy that a sex-only relationship can imitate, and get truly naked with each other. Slowly they began to reveal the tender inner parts of their lives, building on the trust they'd established through their sexual play.

"So you're kinda cute, successful, a great lover and a romantic..." Lena told him.

"Let's keep that romantic part under your hat," Jason teased. "I don't need my players thinkin' their agent is soft."

"Your secret is safe. So basically, you're a catch. Why hasn't some Chicago girl caught you?"

"For the same reason, I suspect, no New York guy has caught you, or have they?"

"I was married for seven years. Divorced now for five."

"Why did it end?" Jason probed.

"Different priorities."

"We've both got our eye on the prize. Work is my wife. I'm never in town long enough to keep any woman happy and after a while they get tired of being number two and move on. I really can't blame them."

"I know that's right. I got divorced because my ex didn't understand why I didn't want to have a baby."

"You don't want kids?"

"I didn't then. I was still in my thirties. I felt like I had plenty of time to start a family. He apparently couldn't wait. Well, he's remarried with two now."

"Are you sorry?" Jason probed.

"Not really. I think it was an inevitable split and the baby was simply the reason *du jour*. So what about you? Do you want kids?"

"I wouldn't mind one more. I already have a son. He's five and lives in Atlanta with his mother."

"Do you see him much?"

"Whenever I can." Jason went on to explain how his last relationship had lasted nearly three years and had produced his child, J.J. (Jason Jr.) but not a marriage. He'd been devastated when his baby's mother had taken their son and moved to Georgia, but he was really in no position to argue, as he spent nearly three weeks out of four out of town. He made a point to visit him at least one weekend a month and had him for several extended stays throughout the year.

"It's a tough life. Like tomorrow, I leave for Europe with Rickie and will be gone for two weeks. You know, Pocahontas, we might have stumbled upon the perfect relationship—gambling buddies. You living in New York, me in Chicago; the two of us making bets and commuting for great sex whenever the desire strikes."

"You might be on to something. So what are we betting on next?" Lena said, playing the game but feeling let down. Maybe, despite his lovely display of "nice," this was only about sex for him.

"I absolutely concur. We need a schedule," Jason said, reaching his own conclusion and presenting it as a done deal. He was willing to say and do anything to keep this lucky, sexy as hell streak going with this beautifully surprising woman.

"Well, let's see, we've got the Masters golf tournament next week, the Kentucky Derby in May…"

"And Wimbledon in June," Jason added. "And the fall is packed…"

"Who do you think is gonna take the Masters?" Lena interrupted his thought, not sure if she wanted to plan so far into the future.

"Tough one; I still think Tiger has something to prove."

"With his life such a miserable mess, I think he's done winning for the year. I say Phil is still the man to beat."

"Nah, Tiger is still the man," Jason insisted.

"Then put your money where your mouth is," Lena teased.

"Baby, where my mouth is going ain't got nothin' to do with money."

Chapter Eleven

"Happy Birthday to you!" The small crowd gathered around a small cake finished singing and began applauding as the birthday boy blew out his candles. The room, filled with Lena's family, looked like a reception area in the United Nations building with all of the shades of the human rainbow represented.

"Happy seventieth, Daddy. I love you," Lena declared, giving her father a warm, loving hug. Despite any relationship strains father and daughter might have experienced throughout the years, nothing could break their bond. Nor would she let any treason on the work front keep her from sharing this moment with her father.

"I love you, too, Sweet Pea. I am so glad you're here."

"You know I wouldn't have missed this milestone. Weren't you at all of mine?"

"And will continue to be for as long as I live."

Lena kissed her father again and then stepped back to watch the family drama unfold. Akira, her Asian stepmother, replaced Lena in her husband's arms and kissed him hard on the lips. Lena witnessed this unusual public display of affection with a grin, knowing it was as much for her mother as for her father. Though their divorce had been amicable and the two remained friendly, Tina and Akira had never warmed to each other. Tina found the Japanese woman meek and submissive, while Akira saw the African-American woman as showy and ostentatious. Lena felt that both viewpoints were incomplete and totally biased, but she stayed neutral while the exes maintained a "keep your enemies close" stance with each other. The thing she did admire about both women was their commitment to Douglas' wish to keep the extended family bond together and strong, despite any differences of culture or opinion.

Douglas Paskin was known as a business pioneer and adventure junkie, but because he was so private, what most didn't know about him was that his true rebellious nature was played out in the women he loved. White-skinned, strawberry blonde and green eyed, Douglas had always been attracted to women of color. Black, Asian, Polynesian, Iranian, the more exotic the better. It had been his nineteen-year, happily haphazard but complicated marriage to his beautiful Nubian queen that had produced Douglas' only offspring, Lenora Macy Paskin.

"Happy Birthday, Son," Macy Turner, Lena's maternal grand-mother, shuffled up to her ex son-in-law to offer. The woman was nearly ninety years old, with soft, velvety skin the color of caramel, and a mind that functioned just as smoothly. Lena loved her grandmother with such intensity and was proud to carry her moniker, each day hoping to prove herself worthy of her namesake.

"Miss Macy, you keep getting better looking every day!"

"Darling, it's in the genes!" Tina DuPree announced drawing both Lena and her mother to her side. "Just look at the three generations of women lighting up this room. The Turner genes are couture, Darling!"

Lena laughed. She might be showy but no one could deny that Tina DuPree was a total life force. Her energy—usually positive and uplifting—was a thing to be reckoned with. But she hadn't always been so lively. In fact, Lena had to admit that her parents' divorce had not only agreed with her mother, but freed her. While married to Douglas, Tina had stayed in the background, dimming her light and keeping the home fires burning while her man was out in the world shining bright. It was only after marrying financier Kenneth DuPree, that Tina had found her place on the philanthropic stage and the spotlight turned on her.

Douglas Paskin looked at his daughter, ex-wife, and mother-in-law and could not dispute Tina's claim. He reverted back to the game he'd used to play with them through the years—which screen goddesses would play them in the movie of their life. Macy, with her soft classic femininity, would be played by the refined and lovely Lena Horne. Tina's striking beauty and fiery personality could only be captured by Josephine Baker in her prime, and Lena, a biracial beauty who had luckily captured all of the loveliness to be found in both her Scottish and African-American strands of DNA, by the beautiful Halle Berry.

"I am a blessed man to be surrounded by beautiful, couture women—past and present," Douglas replied, diplomatically including his current wife in the mix. "Now, Kenneth, Akira, Macy and everyone, into the library. We brought you all gifts from Peru."

"Daddy, I'm sorry but I have to leave soon. I have another appointment," Lena said as the others began to vacate the room.

"By appointment do you mean date? Are you leaving your old man to meet some other guy?"

Lena paused. The last thing Lena wanted to discuss with her dad was the current men in her life. T.J. was totally off limits. She refused to give her nemesis a voice during a family occasion, nor did she want Douglas to detect any weakness in her ability to handle a tough competitor. And Jason, with whom her relationship had been built on a foundation that would be unacceptable and immoral to her very conservative father, was budding in other directions and still had far to go before any introductions would be made. Even then, Lena would be reluctant. Douglas's reaction following her divorce from Michael, had made her gun shy about bringing another man into the Paskin family dynasty.

"Sweetheart, are you okay? You look a bit worn down. Problems?"

"Just work stuff. Nothing I can't handle. But I have to scoot. Let's have lunch next week, okay?"

Lena kissed her dad goodbye at the front door and left to head back to the office. She had to figure out something to get them out of this predicament T.J. had trapped her in.

"Tina, a word, please," Douglas said, as soon as his daughter had left. He gently took hold of her elbow and steered her into a quiet corner of the library.

"How was your trek? All that thin air must agree with you; you look pretty damn good for a man of your age," she teased, giving her ex a kiss on the cheek.

"It was good. Though not nearly as exciting as the time we went back in the seventies."

"Darling, how could it be? Your lovely wife isn't what I'd call a fun time."

"I was referring to my age! Trekking the Inca Trail at forty is markedly different than doing it at seventy. Leave Akira alone. Deep down I know you both like each other."

"Darling, we both like *you*. Each other we tolerate. Now what's with this secret pow-wow?"

"What's wrong with my daughter?"

"Don't you mean our daughter?"

"Ti, don't be difficult. She seems down but is unwilling to talk about it with me, though I get the sense it's about T.J.'s big announcement. I have to give it to him; he's got the town buzzing over this new show. And that's no easy feat. It's a damn good, forward-thinking concept."

Tina rolled her eyes. The truth was biting at her lips to get out, but she refused to break Lena's confidence. "Douglas, surely you must know how this whole T.J. Reynolds circus is affecting her. You could have handled things so much better. Why did you find it necessary to pit them against each other?"

"This was Lenora's idea. I've been grooming her for years to take over the company, but she's always resisted the idea, first with the name change..."

"Your daughter has pride and I admire that about her. You know as well as I do that she shortened her first name and started using my maiden name so people would take her seriously as she tried to get her footing in this business. She wanted to achieve on her own merit; not because of her father's name. You should respect that about her. Most rich kids with her kind of connections want the world handed to them."

"I do respect her, but well, you don't see Ivanka Trump changing her name," Douglas countered. The hurt of Lena's decision to hide her family connections still lingered. "So she went from Lenora Paskin to Lena Macy to find her own way, only to come back and make it quite clear that she wanted no part of PBC. I had to find someone, and T.J. is a damn good man."

"Douglas, that is such horse shit and you know it. She made that decision after you two fell out over her getting divorced. You're the one that made it *quite clear* to her that without Michael in the picture, you were not at all confident that she could handle the job on her own."

"I want PBC to remain a family company. I liked Michael and thought she would need the help once they started a family and all. But the company was always hers," he insisted. "Lena's the one who laid down the stipulation that she would not accept the position until she showed beyond a doubt that she could run it. She has inherited her mama's overwhelming pride."

"Among other things, Darling. But we all know that you needed the proof that she could do it. You had no more of an indication that Michael could run things any better than Lena, other than he was a man. That's why you brought T.J. in, another man, thank you very much, as a Michael's replacement."

Douglas ignored his ex's accusation. He knew that on some level she was right, but would never admit it out loud that had Lena been a son, none of this drama would have happened. Where Tina had it wrong was that it wasn't that he doubted his daughter's capabilities. Douglas knew that the rough and tumble world of broadcasting was tough for a man, and even tougher for a woman who was not only privileged but beautiful. He needed Lena to not only prove it to him, but to herself, that she had the *cojones* to survive in this formidable industry.

"It's all water under the bridge, Tina. We've patched things up and our relationship is back on track. Something more is bothering her. I know my child."

"Well, I'm sure T.J. stealing her show and announcing it to the world like it's his own, has her shook. I told her not to trust him," Tina revealed.

"What are you talking about? This wasn't his idea?"

"Darling, while you were out becoming one with the llamas, your brown-nosing protégé was quite busy undermining your daughter." Tina went on to tell Douglas about the meeting between the two, T.J.'s feigned disinterest, and then his surprise announcement planned strategically while both he and Lena were out of the country. "He ambushed her and now she's left spinning her wheels trying to figure out how to regroup."

"You're sure about this?" Douglas asked, the frown lines on his forehead bringing his eyebrows together. "Intellectual property is tough to nail down in terms of ownership."

"Yes, but don't you dare tell Lena I told you."

"I won't and I appreciate you letting me know. I'm going to have to think about how to deal with this."

"Douglas, please don't interfere. Let Lena handle this. I'm sure this kind of thing goes on all the time."

"True. This happens all the time."

"So let it take its course. Give both Lena and T.J. the opportunity to show themselves as leaders while this thing plays out."

"You really are a smart woman, Tina."

"Darling, tell me something I don't know!"

Chapter Twelve

I give you props, Pocahontas. Looks like you're two for three. So, first dinner tonight, and then your desire is my pleasure. But don't go gettin' a big head about it because when I win again—and I will win again—you, nasty girl, will owe me BIG TIME. Now until then, I will happily and thoroughly enjoy my indebtedness to you. ...MBJ

I look forward to collecting my winnings, Mr. Big Johnson. I'll see you tonight. Bring your A game, lover! Lena smiled as she replied to Jason's email, even though her words sounded much more promising than she felt. Still, she was happy that she had something to look forward to this evening and held high hopes that getting freaky with Big Johnson could deliver her from this depressing work funk she was now mired in.

She sat at the head of the conference table, surrounded by the outraged and scrambling executives in SFN's programming, sales, and marketing departments. The table was littered with the remnants of another working lunch, the third since the news of LiveYou's thievery had broken. Lena and her group of executives were working hard to recover from being blindsided, and come up with a new concept in only a few weeks.

"It's nearly five and I know you all are tired," Lena said. "I do appreciate everyone working so hard on this."

"What Reynolds did was total bullshit," Tony, the VP of sales, declared.

"It seems like such a shame to totally scrap *Sports Watchin' Women*," Aleesa remarked with frustration.

"I know, it was our shining star, but the reality is now that if we air it, it will only look like we are ripping them off," said Jeffery, SFN's VP of programming.

"What if we used parts of the program?" Lena suggested. "Is there a way to turn them into mini segments, have them sponsored by advertisers and then insert them into appropriate programming?"

"Almost like a mini infomercial," Tony offered.

"Won't that still seem like we're copycats?" Aleesa asked.

"Well, they are going after the soccer mom…" Jeffery mused.

"So we'll talk to the girlfriends and wives instead. Make them smart about sports, which we all know most men find sexy. We'll cut out the fashion and food and have one-minute spots on the rules, inside info on the stars…" Lena continued.

"Like injury reports and rules and the ref's signals," Aleesa added.

"I like that, it still gives the women a reason to watch and new advertisers to buy time, which is what we were going for in the first place," Tony concurred. Everyone else around the table added their agreement with the idea, allowing them all to feel as if they were making some progress.

"Okay, I'm feeling just a tad better," Lena admitted. "But we still have a major problem—we have no centerpiece program."

"And time is running out," Jeffery added. "We've got to have this ready to announce at the all-network meeting in early May and then a week later to the advertisers."

"Let's break for today and reconvene tomorrow afternoon. Please, folks, wrack those talented brains of yours. And continue to keep all of this under wraps. Until we find out who's leaking information, I don't even want your staffs to know about any of this. Understood?"

The executives all sounded their understanding as they vacated the room. Aleesa hung back waiting for a word with her friend. "Good call on the *SWW* moments."

"Thanks. I've gotta do something to pull this out of the toilet."

"If you still wanna brainstorm, we can grab a drink."

"I can't. I've got a meeting with some tennis folks," Lena replied, not revealing that Jason would be there as well. Not only was he back in New York to deliver his I.O.U. for losing to her yet again, but she had invited him along so he could meet up-and-coming tennis phenom and potential client, Tracy Clemons. Hopefully, introducing him to a potential new client would help soften the blow of the news she most dreaded delivering. How was she going to tell him about the demise of the show she'd chased his client down for months to host? A show that was defunct before it even hit the air.

"Okay, then I'll see you tomorrow. And don't worry, this will all work out."

"How, Lees? Please tell me how."

"I don't know. It's a surprise."

LENA SIPPED HER WINE AS SHE WATCHED JASON WORK HIS MAGIC on Tracy and his father. She was impressed. They were back at Nobu 57, but unlike the last time he was here with her and Rickie Ross, Jason's demeanor was all business. He knew his professional tennis stats and delivered his progressive ideas with a potent mix of charm and trustworthiness. She was sure that Tracy, just as she had, would soon come to the conclusion that he and his blossoming career would be in good hands with Jason Armstrong and Trinity Sports Management.

As Jason took care of his agent wheeling and dealing, Lena let her mind drift back into the current mess with her own business affairs. T.J. had royally screwed her and it pained her on two levels. First, that she had made a major strategic mistake by going to him full of good will and in the spirit of cooperation and under-estimating his competitive nature. And secondly, someone had told him of their plans. Even though this *SportsMom* show of his was not exactly like *Sports Watchin' Women*, it certainly was similar enough to conclude that it was deeply rooted in her concept. Lena didn't believe for a minute his line about already having a similar show in development. Someone had leaked all the details of their idea. But who? Who would betray her and the network? Until she found out, SFN would remain on lockdown, and everyone would receive sensitive information strictly on a need-to-know basis.

Lena felt her mood sink lower into melancholy. While actually happy to see Jason, she wasn't in the mood for a crazy, sexy, cool evening full of sexual shenanigans. She had won their bet on the Masters golf tournament, and Jason was expecting much more than what she desired, which at this moment was only to be cuddled and consoled.

But that's the role of a boyfriend, not a sex gaming partner, a voice from within reminded her.

He'd also proven the last time they were together that he could do sweetheart nice and do it well, she countered. *Perhaps he'd show her his thoughtful side once again. The rule was winner's choice, so he had to.*

The rules mean nothing if you don't have the nerve to let your desires be known. Lena shook her head to clear the voices, and brought her attention back to the dinner table.

"So we will talk this week when I get back to Chicago and get this all wrapped up," Jason said, extending his hand to the soon-to-be tennis pro. "I promise you, Tracy, you're going to be very happy at TSM and I'm going to do all I can to make you a superstar."

"Lena, thank you for the introduction," Lamont Clemons said, pumping her hand. "I think this has been a good meeting and I appreciate you looking out for my son."

"I'm happy it's going to work out. Tracy is phenomenal and deserves to be represented by the best. I've worked with Jason on a few projects and I can assure you, he always does right by his clients."

Jason stood by smiling and thinking to himself that he and Lena really did make a great working couple. He knew that she was well-connected when they'd decided to do business together with Rickie, but that was the least of it. He was continually blown away by the many incredible sides to this elegant and classy woman. He'd already learned that Lena was sexy, funny, intelligent, as well as being a successful risk-taker. She was the kind of woman that made a man proud to stand by her side and claim her as his own. But now she'd added a generosity of spirit to the mix—a mix that was fast becoming potently addictive.

The four of them stood to say their good-byes and once father and son were out of sight, Jason scooped her up in his arms and gave her a twirl. "Thank you, thank you, thank you for hooking me up like this!"

"No problem. I owed you for working your magic on Rickie," *which I hope you'll be able to do again*, she said without voicing her thoughts. "I hope it all works out." And she really did. She'd met the Clemons last year at a tennis tournament carried by SFN, and was happy to introduce them to Jason when word got around that Tracy was ready to go pro and shopping for an agent.

"I'm glad they're gone. I've been thinking about you and your I.O.U. all night. So Pocahontas, what do I owe you tonight?"

"I'll tell you when we get upstairs," she replied, praying like hell that the Sex Fairy would come sprinkle her with some horny dust on their way up to the suite. "Uh, I really need to talk to you."

"Okay. Let's go," he replied, not at all liking the tone of her voice.

Jason signed the check and then escorted Lena to the elevator. Once inside, he reached for her, planting a hungry kiss of gratitude and craving on her mouth. Lena kissed him back, but they both could feel that the raw passion that had fueled their first two encounters was missing. Jason could only wonder if this was to be a hide-and-go-seek reunion; where an onslaught of seduction and charm would be needed to fan the spark and start the fire, or had the flame that had burned between them been extinguished?

They reached their floor and exited the elevator holding hands but saying nothing. Jason unlocked the door and followed Lena inside. She plopped down on the couch while he mixed them a drink and tried to decipher her mood. He was still so hot for her but not sure if he should push forward or lie back and let her dictate the evening.

"It's good to see you again," he said, handing her a classic martini. "I thought about you the whole time Rickie and I were in Europe."

"Thank you."

"So, what's wrong, baby? You don't seem like yourself."

"I'm not and I'm sorry. I'm just not feelin' it tonight."

"So, are you officially invoking the No4U clause?" he asked, trying to keep his tone light and free of the disappointment welling up inside.

For a moment, Lena considered sucking up her feelings and letting Jason ravish her in hopes that he could lift her libido to meet his. That's what she had done all through her marriage when she hadn't felt like having sex. She'd secretly labeled those marital encounters, "yes, dears" and had spent many a night sexing out of duty and not desire. She decided to go with the truth.

"I guess so, but it's not you, I swear," Lena said, leaning her body into his. "It's something at work. It's got my head all tied up and I'm afraid Pocahontas is not feeling very inspired tonight."

"Tell you what, why don't you and I jump in the bed and drink our martinis while you tell me what's got you all hot and bothered, but not in a good way," he teased lightly.

"Okay," Lena agreed, laughter finding its way to the surface again. She was grateful to have his sympathetic ear. This was one of the few things she did miss about being married—having a pair of willing ears and strong arms at the ready to listen to and console her.

They took off their clothes, slipped into the hotel robes and with drinks in hand, eased into bed. Jason moved in close and put his arm around Lena, gently kissing the side of her head, letting her know that, at least for now, he was down with putting sex to the side and listening to her tales of woe.

"So baby, what's got Pocahontas so down?"

Lena allowed herself to sink back into the comfort of Jason's bed and body. She took a long sip of her martini and began to unload her burdens. She told him about what had transpired during the two weeks he had been overseas.

"Why would the dude do that to you after you went to him trying to hook up and work together? What's in it for him?"

"Without going into all of the details, we're both kind of up for the same job." Lena stopped there, not wanting to get into the specifics.

"Still, that was low."

"Agreed. But this also affects Rickie and his show. I'm sorry, but there is no show anymore."

"That's some fucked-up shit." He took in the news and quickly began going over the ramifications for his client. Lena's sigh stopped the flow of thoughts. At this moment his role was as lover not agent, so he pushed those thoughts aside and gave Lena his full attention. "What are you going to do?"

"Unclear at this point." She went on to brief him about the *SWW* moments, making it clear that she had no intention of wasting Rickie Ross and his talents on some sixty-minute advertisements.

"We're working hard trying to think of a new programming idea. Don't worry; we will come up with something great for Rickie." Lena felt her voice crack a bit and she fought hard to hold the tears at bay. She didn't want to tell him that they'd been wracking their brains for a week with nothing to show for it. The last thing Lena wanted was to come off as some whimpering, well, *girl*, to Jason, a man who liked bold, courageous *women*.

Jason could see and hear the frustration and hurt that had consumed his freaky Pocahontas. And yeah, he was disappointed that his wild night of owed pleasure looked to be totally off track, but he felt for Lena. She was strong and talented and deserved better than some lightweight prick stealing her marbles and trying to pass them off as his own.

"Well, what we need to do is apply some fresh gray matter to this *sitchiation*," he joked, "and come up with something bigger and better that really leaves that show-stealin' punk in the dust and pullin' our high ratings out of his ass!"

Lena laughed as she looked up at him with grateful eyes rimmed with tears.

"Baby, don't worry. You and me...we got this," Jason told her, surprising himself with the strength of his protective feelings for her. Yeah, he wanted like hell to have sex with Lena but at this moment it was her soft sensitive side that was compelling him to calm and comfort her.

"Thank you for understanding and not being mad about the No4U clause."

"Mad? Look, I'd rather you tell me your head ain't in it than pretend and try to fake it all night. In that case, I'd have called the No4U my damn self. There's nothing to understand on my part. It is what it is. But let's hurry and come up with some new show for my client so we can change your mood and you can collect your I.O.U." Jason flashed his twisted and infectious smile, letting her know that he was willing and able to deliver the full Monty— warm friendship and wanton fucking—whenever she said the word.

"Jason, you don't know how much I appreciate you for listening and wanting to help me with this, but I don't want to waste our time together talking about work. I will get it all figured out, but right now I just want to forget that T.J. Reynolds was ever born and chill and laugh with you."

"And maybe a little kiss and a hug here and there, you know for medicinal purposes." Jason flirted while refreshing Lena's drink.

"That goes without saying." She leaned over, meeting his lips with hers and delivering a to-be-continued kiss reminding them both that the incredible passion they shared, while temporarily dormant, was certainly not dead. "So tell me what you and Rickie did while you were in Europe," Lena said, once her lips were free to speak. "Why were you there in the first place?"

"We were over in England for an NFL exhibition and then took the Chunnel from London to Paris to hang out and just chill. But Rickie is so crazy that the trip turned out to be more of a sports smorgasbord."

Lena laughed, trying to understand his description. Finishing her drink, she picked up the olive and gently pushed it between Jason's lips. He accepted the salty orb, capturing and sucking the salt and vodka from her finger, before eating it.

"Is Pocahontas tryin' to come out and play?" He licked his lips.

Lena smiled and shrugged her shoulders, indicating a definite maybe. "So what is this sports smorgasbord?" Jason chuckled, seeing in her eyes that "maybe" was sounding more and more like a synonym for "soon."

"It was pretty funny. After Rickie's football demonstration in London, we went to a cricket match. Well, Rick decided he wanted to try it, so we ended up in some pick-up game. It took him only like twenty minutes to get the gist of it, and then he blew them away. He really is a damn amazing athlete," Jason revealed, enjoying the touch of Lena's affectionate caress on his hand. "And over in France, he wanted to buy a road bicycle for conditioning and then decided to break it in while we were there, so we ended up doing this mini tour de Paris."

"Wait, you two actually entered a bike race?"

"Hell no, well, not officially. It wasn't an actual race. He loves playing tourist so we biked around Paris and checked out all of the tourist sites—you know, the Eiffel Tower, the Louvre, Champs-Élysées and all the rest. But you know with a jock like Rickie, a walk down the hall turns into a competition, so yeah, it kinda became a bike race."

"Should I ask who won?" Lena joshed as she nibbled and sucked on his earlobe.

"Like you don't know. Being an ex-jock, that would be me, is nothing compared to being one of the best wide-receivers in the business; that would be Rickie. And not just that he's a good football player; he's good at *everything*. Dude can even swim!"

"The modern-day Bo Jackson," Lena murmured as the wheels in her head began to turn.

"Yeah, but even more talented. I think he could compete professionally in a multitude of sports—not only baseball and football. He's just that good. He's an all-around athlete plus he's curious and adventurous and smart as hell. I don't think there's a sport he couldn't master if he put his mind to it, and have fun doing it."

Lena's eyes went wide with inspiration. "Omigod, that's it!" she shrieked, grabbing Jason and nearly smothering him in a hug. "It's ingenious and fresh and OMIGOD!" She punctuated her remarks with a scattering of kisses across Jason's astonished face.

"What? Tell me."

"Not now but I will. I need to noodle it around a bit, but I'm thinking—no, I am certain—that I have the perfect show for Rickie and SFN! It's even better than the first and he is going to flat out love it!"

"I can't wait to hear about it. And babe, a suggestion, strategically speaking, when you do figure out a new show, act like the other was a plant all along. Don't even tell Rickie the truth. It will be our secret. That way, when all the cards are played you ultimately come out on top and he is exposed for the jack shit he is."

"Brilliant! Thank you so much!"

Her initial shower of smooches became more direct and singular in purpose as Lena kissed him, long and deep. Her desire, held down by the weighty concerns of work, began to buoy to the surface. Surprisingly, it was not Pocahontas who emerged, but Lena. Even more surprising, was that Jason seemed to understand the difference and treated her as such.

No words were spoken as he proceeded to pleasure her. Jason gloved his dick with a condom and climbed on top, straddling her body while she reached up and guided his hardness into her wet and waiting body. Kindly, gratefully and adoringly Jason made love to her and she to him, replacing the frenzied passion of their past couplings with an exploration into genuine lovemaking. Lust was replaced by longing. Tough demands by tender, caring caresses. Twice before they'd fucked. Tonight they loved.

Her moans filled the room as Lena opened her eyes to find Jason's staring back at her. Their gaze locked, each unwilling or unable to turn away as they revealed their feelings to each other.

The tide was rushing in between them, bringing forth a new level of emotional involvement.

"I'll make you a bet," Jason whispered, trying to divert his dick's wish to unload his cum before she was ready.

"Now?" She sighed back after leaving a hickey below his collarbone.

"Yeah. I bet I can make you cum first."

"Really? And if you do?"

"I don't know. You'll owe me something special."

"Deal," she said, reaching down to tickle and caress his balls, concentrating on the strip of sensitive skin near his anus. Jason's pelvis pushed deeper into her, his rush of "ahhhs" letting her know she'd hit a spot. Jason responded by pulling out slightly and repositioning his rod so it hit not only her clit but way back inside, finding the doorbell to her release and ringing it like a greedy trick-or-treater on Halloween. After several exquisite moments, he turned Lena on her side and lay belly to belly as he reentered her. Starting at her breasts, he slowly ran his hands down the length of her body, stopping a few inches below her belly button. With three fingers, Jason gently and strategically applied pressure to the erogenous area right above Lena's bladder.

It was too much to ignore. Almost immediately, she felt the tsunami begin to roll. They remained in ocular touch as a quiet but powerful orgasm rocked her body with warm and wet waves of bliss and contentment. Jason's came soon after, exquisitely silent but forceful enough to shut his eyes as his face shouted on high the depth of his satisfaction. Momentarily sated, they found a soft and safe place to land in each other's body, catching their breath and regulating their hearts into one beat.

"That was beautiful. Thank you," Jason declared as he lay back on the pillows, keeping her in his arms.

"Beautiful. I like that you think of it that way."

"Oh I do, and I repeat, don't tell my clients that your man is a softy at heart."

Your man? Lena smiled into the darkness. So this wasn't just about sex. Looking into his eyes as they made love, she'd felt him claim her as his own, but now he'd said it.

"Your secret is safe. I never kiss and tell," she said, crossing her fingers, believing that one's best friend didn't count. "But it does appear that I have lost the bet and now I owe you something special, though I think you cheated. That move, whatever you did by pressing my belly, I'm sure is illegal in several states. What was that?"

"You liked it?"

"You couldn't tell?"

"It's an ancient Chinese secret," he said, laughing at her expression of disbelief. "No seriously. It's Chinese acupressure. It's called The Gate of Origin."

"Well, I applaud your creativeness and your international touch to lovemaking, but it's a shame you have to resort to sleight-of-hand tricks to beat me," Lena teased, reaching over to turn on the light and grabbing the hotel pad and pen.

"Please you," he corrected her.

Lena smiled as she scratched her name and phone numbers, both cell and home, as well as her personal email address on to the pad. "I never welsh on a bet," she told him, handing him the information.

Jason's stomach did a somersault resulting in a wide smile across his handsome face. "This really is something special."

"I'm so glad you think so."

"You know, Pocahontas, I think I like you," Jason revealed, punctuating his declaration with a series of kisses across her freckles and down her nose. "A lot," he added with his mouth still on hers.

Chapter Thirteen

What a difference a weekend makes, Rolanda thought as she peered through the glass walls of the conference room. The usual lineup of suspects was present—sales, marketing and programming heads, with one newbie, the bald dude from legal. But unlike her dragging ass of last week, Lena was up and at it, animated like a Saturday morning cartoon. She was smiling. And laughing. And looking like Santa had arrived eight months early. T.J. was not going to like this.

The ringing phone sent Ro back to her desk. Damn, it was only 9:05 a.m. Who the hell could be calling already? Didn't people sit down their asses down, drink their coffee and chill for a minute anymore? It was all hustle and bustle right out of the damn gate these days.

"Good morning. Lena Macy's office," she said, masking the annoyance from her voice and putting on her Suzy secretary voice.

"Jason Armstrong. Is Ms. Macy available?"

Rolanda caught the giggle in her throat before it could escape. *Mr. Big Johnson on the line.*

"I'm sorry, Mr. Armstrong, but she's in a meeting and asked not to be disturbed. Can I give her a message?"

"Yes. Let her know that Rickie Ross and I will be in her office at two o'clock."

FUCK! RICKIE ROSS IS COMING HERE AND I'M WEARING A BLUE JEANS SKIRT AND THIS NO-NOTHING, JACKED-UP BLOUSE! WHY DIDN'T THAT WENCH TELL ME? Rolanda screamed in her head. *Okay, calm down. I can go run out at lunch and pick something up from The New York Look. Something welcoming... and hot.*

"Hello? Did you get that?"

"Get what? Oh yeah. Two p.m. Here at the office. We'll be waiting."

Rolanda hung up the phone, only to have it ring again, this time on her personal extension. *Damn it!* "Rolanda Hammon."

"I like hearing your voice first thing in the morning," T.J. Reynolds cooed in her ear.

"I was just thinking about you."

"Whatever it was, I hope it caused your hand to creep between your legs."

"You're a nasty motherfucker," Ro informed him, dropping her voice.

"Yes, I am and you love it! Now, how's our girl doing this morning? It's going on week two since the big announcement and I haven't heard anything from her camp."

"She must have gotten fucked good this weekend because she's one happy heifer right now. She's got her posse up in the boardroom with the guy from legal, but from what I can tell, it's all good."

"Legal? Ro, what's going on?"

"You know I don't know. Ever since she came back from Montreal we've been on Def Con One. Straight up lockdown. She doesn't share shit with me anymore. Nothing is coming through on her email, no nasty messages, no internal work letters, nothing to give me a clue as to what the hell she has up her sleeve."

"And she hasn't worked on any emails or anything to me?" he probed. Lena had not called to rant, rave or curse him out after she'd heard the news. Her silence was irritating, unnerving and above all, immensely unsatisfying.

"Nothing."

"Ro, you gotta find out," T.J. implored her. This was not good. All smiles in the presence of a lawyer could only mean one of two things: She was coming after him with some kind of legal action and was liking her chances; or she'd come up with something new to replace the sports show. But if that was the case, why the legal eagle?

"I'm trying, but info is given on a need-to-know basis these days. And you know if I ask too many questions, she's gonna get suspicious."

"Baby, I have your back. If she fires you, I'll find you something else. So don't worry."

"I'm holding you to that. It's the only reason I'm risking my job for you." Rolanda put major emphasis on that point. Her current lifestyle, though nowhere near the level she was planning to live, was not cheap to maintain. Ro already had bill collectors unhappy and calling with her skip-a-month bill paying methods. Until she bagged her baller, she could not afford to be without a job.

"Just for the job? I thought you liked the fringe benefits as well."

Rolanda replied with a throaty chuckle, "All I know is that her agent boy toy and Rickie Ross are coming in this afternoon. And I don't know why."

"That could be why the lawyer's there. Trying to figure out what to do about the talent contract. Okay. You call me as soon as you hear something. Now what are you doing for lunch? I'm going to be in the city and I've got a hankerin' for some of your tasty pussy."

"Sorry, but I gotta work through lunch. I'll call you soon, when I find out something. Gotta go; she's coming," Ro lied, trying to ignore her twitching coochie as she hung up the phone. As much as she would have liked to have banged T.J. this afternoon, she had a serious hankerin' of her own. She had to get ready for her meet and greet with the hot as hell Rickie Ross. Besides, it was good to make a brotha wait and work for the poontang every now and again.

Rolanda worked through the rest of the morning doing her usual job of answering phones, checking Lena's email, and dealing with office correspondence. Lena herself was taking care of most of the all-network meeting details, lightening Ro's load considerably, but increasing her suspicions that something big was brewing. By 12:15, Lena still hadn't emerged from her meeting. Rolanda decided to leave early and tack some extra time onto her lunch hour under the guise of dropping off some papers at the printer.

Lena sat at her desk with the door open and a huge smile of anticipation on her face. When she heard Rickie and Jason enter her outer office, she wanted to jump up, run over and plant a big sloppy kiss on Jason's lips. But she pressed down hard on the brakes and behaved appropriately, standing slowly and habitually brushing the wrinkles from her skirt while waiting for them to cross her threshold.

She was so thrilled by everything at this moment. Lena couldn't decide if it was because she was falling in love (as Aleesa was convinced) or if it was that she was sure she now had T.J. Reynolds by the balls. But, once again Rickie Ross was the missing piece. She now had to convince him that the new show, *Rickie Versus the World*, was a bigger, better deal for him, which it truly was. But she had to finesse it so she and SFN didn't come off looking like a bunch of amateurs. Lena knew she had two things going for her: the considerable bump in salary she was offering; and his agent and now her man, would be squarely on her side.

"One o'clock, right on time," Lena said to him, giving him a discreet wink. In one of their now twice daily phone calls, she'd purposely asked Jason to call Rolanda with the message that the meeting was starting an hour later so they could meet in privacy during her lunch hour. Lena trusted absolutely no one at this point, and if playing a few games would help keep this all under wraps until the big meeting at the end of the month, then so be it.

"Rickie, how are you? Please sit down." She directed him over to the sofa. "Can I get you anything?"

"Nah, it's all good."

The three engaged in a little current event chatter, breaking the social ice before they got down to business. Rickie, looking at his watch, finally asked the question that got them all focused on the task at hand.

"So Jason tells me the show I signed on for is a no-go? What's up with that?"

"Honestly speaking, the show concept was so good that another network stole it," Lena told him. "They've even announced that they're putting a 'so similar it's damn near a twin' version of the show on their fall schedule."

"That's f'ed up," Rickie agreed.

"I'm not going to lie, I was mad as hell, but I was expecting it. I'd been a bit suspicious of some practices for a while and well, I set them up to find out if my suspicions were justified. So, after we found out that our show concept had been compromised, we weren't going to put it on the air and risk making you look like an also-ran. Rickie Ross is an original. That's what we love most about you." Lena paused to gauge reaction. So far so good on both handsome faces.

"So what now? Jason had nothing to tell me."

"That's because until today, I had nothing to tell him. I've been working to make sure our Plan B was ready to go before I called you with all of the details. We had to iron out a few glitches but we are definitely going with plan B, a show that is simply amazing. I know you had some reservations about some of the segments we wanted you to do for *Sports Watchin' Women*, but I don't think you'll have a problem with any of these. Honestly it's going to showcase you as the superhero athlete you are. It's a hybrid show— one part travel and one part sports."

"I like the superhero athlete part," Rickie joked. "Seriously, go on."

"When I heard about your cricket playing in England and bicycle sightseeing trip in France, and after talking to Jason about your apparent athletic prowess," she continued, layering the flattery on thick like peanut butter. "I said, 'this is it!' We'll send you around the world learning how to play and then compete in a variety of indigenous sports while at the same time acting as a travel guide. We're calling it *Rickie Versus the World*."

"Now this is dope," Rickie exclaimed, his face lit up with excitement. "I am definitely feelin' this. Seriously. So like what kind of games?"

"Anything and everything that strikes your fancy. Archery in Korea, rugby in England, cycling in Italy, dragon boat racing in Singapore—the more unusual and entertaining the better. You'll have ten days to train for each sport and then compete to the best of your ability. And during the same show, we'll have you and your co-host act as guides, showing viewers the hot spots in each country."

"Co-host?" Jason asked, interjecting himself into the conversation.

"Yes, we've talked to Myla…"

"The babe from the cover of *Sports Illustrated*?" Rickie asked.

"Yep," Lena revealed, knowing that Rickie, like most other red-blooded males out there, would find it hard to resist turning on the tube to see one of the hottest models on the magazine pages teamed up with their favorite NFL superstar.

"Beauty and the beast," Jason chimed in, giving her a congratulatory wink. This was an unbelievably great idea and it was going to blow that dickwad T.J. Reynolds out of the sewer.

"And because of the more strenuous demands on you, we will be upping your salary per episode."

"This just keeps getting better."

"We'll have to get this cleared by the NFL," Jason added, "but it sounds damn good."

The radiance of Jason's telling smile landed on Lena and she took the moment to bask in the sunshine of his pride and respect before continuing.

"The show will be announced at the all-network meeting at the end of the month, and if my meeting later this week pans out, we'll also be announcing that it is completely sponsored. Dick's Sporting Goods is definitely interested, as is Expedia.com."

"I'm really feelin' this, Lena."

"Me, too," Jason concurred.

"Me three!" Lena jumped in. "But I'm going to need you to clear your schedule next week so we can shoot a 'sizzle reel' to present at the meeting."

"And that would be?" Jason asked.

"Honestly, we don't have time to do a full-out pilot, but the concept is so strong and because it's an in-house production, we don't need it. So we're putting together a sizzle reel, which is a fast-moving presentation—another sales tool, if you will, for advertisers. We're going to produce a hot little reel of you and Myla to show your chemistry and introduce everyone to the hottest talent duo out there."

"Cool. I am lovin' this! You tell Jay when you need me and I'm there. Now, I gotta head out. I wanna hit up Mad Ave before we head back. I'll leave and let you two hammer out the dets."

"Great. And Rickie, I'm going to have to ask you not to say a word about this to anyone. Not about the show or what happened to the first one. We really can't afford to get ripped off twice; especially since there is no Plan C."

"You got it. I know nothing." Rickie said his goodbyes and closed the door behind him. Immediately, agent and executive fell into each other's arms, finally able to share the hello kiss they'd both been aching for since they'd set eyes on each other.

"Careful, Mr. Johnson, you're turning me on."

"Baby, join the club. I've been turned on and wanting you since five minutes after we last saw each other." Jason caressed the length of her neck with his lips as his hand gave a welcoming wave to the span of her legs.

Hello turned into a silent, lip-locked conversation on the seductive qualities of the afternoon delight. They made out on the office couch like two horny teenagers; Lena enjoying the simple sweetness of romantic kissing for the first time since her high school bleacher days. There was something about knowing that this office rendezvous was not a prelude to sex, something unheard of in the short history of their relationship, that made the delayed gratification seem as hot and fulfilling as an orgasm.

Lena took the opportunity to practice some old school seduction. She playfully fought with Jason to keep all hands away from any pertinent erogenous zones, while taking the time to experiment with different kisses and touches. Her quest was to make him feel adored and pampered. Jason moaned, pushing her hand down into his lap to feel the hardness of his erection. Playing the role of teenage cock tease, Lena pulled herself away, forcing Jason to marinate in all of his delightful libidinous juices.

"So, who's your favorite to win the Kentucky Derby?" she

asked, pushing the words from her mouth as she tried to settle her breathing.

"Do we have to decide that now?" he asked while leaving a trail of butterfly kisses across her collarbone.

"Yes, we do." Lena ran her tongue cross his lips, leaving them glistening.

"I don't know yet, baby. Who's your favorite?"

"Pammy's Jewel Box. She's the only filly."

"You women always gotta stick together," Jason commented before shutting her up by filling her mouth with his tongue. Rather than protest, Lena allowed herself to melt, lips first, into his body.

The ring of her office phone intermingled with their soft moans and catches of breath. "Let it go," he pleaded through his kiss.

Lena ignored the call, waiting for Rolanda to answer it. It was only after the call hung up and the ringing began again that she remembered her executive assistant was out to lunch. Lena reluctantly untangled herself from Jason, unfulfilled desire leaving her legs feeling like jelly and her heart, and all areas south, pounding.

"Lena Macy."

"Lena, it's Ro. Are you okay? You sound funny," *like I caught you with your ass in the air.*

"I'm good. Just got my hands full," she replied, smiling at her double entendre.

"I know there is a ton of work to do, and I feel really bad about this, but I'm not coming back to the office today. I was on my way back from lunch and started feeling all lightheaded, and like I just wanna get in the bed."

"Maybe…" Lena stopped in mid thought, distracted by the sensation of Jason's tongue running up the back of her neck.

"Maybe, what?"

"Uh, maybe something you ate. Okay, Ro, feel better and hopefully I'll see you tomorrow."

Lena hung up only to have two more lines light up on her phone. She listened and conversed, offered suggestions and then issued instructions, before promising both callers that she would be free in a few moments and down to deal with what needed to be dealt with. Jason looked on with proud eyes as he watched her work, once again impressed by the manner in which this phenomenal woman handled her business. Lena was flexible and yet decisive, creative but practical, giving but knowing when to hold her ground. And the people around her liked and respected her; all traits that made her a formidable partner and a huge asset both in and out of the bedroom.

"I'm sorry but I have to get back to work. There's a lot to do if we're going to get *Rickie Versus the World* ready for the launch. Why are you looking at me like that?"

Jason placed his hands on her shoulders and pulled her close. "Pocahontas," he whispered in her ear.

"Yes?"

"You know that thing I told you the night you gave me your phone number?"

"About the ancient Chinese secret?" She giggled.

"No, the other thing."

"About how you like me a lot?"

"Yeah, and I do like you a lot," he said, repeating the words he'd said to her when they'd last made love, "but I think I love you, too."

Lena's eyes filled with wonder as she reached up and touched his face. "Can I bet on that?" she asked coyly, joy filling her heart.

"Double or nothing, baby. I'm all in."

"In that case, I think I love you back."

ROLANDA NEVER MADE IT TO THE BED. SHE BARELY MADE IT TO the bathroom. Rickie Ross was way too much in a hurry to celebrate his good fortune to wait. She stood in the stall of the men's room upstairs at the Blue Fin restaurant, smiling as he peeled away her new red mini-dress. She felt sexy and sensational, right down to her brand, spankin' new underwear. Lena may have said she couldn't come on to Rickie Ross, but she'd said nothing about him coming on to her! And as soon as he had made her acquaintance, he had. But how could he not want to know her? Not while she was wearing a stoplight red dress that dipped and swerved in all the right places, revealing miles of curves, plus fetish-worthy stilettos. Ro knew she was definitely looking "brake screeching, stop in your tracks, can't help staring" hot.

As the tastiest hunk in the NFL got busy stuffing his hungry mouth with her double D's, Rolanda thanked the gods for her fortuitous timing. It was 1:45, and she had just rounded the corner on her way back to the office. And there he was with his fine ass, coming through the doors of SFN, smiling like he'd already gotten a taste of her good and plenty.

"Rickie, wait!" she'd called after him. She would have recognized that cocky swagger anywhere. "Why are you leaving? Your meeting isn't for another fifteen minutes."

Rickie had turned, caught off guard that she obviously knew something about his schedule; shocked even more by the way she looked. She might have sounded all businesslike, but the way she looked—tits and ass poppin' out all over the place—screamed professional all right. But more like a pro on her way to the club to pick up a night's worth of dollar bills than an executive assistant.

"It's over. The meeting started at one."

"Oh, Lena must have moved it up while I was out," Rolanda had said, not letting her irritation toward her boss show. That bitch was trying hard to keep her from meeting this man. When would Ms. Macy learn that despite being the boss, she was no match for Ro's will to get her way.

"I owe you an apology," she had declared with the promise of make-up sex spewing from every pore. "The boss lady was pretty upset about my note in your swag bag. She misunderstood my message. I hope you didn't?"

"Message?" Rickie ha had no clue what she was talking about.

"From Ro Hammon? Lena's assistant," she had prompted.

"Oh yeah, yeah, yeah. The card."

"I meant what I said. *Whatever* it takes, I am capable and willing to handle."

Rickie had looked her over and licked his lips. Groupies, with their flashy selves and wide-eyed willingness to please, were like the perfect theme park roller coaster where the lines were short and the rides were free.

"As a matter of fact, I was on my way out to celebrate," he had told her, immediately putting his shopping plans on hold.

"By yourself?"

"I know, kinda lame, right? Care to join me?"

"Like I said, capable *and* willing," Rolanda had agreed, knowing he'd be unable to resist.

Rolanda had called the office to let Lena know she'd be out for the rest of the afternoon. She had taken great delight in placing the call, knowing that Lena had not succeeded in keeping her from meeting and mingling with Mr. Ross.

They had walked down Broadway through Times Square, stopping when they reached the front doors of the Blue Fin. "I have to hit the men's room," he had announced.

"I'll wait out here for you."

"No, come with me." Ro had smiled before happily following him inside, stopping at the bar, expecting to share a celebratory drink or two when he returned.

"No, I said come with me," he had insisted, grabbing her hand

and leading Ro upstairs to the men's room and into the handicapped stall.

"So what are we celebrating?" she had asked as he felt her up through a handful of matte jersey fabric. His mouth darted around her neck and ears, never landing long enough to really get her juices flowing but who the hell cared? This was Rickie Fucking Ross. That fact was aphrodisiac enough.

"I'm sure you know all about my new show," he had said as he unzipped the dress, pushing the sleeves from her shoulders and letting it drop to the floor.

"Oh, yeah. They've been working like hell around the clock on it."

Rickie had said nothing, instead pulling Rolanda's breasts from their cups and rolling her nipples in his fingers. They had sprung to life, growing and getting stiff in his hands. That's what he liked about titties—they were interactive and told a man a lot about the woman he was about to fuck. In his expert opinion, a woman with sensitive breasts generally heated up more quickly and generated more pussy juice than those chicks whose weren't. Ms. Willing and Capable was obviously one of those hot and wet, always ready freaky deaks. He had bent down; squeezing and suckling her tit, listening and loving the moans his actions had created.

"You must be really excited," Ro had commented through her theatrics, while ignoring Rickie's rough-and-tumble sexual technique.

"I am, but baby, since you work for the boss, why waste time talking about what you already know," he had replied.

Rolanda had taken the hint and had shut up. Fuck being T.J. Reynolds's spy. She was finally about to get some from what had been the object of her obsession for months; T.J.'s bidding could wait until *after* she got off. Ro had put all her attention back on

Rickie, kissing him hard on the lips all the while unbuckling his belt.

"Now that's what I'm talking about!"

"Well, stop talking and show me what you're working with."

In one swift move, she pulled his slacks and boxers off his hips and slid them down his meaty thighs. His dick sprang free, giving her a big hello. Ro smiled. Rickie's cock was big. It was black. And it was hard as a metal pipe. Just the way she liked it.

He didn't give her much time to admire it. "Let me get just a little taste, bareback," he insisted. With the strength and deftness of the athlete he was, Rickie pushed her against the side of the stall and thrust his rod into her, swallowing the pleasurable growl of penetration that was trying to escape his lips. Rickie proceeded to pump her hard, rhythmically grinding the head of his dick against the rippling walls of her sopping cooch.

"Damn, baby, you got one juicy pussy. It's such a waste not to feel you a hundred percent, but it's time to put on the raincoat."

"Don't worry. I'm on the pill," she told him, as he collapsed against her, pinning her up against the wall.

"I don't worry about that, I had my shit fixed. No more babies for me. I already got three," Rickie let her know. He may be a horny dog but he was certainly not a stupid one; especially with all these crazy chicks out there trying to trick a baller into havin' babies so they could collect support checks. No, it wasn't rug rats he was worried about; it was all the other shit these groupie girls give him. He loved to fuck but not enough to die.

Rickie pulled the rubber from his shirt pocket and quickly stripped off the wrapper, put it on and his dick back inside her. He picked up where he'd left off, pounding her pussy with gusto. Rolanda tried to respond in kind, attempting to put her back into it and make this a memorable "nice to meet you" for them both, but could not proceed under the weight of his body. Rickie moved too fast, his body rocking up against hers as his dick banged her coochie and his hands groped her tits, squeezing them so hard she was sure he'd left fingerprints. She wished she could take off his shirt and run her tongue across those hard, smooth pecs she'd stared at countless times on his publicity photo. She also wished she could kiss him but the only part not in contact with her was his mouth. Rickie held his head leaned back, closed his eyes and stretched his lips tight across his face as he pounded away.

"Yeah, girl, ride this big dick," he grunted into the air.

Rolanda did just that, putting her foot on the toilet to allow him to go deeper. The adjustment in her position agreed with him, as Rickie fucked her harder and faster, squeezing his muscular ass cheeks into her greedy palms. Ro dug her nails into his butt as he shot his jism into her, bucking back and forth against her pelvis, trying to squeeze out every drop. His spasms stopped, and Rickie pulled out, removing the condom and flushing it down the toilet.

"Thanks for the celebration," he said as he pulled on his pants and buckled his belt. "You sure didn't lie, Rhonda. You are hell of capable."

"Rhonda? My name is Rolanda. And you have no idea just how capable I am."

"Sorry. My bad."

"So um, welcome to the Sports Fan Network. I guess, I'll be seeing you around the office," she said, stepping into her dress. "A little help."

Rickie zipped up her dress with one arm while checking out the time on his other. "Yeah, you've got one hell of a boss."

"Yeah, everybody seems to think so, including your agent," Rolanda let him know, using sign language to show him exactly what she meant. Ro left out her suspicion about Lena doing double duty with old man Paskin.

"She's a smart lady."

"Yeah, but she's not the only smart one with some juice," Rolanda let him know, annoyed that he seemed down with the idea. "You should meet T.J. Reynolds; he's over at another network but a lot of folks say he's going to be the head of all of the networks with PBC when Mr. Paskin retires. I know him, if you ever want to meet him. It couldn't hurt you and I'd be glad to introduce you."

"Good to know."

"Yeah, let's keep in touch. I've been around a while and I know a lot of people. And when this whole transition thing goes down, you may need a friend."

"What transition?"

"Douglas Paskin, the guy who owns the entire shebang is retiring soon. He's going to pick either Lena or T.J. Reynolds to run the whole conglomerate. Knowing both of them could only be helpful in the long run, and I can make that happen."

"Good to know. Okay, baby. I, uh, gotta head out. Again, thanks for the celebration. You were great. I'll be seeing you around."

Rickie stepped out of the stall and walked straight out the door, leaving Rolanda in the bathroom smiling. She had just banged Rickie Ross! Was he the best fuck she'd ever had? Not by a long shot, but he had the three F's in abundance—fame, fortune and flamboyance. Now that was one hell of a notch to be proud of and a potentially important pawn to have on her side of the board should Lena pull this thing off and ultimately win. Yeah, T.J. had a great shot, but hedging her bet seemed the smart thing to do. And Rolanda Hammon was no dummy.

Chapter Fourteen

Lena sat across from the breakfast table enjoying brunch with Douglas. It was the first Sunday in a month that she'd felt relaxed enough to actually take a break from work and spend a little time doing the father-daughter thing.

"So why is it such a big secret?" Douglas prompted, smiling broadly and pulling out his considerable charm for his only child. It baffled, and even hurt him, that Lena was holding back on discussing her personal life with him. She still didn't trust him completely, not after the Michael debacle and since the race for his place at the conference table had begun. He hated that they'd lost the special closeness they'd once shared when she was his treasured cliché—daddy's little girl, the apple of his eye, his princess—and he was her hero. It was at times like this that he cursed the business, the family legacy that he held so dear, for getting in the way of his relationship with his beloved daughter.

It was not Lena's fault. If Douglas were totally honest, he himself was to blame. It had always been his creed that the less people knew about him and his feelings, the more powerful his negotiating position would be—in everything, including his personal relationships. This inner directive had cost him his college sweetheart and the love of his life—Tina, and in recent years was taking its toll on his relationship with Lena. But as he got older he couldn't help wonder if it was time to let go and open up. But how does one do that after living a lifetime of holding everything close to the vest?

"Lenora Macy Paskin, I am your father. I am the man who gave you life and would give up his own to protect you. Now, I know that you have a new beau in your life, and I need to make sure he's worthy."

"That's the problem, Daddy. You take overprotective to a whole new level." She smiled at him, loving him for loving her, even if it did feel overbearing sometimes.

"It's only because I love you, Peaches."

"I know," she said, caving to his charm. "Okay, you're right. I have been seeing someone, but it isn't serious. His name is Jason."

"From the way your eyes lit up as his name left your lips, I'd say you're pretty serious. I haven't seen that look in a very long time."

Lena smiled like a kid caught with her hand in the jelly bean jar. No matter how old she got, he could still read her like a well-loved bedtime story. "I like him. Okay, okay, but it's only fun and games at this point," she told him, unwilling to confess her true feelings. "It's a 'something to do' kind of relationship."

"Details. Give your old dad something to navigate the turf with. I'm sure you've already told your mother everything, as you usually do. I'm always hearing things secondhand," Douglas claimed, applying a little guilt to the mix.

"Actually, I haven't. And by the way, it's real mature of you to pull the 'you love your mother more than me' card," Lena teased him. "Jason is a sports agent I met while I was in Miami during the Super Bowl. He lives in Chicago, and we hang out together when he comes to town. I mean, we like each other, but that's all there is to it right now." She hoped her father would buy her explanation and stop digging.

Douglas took a deep breath and exhaled loudly through his nose. Not a good sign. "Sports agents have a reputation for being a rather sleazy breed, don't they?"

"You, of all people, are not believing some stupid stereotype, are you?" Lena felt her hackles rise. "Don't judge Jason, Dad. You don't even know him…"

"How could I? You won't even talk about him, let alone introduce him to your family. If you did…"

"It's not that kind of relationship," Lena insisted, "But if I did, he'd probably drop me like a hot rock. You can be a bit intimidating, old man. Your reputation as an industry giant is a force to be reckoned with. I know that you can be a big old softie, but that's not what most people think."

It was true; few people got the chance to see how tender and caring he was when it came to the people he loved. When Douglas Paskin believed and supported someone, the effect he had on their personal and professional development was long-lasting.

"And Mother, she's comes on like Hurricane Tina. Introduce her to someone and she's smiling and being charming, all the while disarming their defenses. The next thing they know, they're sucked up in the eye of the storm and by the time she's done with them, she knows everything there is to know right down to their shoe size.

"No. I can't risk introducing anyone I really like to you all until I know if he's a keeper."

"Your mother and I are just concerned that nobody tries to take advantage of you because of who you are."

"Daddy, very few people know who I really am, and I like it that way for many reasons. Please, don't worry. Jason is a good guy. He's about to become a partner in his agency and he has a great heart. He really looks out for his clients."

"And my daughter? He does the same for you?"

"Yes, Daddy. I wouldn't be *friends* with him if he didn't. Trust me. Believe it or not, I have great judgment when it comes to men, and many other things as well."

"Do you trust T.J.?" Douglas asked, fishing for information while trying not to break his promise to Tina. He had no intention of getting in the middle of this turf battle, but Lena had been dealt a major professional blow. Corporate waters were rough and shark infested. T.J. had revealed his ability to be cut-throat and competitive—not all bad qualities for the job he was vying for, as long as he knew where to draw the line. Douglas now wanted to gauge how strong and savvy Lena really was when it came to dealing with such a tough adversary.

"Why would I? We're rivals in a high-stakes game. I would be stupid to do so, don't you think?" Lena was so grateful for Jason's idea to make T.J.'s steal look like a part of her plan. It was strategically brilliant and when everything came out next week, she would be the last one standing, hopefully with her very dainty stiletto heel poised delicately atop T.J. Reynolds' crotch.

"Smart girl."

"Daddy, you taught me many business lessons over the years; two that I have built my management style around. First, don't be afraid to surround yourself with the best and brightest, and then let them do what they do best and make you and the company look good. And the second, the old adage of keeping your friends close and your enemies closer. Don't worry. I have T.J.'s number."

"I'm happy you've listened and learned, but you have to also concern yourself with the question: Does he have yours?"

Jason looked around the famous Churchill Downs and couldn't help getting caught up in the sense of pageantry and revelry. Even Mother Nature was in on the party. The robin blue sky contrasted nicely with the bright emerald green field, and the thousands of beautiful petunias and marigolds popping out of all shades of purple, pink, red and yellow, dotted the area like confetti.

The eclectic mix of jovial spectators awaited the arrival of the four-legged stars and their riders.

Despite its billing as a legitimate sports event, it was as much a party as any Super Bowl or NBA Championship Weekend, only this event was infused with Southern gentility and tradition. The majestic steeples stood watch over the multi-tiered grandstand, which were teeming with the colorful fashion-forward display of expensive jewels and outlandish hats covering the heads of famous celebrities and wives of the well-to-do. The stands buzzed with excited anticipation as the rich and well-bred laughed and chatted among themselves, while trying to ignore the gross displays of bad manners going on down below. While the gentry class sipped on mint juleps and Kentucky Bourbon, the common folk were gathered in the infield, swilling down Budweiser and amusing themselves with their own traditional madcap merriment—the Port-a-Potty roof races. Wearing baseball caps and cargo shorts, runners raced each other along the tops of the portable toilets while spectators threw anything and everything at them to impede their progress.

Jason was in Kentucky partying this first Saturday in May with Rickie and several other of his famous clients, but wishing he was there with Lena. He'd tried to convince her to come but she'd begged off, citing the need to finalize her presentation for the all-network meeting the following week. He understood, but was disappointed. Lena would have loved it and he would have loved sharing it all with her.

"Damn, dude. You really do miss her," he said under his breath as he pulled out his cell phone and dialed her number. "Hey baby," he greeted her softly when Lena answered the phone. "I just wanted you to know that I am here in Louisville, and missing the hell out of you."

"I miss you, too."

"You would absolutely love it down here and I would love showing you off. I'd get you one of those big-ass hats and have you strutting around making all the other fillies jealous!"

"You're sweet," Lena said, not telling him that she'd been to Churchill Downs many times with her family.

"How's the work coming?"

"Great. Rickie and Myla's sizzle reel is just that, sizzling! And we're down to fine-tuning the little details. I'm hoping that this all can stay a secret just a week longer."

"Still no idea who leaked the first show?"

"No, but you can be assured head, balls, and a few toes will roll."

"I'm scared of you! So Pocahontas, it's time to place your bet. Win, place or show?"

"Pammy's Jewel Box to show. If my girl comes in first, second or third, I win. What about you?"

"I'd like to see your jewel box," he flirted back.

"Man, do you ever think of anything besides sex?" she asked, teasing him, but really wanting to know.

"Of course, my son, sports, food, clients, vacations, but then my brain always comes back to you and then sex!"

"You're impossible."

"Nah, just a hot, red-blooded Mandingo man."

"Okay, Mandingo man, quit stalling. Who's your horse?"

"My Three Sons, to *win*," he emphasized with authority.

"You do realize that if *your* Three Sons doesn't finish first, you lose."

"Baby, go big or go home. So, like real betting, we should up the ante based on the bet."

"I ain't 'fraid of you or your damn Three Sons," Lena wolfed.

"Okay, nasty girl. I can go with that cuz when my stud smokes your pretty girl's behind, I got some *outrageous* sexual tricks planned for you. Like a…a…an orgy with some lesbian dwarfs? Now whatcha got to say?"

"You are such a slut puppy." She laughed.

"Well, I guess that's better than being a straight-up dog."

"Marginally so. It means you're still a hound but your intentions are good. Of course if you ask my dad, he'll tell you all sports agents are sleazy dogs."

"So you've been talking agents with your dad, huh? Any one agent in particular?" he asked, secretly thrilled that she'd spoken to her father about him.

"I did happen to mention your name when he asked me if I was seeing anybody," she told him, blushing.

"And he called me a sleazy agent? Well, that's not good. Is he in the business? I mean, does he work with agents? What's he got against us?"

"Don't think twice about it," Lena replied, dodging the questions about her father as she always did. "He's just very protective of me. Always has been, will probably always be."

"Yeah, well, remind me to tell you about my folks one day. You want protective? That I got, plus conservative, religious and judgmental, but they love me."

"I'd love to hear about them. Perhaps I'll make that a part of my winnings when Pammy shows your Three Sons her ass as she's crossing the finish line."

"Girl, you can talk some shit. I love it! And I love you! But I gotta go, the boys are back from making their bets. I'll call you after the race. Tune-in though. I want you to watch my boy get all up in filly's jewel box!"

"Nasty ass." She giggled. "I love you back." Lena hung up, hearing her heart sing as she spoke the words.

Jason clicked the phone off, smiling at his good fortune. Her daddy had every right to feel protective. He'd managed to sire the perfect woman—a lady in public, a dealmaker in the board-room, and a freak in the bedroom. And Jason was the lucky man to find her. When the time was right, he'd sell himself to old man Macy, just like he did to every other parent he needed to convince to trust him and put their kid's life in his hands.

"Ready to roll, man?" Rickie asked, slapping Jason hard on the back. "Race is about to jump off. You think Lena will let me try out some horse racing on the show? This shit looks fun."

"Well, I doubt you'd make the weight requirement, but we can ask. If there's a way, she'll find it."

"That's a smart chick, man. Do you know she's close to heading up the whole nut over there at PBC?"

"What are you talking about?" Jason asked, confused by what he thought he was hearing. "Where and when did you hear this?"

"Last time we were in New York and in the bathroom at the Blue Fin while I was bangin' her secretary."

"You fucked Ro?"

"Yeah, I was celebrating my new show. Don't look so shocked. Rhonda says you're doing her boss, which explains the 'hands off' lecture after that first lunch we all had."

"Rolanda," Jason said, correcting the name but not the truth of the rest of his statement.

"Whatever. Trim is trim. It don't need no name."

"Let's get to our seats. They're loading the horses," Jason said, as the call to the post sounded, signaling the imminent start of this year's Run for the Roses.

"Yeah, and I got money to make."

Jason followed his client to their seats, his face a picture of un-certainty. He'd promised to keep their private relationship under wraps so why had she told her assistant? And Rickie had just told him that the "job" she and T.J. were competing for was Douglas Paskin's broadcast heir apparent; why hadn't she? For all the things he did know about her—the hot spot behind her ear, the way her clit responded to the tug of her nipples, how she laughed with joy when she was about to get busy, and how the better the sex the more wide awake she was when it was over, there seemed a lot about Lena Macy that he didn't know. Jason mined his gut for his feelings. Mainly his emotions came down to two: confusion and curiosity. He and his girl had much to discuss during their next go-round.

The bell sounding as the gates opened broke into his thoughts. His attention turned to the flurry of hoofs racing down the track. He watched and listened as the announcer called the race. My Three Sons made his move and jockeyed for an outside position on that critical first turn. Coming out of the turn two horses, Jazzman and Special K, were ahead of his, with Pammy's Jewel Box back in seventh. Coming into the club house turn, Jazzman had taken the lead on the inside rail as the filly made a move to the outside running hard to pull into fifth, with My Three Sons keeping the pace and his third-place spot. It was a grueling half-mile and the tension on and off the track was palatable.

Jazzman continued to lead by a length into the far turn, with My Three Sons on the chase, the outside running half a length behind Special K. A flurry of horse racing and jockeying for position went on during the last turn and going into the home stretch, My Three Sons made his move, overtaking Special K and pulling up on Jazzman. Pammy's Jewel Box fought to remain in contention, but lost ground and fell back into the pack.

The crowd was on its feet going wild as My Three Sons found his stride and raced past Jazzman, extending his lead and winning the Kentucky Derby by one-and-a-half lengths. Pammy's Jewel Box finished practically where she started, in fifth place.

Through the deafening din of jubilant cheers, Jason felt his pants pocket vibrate.

He pulled out his phone and saw that Lena was calling. There was no way he would be able to hear so he let the call go to voice mail and then sent her an instant message.

See what happens when you send a filly to do a stallion's work? Y.O.M. BIG time!

That was pretty impressive, Lena wrote back. *Do you know the chances of actually winning???*

Pretty good if you do research and not just decide by gender or what color uniform they wear! So when do I collect? This was a big win. I'm feeling really nasty. The ante is upped!

Lena took a moment to reflect before typing her response. She loved Jason and she loved the woman she was when she was with him. He had liberated her libido and turned her into a loving freak and made her feel so comfortable in her new sexual skin. And look how he'd helped her spin T.J.'s treachery into strategic gold. Lena's fingers flew across the tiny keyboard.

A bet's a bet. Bring it on, Mr. Big Johnson. P.S. I love you, too.

Chapter Fifteen

"**M**om! What are you doing here? It's not even seven o'clock," Lena asked, opening the door to her Battery Park apartment. Nothing like your mother showing up out of the blue to bring on a little coitus interruputus. Thank God, the doorman had called up to announce Tina's arrival. It had given Jason time to get dressed again and Lena time to do something to sully the freshness of the just-fucked look she was sporting. He'd only arrived a little less than an hour ago, turning their hello kiss into a morning delight.

"I know, but I wanted to have breakfast with you and help steel up that spine of yours for today's meeting. I thought we could go over to the hotel together," Tina said, breezing through the door and pushing into the living room. "Oh my, I see you already have company. Good morning."

"Good morning, Mrs. Macy..."

"DuPree, darling. I haven't been Ms. Macy for ages. Not since brown suits and Jelly Bellies were all the rage. And you are?"

"Jason Armstrong. Nice to meet you," he told her, looking for some sign that she found the name familiar. He found none. Either Tina DuPree was a master at poker or Lena had not yet said anything to her mother about him.

"Uh, mom, Jason is a friend of mine."

"And apparently a very good one to be here at this time of the morning."

Jason laughed nervously. "I actually just arrived about an hour ago. I flew in from Chicago for the meeting."

"Oh, you work for PBC? Which company?" she asked, giving him the once over.

Jeezus. Here comes Hurricane Tina. "Mom, give him a break. Jason is...Jason is my boyfriend. We've been seeing each other for the past four..."

"Actually five," Jason interrupted.

"Five months," she corrected herself with a broad smile. "He's a great guy and an amazing friend. He came in this morning to hold my hand."

"As did I. So what do you say, Jason? You take the left and I take the right and we all sit down over some breakfast and get to know each other." Tina grabbed her daughter's hand and waited for Jason to take the other and together they escorted her to the breakfast table.

"Why don't I whip up a little something, while you two talk," Jason suggested more as a means of escape than to be helpful.

"A fabulous idea, darling," Tina commented as he left the room. "Well, cute, supportive, and he cooks, too! My, my..."

"Will you stop it?" Lena said, her tone a cross between a demand and a plea.

"I'm just saying..."

"Don't say anything," Lena said, listening to the refrigerator and cabinet doors open and shut in the kitchen. This was the first time Jason had been to her apartment and the first meal he'd be making for her. Pity she had to share the experience with her mother.

"Seriously, darling, I wanted to come by and give you a big hug and see for myself what state of mind you are in. What happens today is either going to make or break your future as your father and I have envisioned it. And it looks, as hard as you've been working, like you're finally seeing it as the one you want for yourself."

"Thanks, Mom, I'm fine. I'm feeling good and ready to rumble. It was really nice of you to come by, though next time you might want to call first." Lena's eyes went wide as she used her head to gesture toward the kitchen. The savory smells of breakfast foods wafted through the air, making her smile at his effort.

"Duly noted, though perhaps if you weren't always so secretive I'd have known to do so. I swear, you are just as bad as your father!"

"To hear him tell it, I share all my secrets with you and tell him nothing. Maybe I like minding my own business!"

"Jason, darling, it smells yummy."

"Thank you!" he called out in response, while sprinkling powdered sugar on his culinary creation. It was a good thing that Lena's moms had shown up in the A.M. Breakfast was Jason's signature meal, and it was obvious he was going to have to pull out all his tricks for this charm offensive.

"Keeping secrets is not always a good thing."

"So you're saying there are no scandalous skeletons snuggled up against the fur coats in your closets?" Lena prodded.

"I said no such thing, darling. Secrets and scandals are two different things. Secrets usually come back to bite one in the derriere. But a little bit of scandal makes one's life much more interesting to look back upon."

"You have turned into quite the freak since you and Daddy divorced." Lena smiling broadly. *Fruit don't fall...*

"Lenora, darling, don't be so sure it happened..."

"Breakfast is served," Jason announced, entering the room with two plates piled high with French toast, topped with strawberries and sprinkled with powdered sugar, and scrambled eggs on the side. Usually he'd throw in some Canadian bacon or link sausage or maybe whip up some Huevos Rancheros but pickings were slim around Ms. Macy's kitchen. "I'll be right back with coffee," he told them, wondering why Mrs. DuPree was calling her "Lenora." He added it to his list of questions to ask once the meeting was over and Lena's stress levels had returned to normal.

Jason returned with the coffee and his own breakfast and sat down with the ladies to break bread. Silence prevailed as they all dug in, broken by the satisfying sounds of delicious food being eaten and enjoyed.

"So, Jason, where are you from?" Tina asked as she daintily cut off another bite of French toast.

"Originally from a little town called Vidalia, Georgia, but I live in Chicago now."

"As in the onion?" Lena asked, taking in this new knowledge herself. As much as she loved him and as intimate as they were, there was still quite a bit of personal information she did not know about Jason.

"Exactly. It's about one hundred-sixty miles from Atlanta, which is nice because my parents aren't too far away from J. J."

"And whom would that be?"

"My son, Jason Jr." Jason watched as Tina's perfectly arched, left eyebrow lifted ever so slightly.

"He's five and lives in Atlanta with his mother," Lena chimed in, letting her mother know that she was fully versed on the matter.

"And your parents? Are they retired?" Tina asked. Both Lena and Jason recognized her wording as code for "what do your people do?"

"My dad was the pastor at the St. Paul's Baptist Church and my mother is a retired schoolteacher," Jason volunteered. As the ladies listened, he went on to reveal some of the highs and lows of his life thus far; all things he'd planned to tell Lena and he now decided to share with both women. What the hell, he might as well open up his autobiography and let them see what was inside.

As mother and daughter consumed their breakfast, Jason gave them each further food for thought. He told them about his very conservative upbringing and his roots in the Baptist church and how playing on the church football team was more important to him than attending service. He revealed how upset his parents were when he chose not to use his football scholarship at Penn State to earn his theology degree but instead put his love of the game over his love of God and studied sports management.

Jason spoke of how he'd broken their hearts when he had a child out of wedlock and how they were even more disappointed that he hadn't married the woman and set things right for himself and his son in the eyes of God.

"I didn't think they'd ever get over that," Jason admitted, as Lena's loving hand found his under the table. "The scandal almost killed them, you know, the pastor's son being such a scoundrel. But they did and have been great-grandparents to Jay. I've tried to make them proud while at the same time being my own man and living my own life, but I never want to cause them that kind of shame and disappointment again."

"It's amazing how resilient we parents can be," Tina said softly, speaking both to her daughter and her friend. "But I know we can seem overbearing and unrelenting at times. We only want the best for you kids and sometimes we say and do things that are in direct conflict with whom you've become as an adult. We don't mean any harm, and in time, if we're lucky, most of us finally right our wrongs."

"The sizzle reel is all cued up and ready to go," Aleesa whispered, as she handed Lena her final script. She'd kept everything at home in safe keeping, so there was no chance of information getting leaked before today's presentation.

They stood to the side of the dais in the ballroom of the New York Hilton hotel, waiting for the head from the News Headline Network to finish his presentation so Lena could begin hers.

"You look fabulous in that dress, and blissfully serene, I might add."

"I'm actually feeling that way."

"You must have gotten laid this morning," Aleesa teased.

"That, too, but the peacefulness comes mostly because I know that right now I am holding T.J. Reynolds' scruffy little balls in my hand, and in approximately fifteen minutes from now I am going to be shoving them down his lying, stealing throat. Metaphorically speaking, of course."

"Of course! Damn. You go, Ms. Barracuda! Hanging out with the sharks in the agent tank has rubbed off on you."

"In more ways than you know." Lena smiled. "Have you seen dick for brains yet?"

"Yeah, he's sitting at table thirteen with the rest of his crew. Wearing a gray suit and that oily little smirk of his."

"I'm sure he's feeling pretty damn good about his tired self after the rousing response he got following his presentation."

"I hate to say it, but the show looks damn impressive," Aleesa admitted.

"It should; it was my idea. And before all of this is all said and done, the people who count are going to know about it."

"I was sure he was going to steal the cross promotion idea, too, but he didn't mention it."

"He's not that stupid. Too many people knew that the idea came from our side. Can I tell you how much I am going to enjoy sticking it to that bastard?"

"Girl, it shows. I don't think I've seen you this excited since your little slut romp down in Miami. Okay, showtime," Aleesa said as the master of ceremonies began Lena's introduction.

"Any lipstick on my teeth?"

"Nope, pearly white and perfect. Break a leg, sister."

Lena stepped on to the stage, opened up the folder that held her memorized speech, and took a deep cleansing breath. She wished Jason could have come with her today, and though she could have made it happen, it would have been inappropriate to invite an outsider to their corporate event. As the applause died down, she looked out into the audience to search for the only three faces in the room she cared were there—her mother and father, seated with the PBC Board of Directors, and T.J. Reynolds sitting with his executive staff at the LiveYou table. She gave each of them a smile, saving the brightest and longest lasting one for her irritating nemesis.

"Good morning, everyone. I'm so pleased to be joining you again. This year has zipped by and it's amazing to me that it's already time for us to gather and talk about our respective new seasons. I have sat and listened to your state-of-the-network reports and your new programming plans for the fall schedule with sincere regard. You have been working hard since last year's meeting. You have all done a yeoman job of raising your bottom lines and giving the PBC viewers, listeners and readers programming that is interesting, insightful and entertaining. I am impressed by your professional and creative ingenuity and proud to be your colleague."

Those in the room that loved her, sat and listened, impressed by her command of the podium. Each in their own head, Douglas in particular, was complimenting her decision to come before this audience as a peer and yet, in the most respectful, all encompassing manner, speak to them as their superior. It was subtle and masterful and gauging from the attentive and respectful looks on their faces, highly effective. She was claiming the throne, but without any sense of brash entitlement. Aleesa stole a look in T. J.'s direction, making note of the almost bored expression on his face as he fiddled with his program while pretending to be marginally interested.

"Like all of you, my colleagues at The Sports Fan Network have been working diligently to bring new life and viewers to our channel. Competing with powerhouses like ESPN, the broadcast networks have been tough.

"After taking the helm of SFN, my charge to the programming and sales executives was to find new and creative ways to enhance our programming with two goals in mind: to keep and grow our viewer base, and to bring new and different advertisers to the network. They have not let me down. In fact, they have exceeded my expectations. Over the past year, we have revamped our traditional talking heads shows with new formats, sets and in some cases, talent. This coming season we are producing three major documentaries, including one on the greening of American sports, as well as reviving and revitalizing our biography show, *Sporting Heroes*. We'd like you to take a look now as we give you a glimpse at the new and improved SFN."

On cue, the tape rolled on their first video presentation highlighting the upcoming SFN season and advertising projections, including the sponsored *Sports Watchin' Women* spots. It was an all-encompassing view of the network's new look and schedule, sans *Rickie Versus the World*. Lena was saving that for her big finish. The short presentation ended with interested applause that was enthusiastically polite. It certainly did not match the emotional power following T.J.'s show-and-tell, but it was enough to let her know that they understood the inherent potential of the network's upcoming season.

Lena let her gaze creep over to T.J.'s table. Because of the media splash he and LiveYou had received following the announcement of *Sports Mom*, T.J. had walked into this meeting as the "It" boy. No other network in the group had managed to create such a buzz in years. He sat there applauding away, his "that's all she's got" smirk belying his show of enthusiasm.

Aleesa saw it, too, and shot her boss a concerned look. Lena responded with a smile and an affirmative shake of her head. She was pleased. Were they wowed off their feet? No, not yet. But they would be in a few minutes.

"Thank you. As you can see, we are making great and positive strides to change the direction and fan base at SFN. To this end, I'd like to share with you our upcoming season's jewel. We are so very excited about this program because it branches out into new directions and infiltrates territories like no other network has attempted. We are also forging promotional partnerships with those formally viewed strictly as competition, and by doing so hope to reach new audiences. If they are going to turn the channel, it might as well be to another friend, where they are still going to see and feel our presence. If our season goes as expected, we see it as a future model for many of the networks under the PBC umbrella.

"Great minds must think alike, because like Mr. Reynolds and LiveYou TV, we, too, see the strong value in providing more programming options to the millions of women out there, who not only enjoy the games themselves but the spin-off programming possibilities surrounding them—sports celebrities, food, fashion; the list goes on.

"So in addition to our *Sports Watchin' Women* spots, SFN is proud to announce the premiere of *Rickie Versus the World*, hosted by NFL superstar Rickie Ross and supermodel and actress Myla. This fabulous new show is a hybrid of international sports and travel, and with these two dynamic hosts is guaranteed to appeal to a wide variety of sports, travel, and fashion fans. Watch."

As the Rickie and Myla's sizzle reel rolled, Lena took a long drink of water in hopes of drowning the butterflies. Everything was riding on this show and the buildup started here. She looked out into the audience and smiled broadly. The energy in the room was rising exponentially as the audience watched with rapt attention. This time when the video ended, the applause was long and thunderous. Lena sought out her touchstones. Her parents' faces were both beaming with pride. Best yet, was T.J.'s. It told all. He'd been trumped big time, and he knew it.

That's not all, asshole. The best is still yet to come, Lena assured him telepathically.

"Thank you. Thanks so much," Lena spoke, trying to regain control. "It *is* exciting and it is a testimony to the creativity, *integrity*, and desire by our staff to generate *original* ideas and turn them into advertising and marketing gold," Lena said, looking directly at T.J. "And that is just what my amazing staff at SFN has done. I am happy to announce that advertising for *Rickie Versus the World* is already ninety-eight percent sold out for its first *two* seasons at premium rates. We are thrilled to reveal that Dick's Sporting Goods and Expedia.com are our two main sponsors. Additionally, Samsonite luggage will be sponsoring two thirty-second travel tips during each show, and we will be running special cross-promotion advertising with the Travel Channel and our own *Sports Page Magazine*."

Lena went to reveal the negotiations for a syndication deal going on with the Travel Channel and other channels to run *Rickie*

Versus the World in future seasons. She also stated their plans for an aggressive promotional campaign in women's magazines and on various social networking sites, including an iPhone app for viewers to track Rickie around the world and keep score.

"To close, on the strength of *Rickie Versus the World*, plus our new format changes and special events programming acquisitions, the projection by those who rate our stocks is that SFN's revenue is projected to rise five-point-eight percent to two hundred twenty-five-point three million dollars next year, on a three percent gain in advertising and ten percent climb in affiliate fees. Earnings before interest, taxes, depreciation and amortization may jump six-point-seven percent to ninety-eight-point-four million dollars."

When she finished, the room again pounded their palms in appreciation. These executives, including her father, who'd spent their careers diligently trying to originate or buy programming that was innovative, creative, enjoyable and profitable, knew success when they saw it.

Lena looked over to table thirteen, triumph beaming from every pore in her body, but his seat was empty. T.J. Reynolds had already left the building. She didn't care; all she wanted to do at this moment was to call Jason and let him know how well everything had gone. Better yet, she couldn't wait to add celebration to tonight's I.O.U. She didn't know if it was the thrill of victory or the sweetness of anticipation, but Lena was feeling hot, horny and way impatient to see her lover.

Chapter Sixteen

Lena ignored the ringing phone as she attempted to answer the slew of congratulatory emails that had arrived in her inbox following this morning's meeting. It was nearly five and the phone had been ringing all afternoon as well. The callers, like the writers, were sending her kudos for such a fine presentation, and many were asking questions about the various partnerships she was blazing.

"Lena, that was Mr. Paskin's office. He'd like to see you downtown today at six-thirty." Rolanda stood at the door to inform her boss.

"So, did they say for what reason?"

"No, but she did say it was mandatory."

"Okay. I will see you tomorrow, then," Lena said, trying to leave the exasperation out of her voice while dismissing her assistant. She was pretty sure her father simply wanted to congratulate her in person for the fine showing SFN had put in this afternoon, but she wanted to go home and freshen up before her date with Jason.

"Yep. Good luck tonight," Ro said with a wink in her voice. *Sounds like old man P is horny*, she thought as she hurried back to her desk, picked up her line and punched in T.J.'s cell number.

"It's me. FYI, she's got a mandatory meeting with Paskin at six-thirty tonight."

"Interesting. So do I. Did she have any clue why he wants to see her?"

"Nope. I thought it might be a booty call, but now that you're going, too, I guess some serious shit is about to go down."

"If you hear anything more, let me know."

"And when you have some free time, you let me know. My horns need shaving."

T.J. Reynolds was already in Douglas' office when Lena arrived. She stood in the threshold, unnoticed as T.J. and her father carried on a spirited conversation about the fall of the European economy. As she looked on, two thoughts traipsed back to back through her head: Did Douglas ever think of T.J. as the son he never had; and why had her father sandbagged her like this?

She cleared her throat in welcome as she ventured into the expansive office space. "Douglas. T.J."

"Lena, I'm glad you could make it. Travis and I were trying hard to solve Europe's economic crisis," he joshed.

"Lena, good to see you. Great job today, by the way," T.J. greeted.

"You, too," she replied without conviction.

"Actually, I was wondering out loud how much time you must have spent with your calculator trying to figure out how to offset the high production costs of shooting your new show, which sounds incredible by the way. You know, with the world economy being in such a bad state," T.J. said, loving the fact that he was sure he'd found a flaw in her plan.

"Not an excessive amount; we didn't need to. I mean, of course we took that fact into consideration, but because Rickie is competing against the *world*, that gives us hundreds of options around the globe to choose from. There are so many interesting sports in so many countries where production costs will be considerably lower, that shooting one or two episodes in European locations will not bust the budget at all.

"And the beauty of it all is that we are highlighting local tourism, and folks are eager to have us come and are being quite accommodating. Believe me, we've tried to think of everything—pro and con."

Douglas looked on with interest. The two were attempting to spar with polite barbs, but it was obvious by the tone and energy in the room that the two despised each other. If they weren't careful, it wouldn't be long before the gloves came off and their contentiousness got nasty. Douglas had every intention of provoking them. Before he made his choice, he wanted to witness for himself what each was made of when it came down to the heat of battle.

"Well, Lena and T.J., I wanted to meet you with you and congratulate you both on a fine job, not only today but these past few years. You both have risen to whatever challenge was brought your way, and I am proud of both of you," Douglas told them. He avoided looking Lena in her eyes, not wanting any slip of fatherly pride to show.

"Thank you, Douglas. You are an industry genius and one of the finest men I've had the privilege of knowing. It's been an honor working for you and learning from you," T.J. replied, with a slight catch in his voice.

Opting to say nothing, she smiled at Douglas in response, while screaming at T.J. in her head, *Wipe your schnoz, you brown-nosing dick.*

"I found it interesting today that both of you had decided to go after the female demographic through sports programming. Lena, your show is phenomenal and I love the way that you have spun it out for maximum profit, but while inventive, it seems like a more natural fit for SFN. But T.J., putting a sports show on a channel for women that to date has programmed mainly bridal wars and makeover shows, while risky, still shows creative genius on your part. How did it happen?"

Lena's antennae went up. Her father was fishing for information. Did he know what had really gone down between the two of them?

T.J. beamed at Douglas' statement, so caught up in the compliment he didn't see the trap that Douglas was laying for him.

"Honestly, Douglas, it was all in the research—a study that showed women are more likely to be watching sports than soap operas. It was such a coincidence when Lena and I met and she brought up the same study."

"Oh, so you two met about the idea of programming sports to women?" Douglas asked, turning to Lena.

"Yes. I had set up a meeting with T.J. to discuss the idea of cross promoting a sports program for women that SFN was developing for next season," she said, looking directly at T.J.

"And as I told Lena at that meeting, LiveYou already had a show, *SportsMom*, in development."

"He said that?"

"Yes, he did, though he didn't name or describe anything specific; just that he already had a sports show for women in development and felt that I might be a bit naïve in suggesting two competing networks work to cross promote their programming," Lena revealed, planting a little dig. She was trying to walk the line carefully. She did not want to come off like a tattling kid, literally running to Daddy. At the same time, she was not going to let this asshole get away with stealing her idea without Douglas knowing the truth.

"Sounds like a pretty progressive idea," Douglas remarked.

"I agree, and I believe what I told her was that it was a bit premature to discuss before the programs were fully developed." T.J. pursed his lips slightly, a nearly invisible nervous tick that would normally go unnoticed, but today, with four eyes in the room watching his every move, it did not.

"And how did you come up with your concept?"

T.J.'s lips twitched again. "I really don't know how it happened.

I had nothing to do with it. My staff came up with it. My programming VP, who is a soccer mom herself, thought it was just what the viewer and the network needed, brought it to me and I enthusiastically concurred."

Lena watched him lie with such ease, it got her ire racing. She had no idea how it exactly had gone down, but she did know that he was lying through his teeth.

"With all due respect, Douglas, do you have something to ask me? If so, sir, I prefer you come right out with it."

"Okay, that is fair. Lena, do you have any questions?" Douglas asked.

T.J. shot a glare at Lena, who returned his look with one of her own, a revealing mix of "gotcha" and "don't blame me."

"All right. Let's get this all out on the table. I believe, strike that. I *know* for a fact that you had no such sports show in development when we met. I believe that somehow you learned the details of our original show, *Sports Watchin' Women*, and poached it. Sure, you tweaked it a bit, but it is basically the concept I shared with you at our meeting."

"You have no proof of any such thing."

"And why didn't you wait to announce it today at the all-network meeting? Seems to me if you hadn't stolen it, you wouldn't have felt the need to get the press involved. But you had to make sure you got it out there before me, so you could claim it as your own."

T.J. sucked his teeth, trying to hide his guilt with faux indignation. His subtle admission gave her the courage to continue on with her own slight embroidery on the truth.

"You may have taken me for naïve, but I have great instincts, and I left that meeting knowing that I couldn't trust you, and that I had made a tactical error in trying to team up with you. But as my father once told me," she said, consciously avoiding Douglas' eyes, "a mistake is only a mistake if you don't learn your lesson. What you didn't know is that as soon as I got to my office, I started working on a bigger show that better showcased my host, which is what we presented today. So all told, I'm happy. I have a better program, with a much better payout to the bottom line, and you and your brand of doing business have been exposed."

"Hmmm, interesting though faulty logic on your part. All I can say is that your claim is preposterous and is verging on paranoia. As we all know, there are no new ideas and that similar concepts appear all the time." His jawbones clenched, silently revealing his anger. T.J. couldn't believe that this bitch had played him like this.

"That is true, and I'm not surprised that is what you offer as an excuse, but it really doesn't matter because you and I both know the truth."

Douglas watched their exchange with amused interest. T.J. did not budge from his position, though it was clear by his need to debase his competitor, however left-handed, that he was lying. But he was most impressed by Lena. As an executive, she remained cool and stated her position without the need for personal attack. And her critical thinking skills were outstanding. Her instincts had led her in all the right directions and her know-how made sure there was a payoff in the end. As a daughter, she had made him proud, all the while proving herself as a capable and brilliant leader.

"I have worked both of you to your limits these past years. I thought you each did a fantastic job this afternoon inspiring enthusiasm among your colleagues. With very divergent styles, you both lead by example, and have proven yourself to have the ability and foresight needed to run this company. But now I must decide which of you has the ability to lead PBC into the future.

"T.J., tell me, what is your vision for PBC?"

"Uh…well….uh, you know off the top of my head…" Lena and Douglas watched with surprise as the usually unflappable T.J. Reynolds floundered with his response.

"Uh, like I said, I have been honored to work under and learn from you, Douglas. If given the privilege of running PBC, I want to retain *your* vision. To maintain the high standards and quality products that this company is known for, thanks to your hard work and commitment to excellence, and of course keep it growing in the right direction."

"Thank you. I appreciate the compliment. And Lena, what do you see in the future for PBC?"

"Well, Douglas, maintaining your commitment to excellence would be a huge part of my commitment to PBC, but I also believe that for PBC to continue to thrive it has to continue to grow. My vision is to make us stronger by continuing to diversify. In the future, I see PBC becoming a larger lifestyle network. We have LiveYou for women, but if we could add food, shelter and travel to our roster, it will get us into more households and give us a stronger position when it comes to negotiating with advertisers and affiliates."

The paternal pride he had tried so hard to keep under wraps came bursting forth. There was no residual doubt in his mind. Lena was ready to take his legacy and run with it.

"Travis, Lena, I have made my decision. I will be holding a press conference sometime next month to announce Lena as my successor," he said, shaking her hand and looking his daughter dead in her eyes. "Congratulations. You definitely *earned* it. And I am very proud of you."

And for the first time in public, Lena hugged her father. "Thank you," she whispered in his ear.

T.J. stood by feeling like the fucking first runner-up at the Miss

America Pageant. Rolanda had been right. It was obvious by the flow of emotions passing between the two, that the bottom line on their relationship was way deeper than anyone ever suspected. He had worked his ass off for years only to have it snatched away by some bitch who'd fucked her way into the executive suite.

"T.J., you've been quite an asset to PBC. This race for my successor was neck and neck down to the end. It was not an easy decision and I hope you will continue to share your insight and brand of leadership with PBC for years to come," Douglas said, turning to shake his hand.

"Truthfully, Douglas, I am very disappointed and need time to consider my options. But I thank you for the consideration and opportunity," he replied, managing to keep his anger in check. He was not about to go off now because he had no intention of throwing up the white flag. "So, if you will excuse me. We'll talk soon."

Douglas and Lena stood silently as T.J. departed. From the corner of his eye he saw her checking her watch. "I'm sorry; am I keeping you from something? Someone?" he asked, his teasing tinting every word.

"I am sorry, but Daddy, but I have to leave. I have a previously scheduled appointment."

"You mean a date." He laughed, amused by her professional demeanor.

Lena replied with laughter. "Okay, okay, no putting anything past you! I have a date with Jason," she admitted before giving her father a warm and loving hug. "I love you."

"I love you, too. Still just fun and games? You have plenty of reason to celebrate."

"Oh I do. Dad, you won't be sorry, I promise. I will not let you down. I am going to make you and our family so proud."

"Lenora, you already do. As a daughter, you always have. But as a businesswoman, I have never been as proud of you as I am today. I will admit that it may not have always been so, but there is no longer any doubt in my mind that you are the right person for this job, daughter or not."

Lena felt the tears begin to gather. "Thank you. I can't tell you how much it means for you to admit that. Now I really have to scoot. I will talk to you soon," she told him before delivering another hug and kiss to his cheek.

Feeling light and joyful, Lena breezed out of the office and made a beeline to the elevator, only to find T.J. waiting for her. He said nothing until they stood inside the executive elevator, where he offered his version of a congratulation. "Nicely, done, Lena," he hissed in her ear. "Not only did you manage to tattle without looking like a complete bitch, you pulled off looking surprised when Douglas asked you that final question, which *you* obviously knew ahead of time and were prepared for. But I guess that's one of the perks of banging the boss."

Lena replied with a swift slap to his face. "You lying, conniving son-of-a-bitch, how dare you! You don't know what the hell you are talking about. Douglas is not my lover, you sick ass, he's..." Lena stopped herself for revealing more. She was sure that eventually their relationship would be revealed, but not this way.

"Well, you enjoy your new title tonight," T.J. said, rubbing the sting from his cheek. "But don't get too comfortable with the idea. This shit ain't over. Not by a long shot."

The doors opened, depositing them both into the impressive lobby of the PBC headquarters. They stepped forward together, exiting the elevator and going their separate ways. T.J. walked away vowing to get what was his, however he had to do it. Lena moved forward, putting all of the business drama behind her. She wanted to let the happiness of this day bubble to the top so she could celebrate and enjoy her sexy evening with Jason.

Chapter Seventeen

"And then he said, 'congratulations,'" Lena said, munching on her Asia de Cuba calamari salad as she recapped her meeting for Jason.

"So this job you were competing with T.J. with was for the head of the entire network?"

"Yes."

"Why didn't you tell me?"

"For a million reasons, but mainly because I didn't want to scare you off. And I knew that if we stayed together, you'd eventually know."

"Good answer," Jason declared as he raised his glass. "A toast to the sexiest, smartest, hottest CEO I know." The two touched the rims of their champagne flutes and took a sip before sharing a long congratulatory kiss at the table.

"As long as we've got this Q & A going, why did you tell me not to tell anyone about us, but you told your assistant?"

"I did no such thing. The only person who knew about us, before my parents, was my best friend, Aleesa, who doesn't count because..."

"Best friends and sisters never do."

"Exactly. I see you know the girlfriend rules." She giggled. "But seriously, what makes you think that Rolanda knows about us?"

"Rickie told me. Apparently, he did a little celebrating with her after our last meeting together."

"When she got 'sick' and didn't come back to the office."

"I guess. But it appears that she's not only prone to opening her legs but her mouth as well."

"What else has she been telling people," Lena wondered aloud.

"What? You think she told T.J. about the show?"

"I don't see how. As far as I know, I don't think they've ever met," she replied as Jason ran his finger up the inside of her thigh.

"One more question before we turn the conversation to how much you're looking forward to me making you come in all kinds of new and interesting ways."

"Hmmm...sounds promising. Okay, so hurry up and ask. We obviously have better things to talk about. What else do you want to know?"

"Why did your mother call you Lenora this morning?"

Lena felt her breath momentarily catch in her throat. In the scant seconds that she had before it seemed obvious she was hiding something, she had to decide how much to reveal. Now that she had the job on her own merits, was there any harm in revealing the truth? At least to the man she now loved?

"It's my real name," she admitted, deciding to stop there unless Jason asked more. She wanted to celebrate and have their sexy evening. Revealing everything might lead to a hot and heavy discussion that had nothing to do with her achieving orgasm in novel and exciting ways.

"I get it. Lenora is kind of old-fashioned sounding and you're a modern hottie. But let's not worry about Lenora or Lena right now. I wanna talk to Pocahontas. She has quite an I.O.U. to pay off."

"Well, I'm going to go to the ladies room, and then why don't we go back to my apartment so Pocahontas can begin to work off her debt," she suggested, nuzzling his neck.

"We can definitely hit your place first."

"First?"

"I have ah, kind of a field trip planned for us."

"Really? And where are you planning on taking us?"

"To a show. At a club."

"What kind of club? A strip club?"

"Yep. You up for a lap dance? Cuz if you are, I'd love to watch. I can't tell you how fucking turned on that would make me, *is* making me just thinking about it." Jason moved his napkin to reveal the rising boner in his lap. "Or would you like to invoke the No4U Clause?" he asked, hoping like hell that he hadn't pushed too far by introducing another woman to their equation.

Lena looked at Jason with curious eyes. Having a woman give her a lap dance was something she'd thought about only in her fantasies. She'd watched shows like *G-String Divas* and other movies with exotic dancers, and the women always intrigued her. But did she have the balls to actually make this fantasy true?

What would it be like to have an attractive and sexy woman in her lap trying to excite and entice her? And how much fun would it be to take all that juicy pent-up desire and fuck the hell out of the very sexy Jason Armstrong.

"When do we leave?"

"You're sure?" Jason queried, his dick coming to life again at the suggestion that she might be willing to play his game. "You're up for a night out at a club?"

"You won the bet fair and square so, as per our rules, your wish is my pleasure."

"*Our* pleasure."

"That, Mr. Johnson, goes without saying!"

The nasty girl spark was back in her beautiful eyes and Jason wasted no time dithering. "All right, Pocahontas, you go on to the ladies room, but hurry back. The limo leaves in ten. We're going to Queens."

IT WAS NEARLY MIDNIGHT WHEN THE TWO WALKED IN TO Riviera
Gentleman's Club in Astoria, Queens. "Hey dog. Long time,"
the large Randy Jackson look-a-like bouncer-slash-host at the
door greeted Jason.

"'Sup, man," Jason replied, extending his hand for a fist bump.
Lena kept her eyes down and waited. She felt her body stiffen
slightly, taken aback by Jason's choice of venue. This was nothing
like the sparkling strip clubs she'd seen in movies or on television.
The Riviera was much seedier than she'd expected, being a
"gentleman's" club and all. *It's a titty bar, not the Harvard Club*,
Lena quickly reminded herself, repelled but curious nonetheless.

Jason held her hand as they walked further into the club. "Red
Light Special" by TLC blasted through the space, providing the
background rhythm for a tall, tattooed brunette dressed in a tiny
thong, sporting full and faux breasts, snaking down the pole headfirst. The girl made no eye contact with the audience and seemed
to be in her own little world, oblivious to the leers and cheers
around her. While she danced, her sisters in the trade milled
about the room chatting and flirting with the customers.

"That's kind of rude. Why are they talking while the girl is on
stage?"

"You're cute. This is your first time, isn't it?" Jason laughed. He
found it both refreshing and sexy that Lena was inexperienced
with this world. Innocence and curiosity were a rare and hot-as-
hell commodity to find in most women, let alone someone as
experienced and worldly as Lena. "They're working, too—
soliciting drinks and private lap dances."

"Oh." Lena, feeling naïve as hell, closed her mouth, and checked
out the clientele. Scattered around the bar and tables was a mix of
Wall Street Willies and Average Joes. Among them sat several
couples, many of the women looking like she felt, wide-eyed and

slightly uncomfortable, but all were united in their desire to be titillated and entertained by tonight's roster of erotic dancers.

"Hey, Jason," a petite Asian hostess greeted him, with a wink of her eye and tug of her lip. She was wearing a red lace balcony bra and matching thong covered by a long black sheer robe that revealed her small but impressive assets.

"Hey, Mimi."

"A regular, are we?" Lena asked, her tone shimmering between amusement and reproach.

"This is one of Rickie's favorite spots when we're in town," he explained while ushering her over to the main bar area. "So, yeah, I've been here a time or two. Plus they remember the big ballers, or in my case, the people hanging with the big ballers."

Jason found them two seats right at the leading edge of the action. The stage was momentarily empty and the girls on the floor stepped up their invitations. Lena looked on as Mimi hooked her next dance partner and disappeared into the back.

The two settled into their seats. Jason ordered a bottle of over-priced champagne and then handed Lena a wad of bills.

"These are twenties! You are a baller! No wonder they all know you. But I don't need these," she informed him, pushing the money back into his palm.

"Yeah, you do. It's club etiquette. If you sit at the stage you gotta tip or give up your seat to someone who will."

"Who knew a place like this had its very own version of Emily Post," Lena joked, taking the bills back.

"The rules are simple: *do* tip and *don't* touch."

"So tell me again why guys like these places?" Lena asked. "You spend a lot of money on these girls just to ogle them. And then spend more to have one sit on your lap and grind all up against you with her boobs in your face, and you can't even touch them."

"It's a guy thing. For me, half the fun of a lap dance is the restraint and frustration. It's the ultimate cock-tease made all the better if you have your own hot piece of ass waiting for you at home, like I do," he explained with a wink.

"Oh, okay, that part of the joke I understand. It's like she's the fluffer in a porn movie."

"Exactly. And how do you know so much about porn movies?" Jason asked, intrigued and delighted.

"You don't worry about that," Lena teased. "So there really is no sex in the champagne room?"

"Well, technically no, but you'll see. With the right girl, the right bouncer, and the right price…well, some of the rules do get bent," Jason finished his thought with a sly smirk and shrug of his shoulders.

Lena's Strip Club 101 tutorial was interrupted by the pulsating, attention-grabbing beat of the song introducing the next dancer. A leggy, bronze Latina, wearing a lavender, whisper sheer baby doll that showcased her beautifully sculpted breasts, and tiny panties, sashayed onto the stage. Wearing clear platform sandals, she strutted gracefully and purposefully to her pole, walked around it several times and stopped with her back to the audience as she gyrated and suggestively wiggled her ass. She turned, flipped her hair and looked over her shoulder, catching Jason's eye and smiling. A few more kicks and turns allowed the room to see what she was working with before she took a slow and sultry spin on the pole.

As the music played on, Lena recognized the opening lyrics to the singing group 112's very sexy song, "Peaches and Cream." It was a song about eating pussy and between the suggestive lyrics and body movements going on before her, Lena could feel the horniness she'd brought with her into the place, kick itself up a notch. Again, the girl, while clutching the pole and licking her tongue against it, sought out Jason's eye.

"Do you know her?" Lena asked, jealousy sprouting like weeds around her disposition.

"That's Jordyna. She's danced a few times for Rick and me. Nice girl," he replied, smart enough to look earnestly in her face.

"Humph," was all Lena could say as jealousy and desire caused a steady drip, drip in her underpants. Jordyna was beautiful and classy. Not only was her body in tip-top condition, but she hadn't marred her gorgeous bronze skin with gaudy tattoos like so many of the other girls.

"Baby, no need to be jealous, though it's cute as hell. First of all, of course I think she's hot because she kind of favors you. That said, she's got nothin' on you. And secondly, she's only hot for the wad of twenties I got in my hand, not me."

As 112 sang about loving the smell and taste of peaches, Jordyna effortlessly pulled herself off the floor and then gracefully flipped onto the pole, stopping spread eagle, to show her own scantily covered passion fruit to the admiring crowd. She closed her legs around the bar, laid out flat, and using nothing but her core strength spun herself around the pole. Lena sat amazed by the girl's abilities. Seeing it so up-close-and-personal like this, she realized how much power, physical strength and athleticism was required to make it look as if you were effortlessly flowing around that metal pole.

She'd always been fascinated by the idea of strippers and the power they commanded. Lena watched the woman move, and unlike the dancer before her, every eye in the place was on Jordyna, mesmerized by the seduction of the tease. Her cool was hot and her detachment, maddening. There was something about her blend of sensuality and cockiness that made this woman so sexy. Yes, much of it came from the way her body slithered and shimmied around the stage, but so had the other woman, and she hadn't been nearly as captivating. There was a look in Jordyna's eyes that came with the knowledge that she was desired, that every dick in the room, and a few clits as well, were hard and at the ready for her bidding. However she felt about herself once she left the stage was one thing, but it was clear to everyone in the room that when she had her legs wrapped around that pole, Jordyna owned the fucking world!

She was coming to the end of her routine, evidenced by the fact that she was now slithering down the pole headfirst, while at the same time managing to remove her baby doll top. Completely naked but for a barely there g-string, she touched down on the floor into a split, and immediately moved to the edge of the stage. The crowd, giddy as paparazzi at a Brangelina sighting, called her over by waving bills in the air. Taking her time, and with the grace of a cheetah, Jordyna moved toward each of the clamoring voyeurs, seductively squatting to accept their dollar bills between her breasts, ass cheeks and panties.

"Nice to see you again, sugar," she said as she thrust her breasts in Jason's face to accept his $20 bill. Her voice held the tone of an "ask and you shall receive" promise.

"You, too."

"And is this your girlfriend?" she asked, smiling mischievously as she looked Lena over. Lena smiled shyly as she tucked a couple of twenties into the front of her panties. Her fingers accidentally brushed against the lace triangle, but Lena felt no spongy resistance from pubic hair. The idea of Jordyna being bald down there made Lena's clit twitch.

"Yes."

"She's gorgeous," she told Jason while her smoky brown eyes focused on Lena.

Lena felt her face and body flush from both embarrassment and uninvited desire. Her eyes dropped from the girl's face, stopping on her fantastic tits. She had the most beautiful, perfectly symmetrical areolas and nipples that Lena had ever seen. They were the size of a quarter and milk chocolate with a chubby nib that screamed to be sucked. Her gaze traveled down her toned tummy, settling itself on the tiny angel dangling from her belly ring. Lena licked her lips before realizing that she was staring.

"Oh, my God! I'm so sorry. I didn't mean to stare...it's just that..."

"I'm Jordyna," she said with an amused smile. "How about we go into the VIP room and I do a private dance for you?"

Jordyna was no dummy. Even if she hadn't already known Jason to be a huge tipper, she would have picked him. Like all the girls, she'd trained herself to recognize the A.T.M. (Always Throwing Money) males in every crowd. It wasn't just the twenties he and his girl had tucked between her tits; both of them looked, smelled and acted like big bucks. And besides making money, she was feeling bored and a little bit naughty tonight. Judging from tonight's crowd, plucking the cherry from this obvious club virgin would be the most fun she'd probably have all evening.

Jason looked over at Lena, checking her eyes in the dim light, searching for her approval. There was a cocktail of confusion and interest looking back at him. He smiled at her, letting her know that she was in good hands, and that he would keep her safe.

"So, baby, what do you think? Can you handle it?" he questioned while at the same time daring her.

"Uh....um...I don't know," she balked. Lena was turned on and curious as hell but still wasn't quite sold on the idea. She sat quietly and took a quick gut check. It wasn't like anyone would know. This would be another intimate secret treasured between

Jason and her—a shared memory that would be theirs forever.

"I'll tell you what, why doesn't she give us both a dance together. I'll stay with you the whole time. Would that make you feel more comfortable?"

"That and a bottle of champagne," she said, smiling at her boyfriend and accepting the challenge. She felt safe, as she'd grown accustomed to feeling when she was with Jason. "But on one condition—"

"Name it, baby."

"No matter what she does, you don't get to touch," she declared. Her condition was based on two factors: Jason's stated enjoyment of a good cock tease, and her lack of interest in seeing another woman groping all over her man.

"Done," he readily agreed.

"Jordyna, why don't you bring us a bottle and meet us in the VIP lounge? But first, where's the ladies room?"

"I'll show you myself," the dancer volunteered. She didn't want to let this one slip away and into the hands of another girl. The woman's embarrassment alone spelled big tip, and she was sure if she warmed her up and turned her into a hot gooey mess for her man, his grateful dick would tip her large as well. "You go make yourself comfortable," she told Jason. "We'll be right back."

As he watched both of their fine asses switch away from him, Jason felt a surge of excitement in his pants. He made his way to the V.I.P. Lounge, smiling, knowing that he was one lucky motherfucker.

"Dude, you know you can't come into the lounge unescorted," the same bouncer from the front informed Jason.

"Jordyna sent me back to wait. She and my girl went to the ladies room."

"Cool, but you'll have to wait outside until Jordy gets here. So, where's your partner? Haven't seen you two in a bit, but I swear you all turned the lounge out last time. In fact, I got something here for him."

"Yeah, well, what can I say about my boy."

"That he hooked you up right, cuz you're back for more."

"True dat."

"So you want the same deal as last time? A thousand dollars, including tip. The lounge is yours for three songs. Another five hundred and you get the goody bag."

"A thousand's cool," Jason agreed, peeling off the requisite bills. He remembered the good time he and Rick had had with Jordyna and her friend, knowing this time with Lena would be even better. He had no idea what was in the goody bag, but turning his own loving nasty girl on and out was goody enough. Anything else was icing.

Jordyna returned with Lena and purposely led them both over to a pair of side-by-side leather easy chairs. As the dancer took Jason's sports jacket and hung it on a coat rack across the room, Lena took a quick look around. The room was dark and shadowy, filled with identical chairs set around the room. The only light source was pink and dim and set a mood that screamed illicit sex. Moving slow and feeling horny, Jordyna stood before them both and invitingly caressed her body to the sounds of Alicia Keys' "Un-Thinkable." In her mind, she decided to get to the pretty girl by first going through her hunky man.

Lena felt the strings of seduction pull her desire to the forefront while pushing away her inhibitions. She watched as Jordyna backed her near naked ass up in Jason's face. The stripper slowly gyrated and pushed her butt close enough for Jason to do what he would have done to her: kiss the small of her back and the slap her ass. But true to his word, Jason's hands remained at his side, until Jordyna picked one up and rubbed it inside her inner thigh. Lena's eyes registered her confusion. *What happened to no touching?*

"It's okay," the dancer whispered, catching Lena's gaze. To emphasize her point she slid down Jason's torso and began grinding her ass into his lap while she rubbed his cock. Jordyna moaned and licked her lips. "See, it's okay," she repeated as she turned around and dropped into a squat, her head between Jason's legs. In one smooth, fluid move, she snaked herself up between his legs, thrusting out her chest and rubbing her full exposed breasts against his dick and torso before offering them to his hungry mouth.

Jason looked over at his girlfriend, the man in him wanting to pounce on those beautiful breasts and suckle them 'til they gave milk, but the mate in him hesitated. He didn't want to do anything to upset Lena; especially since she'd been such a good sport about indulging his fantasy. He decided to stay with the no touching rule, but neither male nor mate could keep his hips and pelvis from following the rhythm set by Jordyna's pussy grinding into his steadily rising dick.

Lena watched, her emotions an equal mixture of lust and envy for both of them. Sitting there, seeing her man getting all hot and bothered by the wiles of another female, was both irritating and arousing at the same time. And Jordyna, with her free and unconstrained libido, exuded the kind of steamy sexuality she craved for herself. Jordyna had the ability to evoke raw desire that was not in any way gender specific, but was natural and universally enticing. She felt her body blush with the heat of her sexual want. She squirmed in the chair, wondering if the ever-present bouncer in the corner could smell the scent of arousal as it began to rise.

Jordnya took notice of Lena's curious lust, and gracefully disengaged herself from Jason to turn her attention to the true object of her cravings. Jordy crawled into Lena's lap. With her legs straddling Lena's hips, she leaned forward and brushed her lips past her cheeks until they rested on her earlobe.

"It's okay to touch. I like it," she whispered, her warm breath caressing Lena's neck. "You will, too," she promised. Jordy held her gaze as she purposely unbuttoned Lena's blouse to her navel, and pushed back the fabric to reveal the curvy, succulent flesh of Lena's breasts. The breath of both women clutched in their throats at the revelation.

As the music changed from Alicia Keys to the slow and highly evocative voice of Maxwell, Jordyna suggestively massaged Lena's pussy with her own for several beats before lifting and leaning her body into Lena's and giving her a slow tit massage. Lena felt her entire body tense with her brain's confused indecision before relaxing into the moment at her sex center's command. She closed her eyes and gave into the glorious sensation of pillowy pleasure. Their breasts, while different in shape, were similar in size and Lena could feel not only her nipples stretch and grow hard in search of additional stimulation, but Jordyna's do the same.

A low, hungry moan escaped into the room, and Lena was unsure from whose mouth it came, but she didn't care. How different a woman's chest pressed up against her own felt. She loved the skin-on-skin sensation she experienced when Jason pressed his body to hers—soft mounds of flesh meeting hard, pectoral mass. But with tit-on-tit, it was about a soft and smooth encounter with its equal with a cushiony, sexy sense of give and take that was deliciously appealing.

After several more beats of glorious rubbing, Jordyna pushed herself off of Lena's lap, and in a smooth as butter move, parted her legs and dropped down between them. She bent her head forward, throwing her toffee-colored hair against Lena's torso and slowly brushing her bare chest with her silky mane. Lena felt the sensation of a thousand tiny feathers tickling each individual nerve ending. This was a new and exciting tactical uproar that sent Lena's pussy into a juice-producing whirlwind.

Before she could get used to the experience, the stripper moved again, turning her back to Lena and placing her apple ass in her lap. She rocked her pelvis to and fro, causing Lena's skirt to ride up, exposing her naked thigh. Again, she rubbed her barely covered coochie up against Lena's, making both ache with an unprecedented urgency.

"Oh. Oh. Oh," Lena moaned softly as she curiously ran her finger up Jordyna's spine as she watched another woman's backside beckon her.

With the agility of an acrobat, Jordyna turned and moved to the side, riding Lena's right thigh and once again offering her tits to her virgin mouth. Lena could feel the juicy crotch of Jordy's g-string dampen her naked leg. For the first time in her life, Lena seriously wondered what it would be like to taste the pussy of another woman. The devilish thought raised her wantonness to another level, and without questioning her impulse, Lena captured Jordyna's chocolate-colored areola with her mouth. She pulled at the woman's nipple, alternating the suction, and tickling her own tongue, as the nip grew longer and harder. Lena's boldness had a direct effect on Jordyna's libido. She once again straddled her lap and purposely began to grind her pussy deeper and longer into Lena's. She was getting to the newbie and it was turning her on. Jordyna pushed her breast deeper into Lena's mouth while her hands reached to reciprocate. Her fingers tweaked and twisted Lena's tips and massaged her tits until she got the desired reaction.

Jason watched his woman ravishing and being ravished by another and felt like his dick was about to blow the fuck up. As the song changed, and Maxwell was replaced by Prince, demanding and begging at the same time for someone to do him, Jason slipped into another chair across the room to better enjoy the view. He'd promised not to touch Jordyna, but had said nothing about doing his own handiwork. He slipped his cock from its denim confinement and began to fondle himself as he watched the show.

"I see you, baby," he called out to her.

Lena looked over toward the sound of his voice, but said nothing. The breathing around the room was getting shorter and much more vocal. Another set of moans escaped Lena's mouth, echoed by the others, and heightening the urgency of their actions. Lena disengaged her mouth from the woman's tits, and threw her head back to simply revel in the moment. Jordyna increased the cadence of her dance, moving her game of seduction across the line to the pursuit of satisfaction. Lena became a willing partner, lifting her pelvis to meet Jordy's while her hips picked up the rhythm and moved when and where hers did.

Do me, baby, Lena sang the words in her head as she felt the tingle of imminent orgasm simultaneously creep down her torso and up her legs, meeting in the middle. Her coochie began to pulse and contract with a new-found intensity. Jordyna closed her eyes and maintained her steady rhythm, rocking back and forth, occasionally moving her groin in a circular motion, while always maintaining contact.

As the two women continued to tease and tantalize each other toward release, Jason's hand furiously tugged at his dick. The pleasure he felt knowing that Lena felt so deeply for him that she would give him this moment, was temporarily pushed aside by the sight of these two beautiful women together. It excited him to see Lena damn near having sex with another female while he watched.

Jordyna reached up and pinched and rolled Lena's nipple, detonating the force between her legs. Lena's body began to buck and roll as she gave into the exquisite finish of this forbidden pleasure. Jordy closed her lips to catch the chuckle threatening to escape as she rode the wave. There was no hotter feeling than turning a cherry out.

"You are beautiful," she whispered in Lena's ear as she climbed off her lap. Like the pro she was, Jordyna's timing was perfect. Prince sang his last note, accompanied by the not so subtle clearing of the bouncer's throat. The forbidden fantasy was over. Her I.O.U. paid. Lena, her rapture now tinged with embarrassment, quickly buttoned her blouse, smoothed her skirt, walked out of the lounge and continued through the club doors and into the waiting car.

Jason quickly got himself together and got up to follow. He bolted out of the club in hot pursuit of his woman. He had to get to Lena and find out how and what she was feeling. She'd run off so fast that he was afraid that his selfish desires might have ultimately caused the woman he loved more remorse and regret than it was all worth.

The limo was at the entrance and he slipped into the back seat expecting to find Lena in tears, but instead she was buck naked, legs open, lying in wait.

"Girl, I do love you," he said as he quickly unbuckled his belt and lost his pants on the floor of the limo. Within seconds, he was inside her, providing a most fulfilling end to her lap dance.

Chapter Eighteen

Lena walked into her office feeling powerful as hell and with a new sense of purpose. Yesterday, when she'd arrived, she was the president of the Sports Fan Network. This morning, though it was yet to be announced, she was the head woman in charge of the whole damn company. It felt good to know that she had won her spot fair and square and the old-fashioned way—through hard work and without nepotism. Had it helped that Douglas was her father? It sure hadn't hurt, but at the same time, it hadn't helped in any significant way either. She could look anybody in the eyes and feel confident that she had worked her ass off to earn the right to sit at the head of the Paskin Broadcasting Company table.

But winning the top spot at PBC wasn't the only source of her power surge. Her and Jason's deliciously scandalous and highly invigorating night of incredible sex, had left her not only smiling and momentarily satiated, but feeling empowered. Who knew that sex could do that for you? Lena certainly hadn't. But there was something about giving into temptation last night, and liking it, that made her feel like for the first time in her life, she was in full control of her destiny.

She looked at the calendar on her desk, still turned to yesterday's date. All things considered, May 25th was going down as one of her top five greatest days ever.

"You are a bad bitch, Lenora Macy Paskin," she complimented herself in a fully swaggered murmur.

She still couldn't believe that she'd been so incredibly bold to not only accept a lap dance, but also to taste the breasts of another woman. And then with Jordyna's pussy rubbing up against hers, she exploded into a long and toe-curling orgasm while Jason watched. Last night had been a once-in-a-lifetime experience, and definitely one she'd be putting down on her private scandal sheet to reminisce about for years to come.

Lena considered calling Aleesa to fill her in on last night's happenings, but after further consideration, decided against it. Her scandalous behavior was nothing she needed to share with anyone else but her man. It would stay between them and be the fuel for their delicious "I've got a secret smile" for the rest of their lives.

"Lena, your mother is on line one," Rolanda buzzed in to inform her.

"Hey, Mom, I guess you've heard."

"Yes, darling. Your father called me after you'd left his office. I tried to call you last night, but you were out very late. Celebrating with Jason, I suppose?"

"Yes," Lena agreed, blushing at the thought of talking to her mother while the memories of her erotic celebration were so fresh.

"Good. I like that young man. And I'm very proud of you. And Douglas, for that matter. He finally did the right thing, though I still don't understand why he didn't name you from the beginning and avoid all of the ensuing hoopla."

"You know that I had as much to do with that as he did. This company means everything to Daddy. He built it; it's his life. And I wanted him to be comfortable with his choice and not spend the rest of his days second-guessing that his company is in good hands. So it really did work out."

"I suppose you're right, but PBC is *your* company now. You run it the way you see fit."

"Okay, Mom, but right now I have to run SFN, and I have a meeting in ten minutes. Let's have dinner soon and celebrate. All of us. I want the whole family there."

"The *entire* family?"

"Yes, Mother. You, me, Daddy, Akira and Kenneth, too."

"All right, if you insist on her being here, it's done. We can do it here, Friday. I'll call the wife now and let her know. We have to give her plenty of advanced warning so that she can try to find something decent to wear."

"Whatever, Mom" Lena replied, ignoring Tina's slight. "Thanks for calling. Let me know when it's all set up."

"Will you be bringing Jason, darling?" Tina probed.

"It's possible. Why?"

"Just checking to see if I should be considering him family yet."

"Good-bye, Mother!" Lena shook her head in amusement as she hung up the phone.

"Lena, Jason Armstrong and his client are here," Rolanda interrupted again to let her know. She refused to say his name and tried to keep the petulance out of her voice but was unsuccessful. Fuck Rickie Ross for pretending he didn't know who the hell she was.

"Can you please escort them into the conference room? I'll be right in."

Rolanda sucked her teeth in response. Lena chuckled to herself. Clearly, Rickie hadn't brought flowers to this reunion.

Lena gathered up the new contracts and exited her office.

"What's so funny?" Rolanda asked as she passed by, her irritation clear.

"Funny?"

"Yeah, you have this goofy smile on your face," she informed her boss.

"I don't know. Something my mother must have said." She had

no intention of revealing how much her mother's comment about Jason being family had thrilled her. She also was damn happy she was about to see the face of the man she loved.

"Whatever," Ro hissed under her breath, pissed off that anyone could be smiling after that jackass had dissed her so badly.

"What's this doing here?" Lena asked, noticing a man's jacket thrown over the reception area armchair.

"He left it here."

"He who?"

"The football player's agent," Ro informed her, refusing to say Rickie's name.

"Well, hang Mr. Armstrong's jacket in my office," she directed her assistant on the way out.

"Gentlemen," Lena greeted the pair as she came through the conference room door. Both men stood and returned her hello with a hug. She allowed herself a quick second to breathe in Jason's essence before releasing him and resuming their professional stance. "Rickie, what did you say to my assistant to ruffle her feathers so badly?"

"That girl is big trippin'," he replied, brushing it off.

Jason and Lena shared a knowing look.

"What, man? You told her?" Rickie asked, looking at his agent.

"She knows."

"Well, she came throwing it at me. What was I gonna do? Anyway, now she's all pissed off, acting like I was supposed to propose or something."

"Again, I apologize for my secretary's behavior."

"And again, like I said, she's trippin'. The whole time we were getting busy she's talking about how much she could do for me around this company. Introduce me to the new head of PBC…"

"Really? And who was that?" Lena asked, suspicion causing her ears to perk up.

"Some dude with just initials. I don't remember."

"T.J. Reynolds?" Lena probed.

"Yeah. Rhonda said that she knew him and a lot of other people. And when some big transition went down, it would be good for me to know the players around the company and she could make it happen."

Lena immediately shot Jason a look. She could tell by his face that he was thinking the same thing. Rolanda had been the source of the leak. That whorish little sneak.

"Well, let's get these signed and you two on your way. I know you have a plane to catch, Rickie," Lena said, pushing the contracts across the table. *And I have to deal with Ms. Hammon.* She picked up the phone and dialed her office extension.

"Ro, could you please join us in the conference room?"

"Now? I'm sort of in the middle of something." Work was definitely not keeping her from joining them. Disgust was the culprit. At this moment, Rolanda wanted to be in the same room with Rickie rat about as much as she wanted to pluck her pubes clean with a rusty pair of tweezers.

"NOW!"

Rolanda reluctantly got up from her desk and walked the short distance from Lena's office to the executive conference room.

"You wanted to see me?" she asked from the threshold, careful to avoid Rickie's eyes. She needn't have worried, as he was too busy on his phone texting to look up.

"Yes, come in. I need a couple of things clarified. Rickie here tells me that you two recently spent some time together, and that you offered to introduce him to T.J. Reynolds. Is this true?"

"Uh...well...I uh...." Rolanda stuttered while trying to think of an explanation.

"I wasn't aware that you and Mr. Reynolds knew each other."

"Uh, well, I met him once when he came to the office."

"T.J.'s been to the office? When? You never told me that," Lena grilled her, growing increasingly angry.

"I don't know. I must have forgotten."

"Interesting memory lapse. When was this?"

"I don't know—weeks ago."

"Just how well do you know T.J.?"

"Uh, not that well."

"Girl, you told me that you and he were like that," Rickie said, looking up to intertwine his middle and index finger.

Ro simply sucked her teeth in response.

Lena knew she had found her mole and the knowledge that it was her assistant disgusted her. She had always suspected Rolanda of being sneaky and nosy, but it never had occurred to her that she was disloyal to boot.

"We'll discuss this later," Lena said brusquely. It was clear what "discuss this" meant to everyone in the room. "In the meantime, will you please go back to my office and get Jason's jacket and bring it here? Thank you," she said, curtly dismissing the girl.

Rolanda trudged back to her office even more pissed off than she'd been. How dare that bitch embarrass her by calling her on the carpet in front of Dickmo and his sorry-ass agent! Lena Macy, Rickie Ross and this whole band of sorry motherfuckers could kiss her ass. She walked into the inner office and furiously grabbed Jason's jacket from the chair back where she'd thrown it, turned and swung it hard in the air. She heard the thud of something hit the wall and then drop to the floor. She looked over and saw a silver pen on the floor.

"Fuck it. I hope it's his lucky pen and that bitch never signs another damn contract," Ro declared, not giving a shit about Lena's favorite fuck buddy's possessions as she walked out of the office and back to the conference room.

"Thank you," Lena said, accepting the jacket with an icy tone. "I'm going to walk them out and then I have a meeting with programming. I need you to print out all the Samsonite print materials for Rickie's show. It's on the flash drive. Please leave them on my desk. When I get back from my meeting, we will have a meeting of our own."

Rolanda returned to the office and walked over to Lena's desk. Her foot stepped down on something hard and when she lifted it, she saw a small flash drive lying on the floor. She picked it up and inspected it. The drive was nondescript and unlabeled. Assuming it to be the Samsonite drive, she plugged it into the computer and tried to find the documents. There were no Word documents to be found, only a video entitled Riviera. Curious, she clicked on it.

"Holy Mother Fuck!" she shouted into the air as a dark and grainy image of one woman sucking some lusty dark-haired stripper's titty while the girl was sitting on her lap and tickling her coochie with her own appeared. The lighting was too poor for positive identification, and Ro couldn't tell one hundred percent, but she was pretty sure that the woman sitting in the chair was none other than Lena Macy. And was that her boy toy agent sitting over in the next chair with his hand down in his pants?

Ro sat and watched the video for the next ten minutes or so. Lena did more taking than giving, but clearly she was into the girl-on-girl action. As was she. Ro felt her vagina begin to mist and seize as she watched the two women fondle, kiss and rub up on each other.

The laughter that began in her belly and exited her mouth with a roar was the sound of pure revenge. Rolanda felt like a desperate 49er who had just struck gold. Screw the spicy emails. They were tame compared to this find. The video drive proved beyond a shadow that Lena Macy was a serious freak. Proof Ro could practically guarantee Lena would not want made public. Now, there was only one decision that remained to be made: What to do with this information? Now that she'd lost her job, should she get paid in exchange for this? Or should she insist on a new, totally perked-up, bigger, better job somewhere else in the company? Oh, the possibilities were endless!

LENA IMMEDIATELY DETECTED A MOOD SHIFT WHEN SHE RETURNED to her office. There were several files sitting on her desk, including the work she'd requested. And Rolanda was waiting and looking quite willing to talk. The anger and embarrassment of getting caught undermining her boss was replaced by an almost defiant sense of amusement. Had she been chatting and consorting with T.J. again?

The idea of Ro and T.J. scheming to undermine her together fired up Lena's wrath and determination to deal with both of the conniving and untrustworthy weasels for once and for all.

"You wanted to see me?" Rolanda asked.

"Yes, I've just been down to Human Resources, letting them know that you have been terminated. Today is your last day."

"You're trying to fire me? For what?"

"Surely, you can't be that dense," Lena shot back. "You pick your offense: insubordination, breaching your confidentiality clause, disobeying directives, soliciting sex...any one of these is grounds for dismissal and you've done *all* of them."

"You've got nerve; especially on that last one."

"What are you talking about, Rolanda?"

"Soliciting sex. You're going to fire me for having a little office romance when you're doing the exact same thing?" Rolanda watched Lena's face for some sign that she was getting to her, but the bitch's poker face was intact as ever.

Knowing already that Rolanda was aware of her relationship with Jason allowed Lena to save giving Ro the pleasure of one-upping her.

"Surely you don't consider your dalliance with Rickie Ross an office romance, as he doesn't even know your name..." Lena's words stopped as a bolt of enlightenment momentarily left her mute. Office romance? Rolanda was not speaking of Rickie but rather T.J. She'd not only been feeding him information all this time, but had been fucking him as well!

"Ah, but you aren't talking about Rickie now, are you? Your office lover is T.J. Reynolds. Why else would you be willing to cheat and lie and betray SFN and me?"

"Like you and Jason, or should I say *Mr. Big Johnson*, never talked about any company business during your pillow talk sessions. Though I must say, you two were so busy talking dirty that work was probably more of an afterthought. Isn't that right, *Pocahontas*?"

This time the emotional shift on Lena's face was blatantly noticeable. How did Rolanda know what she and Jason talked about and for that matter, their pet names for each other? Rolanda couldn't keep herself from voicing a small "gotcha" chuckle. This was going to be way too easy.

"You might want to check the insurance file on your desk. I think you'll be amused. I was."

Lena took a few seconds to stare her assistant in the face, before opening the manila folder and glancing over the printouts. She grimaced as she recognized the sexy emails, including their favorite things lists that she and Jason had exchanged following their lunch at Nobu 57 and in the weeks that followed.

"Where did you get these?"

"Right from your computer. I printed them out like I do all of your emails. That's part of my job. I guess you forgot that all your emails, even the nasty ones, come to both your BlackBerry and this computer."

Fuck! Rolanda was correct. Because she'd so rarely used her work email for private correspondence, she had completely forgotten that the two were connected. Why hadn't she given her personal account information to Jason immediately?

"Still want to fire me?" Rolanda asked, fingering the flash drive in her pocket.

"Absolutely. In fact, this conversation is done."

"I don't think so, because I know a lot more that I'm sure you wouldn't want to get out. Like how you got your new job."

"Now what are you talking about, Rolanda? What line has T.J. been feeding you? I got that job on merit, despite you and T.J. scheming to steal my show and one-up me."

"Merit, my ass. I know you're sleeping with old man Paskin. You're such a hypocrite. You accuse me of soliciting sex when you've been fucking your way through this company all along. And now you've scored large. I have to say, though, I never saw that coming."

"Who told you that mess? T.J.?" She laughed. While she'd been angered by T.J.'s suggestion about her and Douglas, she somehow found Rolanda's misconception amusing.

"No, I saw it with my own eyes. I've seen you two hugging up on each other, whispering in each other's ears when he comes up here. And he's the only meeting you have where the door is always closed. And why is he always calling you downtown for 'mandatory' meetings? It doesn't take a rocket scientist to figure out what's going on."

"Apparently it does." Lena chortled. Rolanda was confused when Lena's response was a burst of uncontrollable laughter. This was not the reaction she was expecting.

"You and T.J. are perfect for each other," Lena stated in between chuckles. "You both think you're so much smarter than other people. But you're not. Not by any stretch of the damn imagination. It's really sad how idiotic you both are."

"Save your lecture," Rolanda told her, insulted and annoyed by Lena's lack of shock that she'd been outed. "Your best defense is a great offense tactic that is as old as dirt or at least as old as that white man you're screwing."

"Rolanda, this is the last thing I am going to say to you before you walk out of here, escorted by security if need be, never to return. It's going to come out eventually, so you might as well know now. Douglas Paskin is not my lover. He's..."

Just like with T.J. Reynolds, something told her not to continue. "...he's a family friend and my professional mentor. He's wanted to put me in charge of PBC for years, but I wanted, no needed, to prove to him and all the knuckleheads out there, like you and T.J., that I could earn the job on my own merit and not just my family connections. I have worked my ass off for the past ten years and now that I have proven myself, I am happy to accept his offer. I don't give a damn about what other people think about it.

"Now, as head of SFN, you are fired for all of the reasons I stated; plus I can't stand having your sneaky behind around me any longer. And don't go running to your boyfriend, because he won't be working for this company much longer either. He'll either go on his own now that he's no longer in competition for *my* job, or once I'm the official head of PBC, I'll give his ass the boot as well.

"Now get the hell out of my office. You have fifteen minutes to exit this building before I send security up to get you."

Rolanda could only stare back at the woman she'd assisted for nearly two years, but obviously didn't know at all. The secret life of Lena Macy ran deep and wide. Ro didn't believe one word of this "prove myself" bullshit that Lena was spewing. What a bitch to let people believe she was truly in the hunt when the deck was stacked against T.J. all along. Okay, so *maybe* she wasn't fucking old man Paskin, and that was still a big maybe, but she had the ultimate "in" all along. And now she, and T.J. for that matter, were thrown out on their asses.

"You don't have to call security. I'm going to leave now and let you get back to work. I'll give you a couple of days to think about all this and then we'll talk again. I wouldn't be too rash, if I were you," Rolanda said, calmly looking her boss in the eyes. "Not till you know the extent of what I know."

Ro said her peace and didn't bother to look back as she exited the office, clutching the video proof of Lena in her hand. She'd hate to out the new head of PBC as a bona fide freak, but certainly would if pushed. Hell, this was a fucking eat or be eaten situation. Rolanda could not afford to be fired. Not with all those damn bill collectors blowing up her phone with their threats. She couldn't afford for T.J. to be let go either, as she was counting on him to keep her employed with an even bigger and better-paying job.

She gathered up her personal belongings and threw them into her tote bag. As soon as she got down into the lobby, Rolanda pulled out her cell phone and dialed T.J.'s number.

"Give me twenty minutes to get home and then check your private email. You're not going to believe what just fell into our laps."

Ro hung up and began walking toward her subway stop. For a woman who had just gotten fired, she was smiling like she'd won the lottery. And in many ways, Rolanda felt like she had. After T.J. got a look at Lena's little porn adventure, they would put their heads together to determine the best way to put Ms. Macy back in her place and the two of them back behind the wheel.

Chapter Nineteen

T.J. felt his dick get hard as he checked out the two chicks getting frisky in the champagne room of some dive strip joint. He yanked at his cock, pulling and pushing it to the same rhythm of the action taking place on his computer. Yeah, it was all sexy as hell, but what was really getting him off was the realization that Rolanda may be right in assuming that this was a video of Lena in action. He now had the evidence needed to convince Douglas Paskin to reverse his decision to make this slut the head of his company. As persnickety as Douglas was about his personal and business identities, there was no way he was going to trust his well-earned reputation to a budding porn star.

He shot his wad into a Kleenex and took a minute to regulate his breath before dialing his friendly accomplice. The best thing that had happened to him in recent years was walking into Lena's office and joining bodies and forces with her horny assistant. Surprisingly, Rolanda Hammon was turning out to be the key component in assuring his ascension. She'd proven herself to be a valuable ally, and T.J. fully intended to fulfill his promise of setting her up a well-paying gig somewhere within the company. What remained to be seen was how closely she'd be working with him in the future. The girl was an incredible fuck, but about as trustworthy as a condom with a pin prick.

Before he could dial her, Rolanda's number came up on his ringing cell phone.

"Well, did you see it?" she blurted out.

"Yes. Are you sure that it's her?" he asked. "I mean it kind of looks like her, true, but you can't tell one hundred percent that it is actually Lena. What proof do you have?"

"The video is too dark to see the faces clearly, and at first I wasn't sure, but then after I watched it a few times, I'm sure. I recognize the diamond hoops she's wearing."

Personally, T.J. didn't give a shit if it was really Lena or not. The woman in the video looked close enough to show reasonable doubt in Douglas Paskin's head. "Where did you get this? Does she know you have it?"

"No, she doesn't. I thought we could use the element of surprise to our benefit, and don't worry where I got it from. Just be glad I got it." Ro saw no need to reveal any more information than necessary. T.J. didn't need to know that securing this damning evidence was simply the result of a hissy fit gone terribly right and not some secret connection. "The bigger question is what are we going to do with it? I'm thinking that we put it out there and let the chips fall where they may."

"What? Like on YouTube?"

"For starters, and then email it to the heads of all PBC subsidiaries."

"Hmmm….perhaps. I guess we could also make sure that the emails you found on her company computer get into the right hands as well."

"Yeah, well…"

"What? You still have those—right?"

"Yeah, I do, but she knows it. I left her a copy to help her reconsider firing me, and you, by the way."

"Shit. That means she'd know that you were the one who fed them to the media, but if she's already fired you, I guess it doesn't matter that she knows."

"So, I'm taking the hit on this alone?"

"Baby, you have to. I cannot be attached to any part of this—at least not the leak. If I am, Douglas is not going to hand the keys to the kingdom over to me. You understand that, right?"

"Yeah, but I'm telling you, T.J., if you fuck me, I will go to all of them and let them know everything."

Is this round-the-way bitch trying to threaten me?

"Not to worry, baby. I told you, I got your back," T.J. promised, his calm voice belying his annoyance. "You help me get this and you'll be sitting in some office trying to figure out how to spend your signing bonus and new salary." T.J. placated her while making up his mind that she'd never work for him.

"Okay, but I'm just letting you know. So how are we going to do this?"

"I'm not really sure, but let me handle this. I'll figure out a way to get all of this news to Douglas. For now, hold off on sending this or the emails anywhere else. We don't want to throw everything at them all at once. We need to have more in case he doesn't get our point immediately. What I want you to do is upload this on YouTube. We need to scare him into thinking the downfall of his company's reputation is imminent," T.J. said, not caring about any libelous fallout that could occur. "And give his secretary a call and insist that you meet with him ASAP. You do that, and leave the rest to me."

T.J. and Rolanda stayed on the phone for another few minutes, plotting Lena Macy's unfortunate fall from grace. By the end of business tomorrow, the secret life of Lena Macy would be secret no more. The pristine image of Douglas's golden girl would be tarnished beyond repair. No amount of public relations spin could polish it up in time for her to reclaim what was always destined to be his.

"YOU CAN GO IN NOW," DOUGLAS'S SECRETARY INFORMED HIM. T.J. gave Margaret a sunbeam smile and strutted confidently through the doors of what was soon to be his office.

"Travis, what can I do for you? You made it sound like there's some urgency surrounding this meeting. Is this about my decision to name Lena as my successor?"

T.J. exhaled deeply, hoping his sigh conveyed the right amount of angst and concern. "Yes, in a way it does, Douglas. This is a hard subject for me to broach, particularly because of your recent decision regarding your successor. I hope you will understand that, even though I don't agree with it, what I am about to tell you has absolutely nothing to do with that decision."

"Why don't you say what you came here to tell me?"

T.J. sighed again for dramatic effect and began to unwind his tale. "I had a call from Lena Macy's former assistant, Rolanda Hammon. Apparently, she's been fired."

"Yes, she called my office as well, wanting to meet with me. I had Margaret put her off. Surely she knows I don't get involved with personnel matters at the various networks."

"I'm sure she does, but this matter is a bit more serious. I guess when she couldn't get an appointment with you, she called me. I must say that what she had to share is most disturbing. It was my intention to handle this myself, and to keep you from having to dirty your hands, but I couldn't deal with this alone. Douglas, this is a very delicate matter and I truly regret being placed in this position, but I feel that you need to know."

"Know what, damn it?!" Douglas asked, his intuition telling him that he wasn't going to like what he was about to hear.

"Ms. Hammon came to me alleging that Lena has been...been... well...trading sexual favors to sign talent."

"What the hell are you talking about, T.J.?" Douglas asked, a fire lit in his eyes.

T.J. continued, revealing to Douglas that Rolanda had come to him, distraught over her firing. She'd claimed that Lena was so desperate to add Rickie Ross to the SFN talent pool that she once revealed to her that "she'd do anything necessary to get him."

"That's the basis of her claim? An obvious bit of exaggeration? Hearsay?" Douglas commented gruffly.

"No. Unfortunately, there's more. Ms. Hammon says she thought nothing of it until she was printing out Lena's emails, as apparently was part of her duties, and she ran across, uh...um... sexually explicit emails between Lena and Rickie Ross's agent, left on the company's server. She claims that's when she put all of it together. Lena took a trip down to Miami specifically to hook up with Rickie, but ended up meeting his agent instead and becoming..uh...well, intimate with Mr. Armstrong, and has been sleeping with him in order to get Mr. Ross to host her show."

Douglas felt his jaw clench as he digested the information. T.J. had no idea of the thoughts barreling around his head, making it feel like it was going to explode. He knew all about Lena's relationship with Jason, and she herself had painted it as a fun and games friendship. Was his daughter playing the sex game? Could there possibly be any truth to this vicious accusation? Or was this the angry spittle spewed by a rejected employee?

"You've seen these emails?"

"Yes. Ms. Hammon gave them to me," T.J. admitted, holding the manila folder out for Douglas to see.

"They are what she says they are? Proof of what she is accusing?" Douglas said, stepping back and away from the trashy evidence.

"I think that based on the exchanges, one may construe that Mr. Armstrong was helping to influence his client on Lena's behalf."

"Well, unless they outright prove these allegations, they are nothing more than personal emails, that yes, should not have been on the company server, but all they really prove for *certain* is that Ms. Macy and Mr. Armstrong are involved in an adult relation-ship. I think they provide a pretty flimsy basis to accuse a well-respected executive in our company of such heinous behavior."

"I'm sorry to say, Douglas, that there is more. A video." T.J. put a flash drive down on the CEO's desk. "It may not prove her reasons for being with the agent, but it certainly does violate her morals clause...and frankly, leaves PBC wide open for less than desirable media scrutiny. It's already been posted on YouTube, with the unfortunate title, 'TV Exec in the Lap of Lust.'"

T.J. noticed Douglas's nostrils flare as he walked over to the computer and logged on to YouTube. He entered the title that Rolanda had given to him and pulled up the infamous lap dance video. He hoped the old boy enjoyed watching his girl get her freak on.

Grunts and sexy moans sprang from the speakers, assaulting the elderly man's ears and creating a fissure in his heart. Douglas sat with his eyes on the screen while the blood drained from his face, taking with it every vestige of vitality, and leaving him looking every bit of his seventy years. T.J. kind of felt sorry for the dude as he watched his protégé's stellar reputation being destroyed. Less than ninety seconds in, Douglas turned away from his computer; pain the only expression on his face.

"What does the girl want?" were the only words to leave his mouth.

"I asked the same thing. This is the tough part. She's a loyal employee who feels that she was unfairly fired when Lena found out that she knew everything. Rolanda has been with SFN for nearly seven years. She doesn't want money. This is not a blackmail situation. But she's a whistle-blower, not a criminal. She wants what's best for the company."

"Sounds like she's a disgruntled employee who wants revenge."

"I don't disagree with you, but revenge makes people do ugly things. She says she's prepared to not only send it to all the tabloids, but also to the heads of all the PBC networks. If this gets out that wide, PBC is going to become the center of the latest sex scandal to hit the media. Do we really want that?"

Douglas could not answer. His thoughts were a jangle of confusion and heartbreaking questions. The woman T.J. was talking about, the one in that tawdry video, was not the Lenora he'd raised. Or was it? He had no clue, nor should he, of what went on in his daughter's personal life. Still, he never imagined that the little girl who used to run from boys because they had cooties and had declared kissing gross, had now been videotaped doing unspeakable things with another woman. In public. Had this agent fellow corrupted her to this point? Or was Lena's judgment so skewed she didn't realize what a horrid influence he was on her?

And what was T.J.'s role in all of this? Was he really the innocent bystander he portrayed? The hero trying to save the company's image? Or was he simply trying to take an unfortunate circumstance and turn it to his advantage?

"Douglas?" T.J. called out, taking his silence for shock.

"I have to think about this. I need time to sort it all out," Douglas finally spoke. "Thank you for bringing this to my attention."

"That's totally understandable. I will do my best to keep Ms. Hammon quiet and squash any further exposure while you sort all of this out."

"I'd appreciate that, Travis. And is there any way to get this thing off of YouTube?"

"I'll try to get it removed as soon as possible."

"Thank you. I'll be in touch," Douglas replied.

I know you will, T.J. thought as he strutted out of his office, leaving the head of the Paskin Broadcast Company, slumped in his chair looking like he'd just been informed of the death of his best friend. T.J. hated being the bearer of such shocking news, but could only feel but so bad. As they say, everything done in the dark, comes out in the light. Girlfriend should not have been so damn sloppy, but lucky for him she was.

Chapter Twenty

L ena was as excited as she was nervous walking up the front door to her mother's Upper East Side apartment with Jason on her arm. This was the first man she'd "brought home" in over four years and she wasn't sure how Jason would fare under the loving scrutiny of her blended family. Her stepparents were no worry. Kenneth and Akira would be as hospitable and friendly as they always were. Her mother had already met and liked Jason, so hopefully things would continue to go smoothly between them. Even the ever present, passive/aggressive back and forth between Tina and Akira didn't concern her. She was sure Jason would find the two women amusing as they traded left-handed compliments. It was only Douglas and his opinion of Jason that gave her pause and made her second-guess her decision to bring him.

"You're sure you're ready for all of this?" she asked before turning the knob.

"I'm looking forward to celebrating your big job with the family. I'm honored to be included. Don't worry about me. I'm a charmer." Jason winked and gave her a quick kiss on the lips.

"This is true," Lena said, kissing him back, "but my family isn't quite like most you're probably used to down there in the South," she only half joked. "It's a bit...well, eclectic."

"Eclectic?"

"Think Tiger Woods meets Barack Obama and you get the picture."

"I'm beginning to understand."

"Once when I was little and asked why everyone in my family wasn't the same color, my Grandma Paskin told me that we were a bit of a 'swirl.'"

"Grandma Paskin? As in the mother of Douglas Paskin?"

"Yep."

"You're *the* Douglas Paskin's daughter?" Jason tried to rein in his shock. This woman was full of surprises.

"Yeah, so I'd turn that charm up on high, if I were you. Okay, we're going in!"

She turned the knob and opened the door and was greeted by the deep and sexy sounds of Kenneth's favorite baritone jazz singer, Johnny Hartman. Inside, Kenneth, Akira and her Nana Macy sat among the huge bouquets of hydrangeas in the all-white living room, chatting quietly and sipping champagne. Neither Tina nor Douglas were to be found. Lena stepped further into the room, and was immediately hit by the low-key energy buzzing around her. The collective mood in the room did not feel at all celebratory. Instead it felt more like a wake. Something was wrong.

Jason stepped inside and immediately understood Lena's swirl comment. Based on the live family portrait sitting in front of him, it was totally appropriate that Tina DuPree lived near United Nations Plaza. This multicultural mix of rich folks definitely did not look like any of the folks at the Armstrong family reunions he'd ever attended.

"Darlings! Come in," Tina breezed into the room to greet them. "Jason, please do come in and make yourself at home. Let me introduce you to the rest of the family."

Lena stood back while her mother hijacked her lover and led him to the couch to meet her relatives. The funky feeling in her stomach was getting worse. Tina was too sedate and her cheerful nature felt forced. And that smile on her face was as faux as they come. Where was her father? Had something happened?

"This is Lena's lovely stepmother, Akira Paskin; her stepfather and my husband, Kenneth DuPree; and her grandmother, Macy Turner. Everyone, this is Lena's friend, Jason Armstrong. You all chat and make him feel welcomed. Darling, do sit. Kenneth, please get Jason some champagne," Tina directed.

Lovely stepmother? Oh hell no, something was definitely up. Lena caught her mother's eye and waved her over.

"Excuse me, darlings. I need to check on dinner," Tina said, excusing herself and grabbing her daughter's elbow and escorting her into the kitchen.

"What's going on? Where's Daddy?"

"He's in Kenneth's office. Totally distressed. I've never seen him like this. He just told me what happened."

"Mom, you're scaring me. Is Dad okay?"

"Lenora, how could you?"

"How could I what?"

"You know how he feels about scandal of any kind. What were you thinking?"

"What the hell are you talking about? What scandal?" The look of confusion on Lena's face said it all. She had no idea what was going on.

"You really don't know about the video of you and Jason on the Internet? Lenora, it's a sex video." Tina's face lost all its animation as she wrapped her arms around her daughter. Lena leaned into her mother's hug, grateful for the love and the absence of judgment.

Lena felt weak and disoriented. There was a video of her and Jason having sex? Which time? Her mind quickly went into rewind mode, trying to recall the many lusty scenarios they'd performed throughout the months of playing their private, I.O.U. game.

What had been her treasured sexual adventures now felt dirty and deviant. When had they been videotaped? Lena felt ice cold as panic replaced the blood running through her body. "I've never made a sex video."

"Could Jason have done so without your knowledge?" Tina asked, giving voice to Lena's thoughts.

"I don't know." Lena spoke the truth. "Have you...? Has Daddy... seen..." The idea of her father seeing her sex, let alone such creative sex, sickened her.

"I have not. But he has, though he won't discuss it. Apparently, your secretary is threatening to release it to the media. Darling, I hate to tell you, but it's already on YouTube."

Lena's tears began to flow. She had finally done what she'd tried to avoid doing all of her life—disappoint her father. But somehow she'd managed not only to disappoint, but embarrass and humiliate him as well.

"Oh, my God, look at you. You're white as a sheet. Come with me."

"Is everything okay?" Jason asked, as the two women skirted the living area on their way to the back of the apartment.

"Yes, Darling. Don't worry about a thing, I'm taking Lena to say hello and check on her dad. He's a bit under the weather. Kenneth, more champagne for everyone. Akira, darling, would you please take over for me with the caterer? We'll be right back."

As the two women disappeared into the hallway, Jason resumed chatting with the others, despite his rising worry over Lena. So far her celebration was not starting out on a good note. Judging by the look on Lena's face, Douglas must have been more than a bit under the weather.

Tina led her daughter into Kenneth's office. Sitting on the couch, truly looking ill, was Douglas. For the first time in his life,

Lena thought her father looked elderly. The life force that usually emanated from his pores was absent. In its stead, sat a broken old man. Had she done this to him?

"I'm going back out with the others," Tina informed them. "Douglas, listen to your daughter. Do not judge. Lena, tell him everything. Do not lie. You two work this out," she told them, her heart breaking for both of them.

Lena, feeling like she was a ten-year-old in trouble, made the walk of shame across the room and over to her dad. "Daddy, I'm so sorry," she sobbed. "I don't know how this happened."

Douglas shifted uncomfortably in his seat. He'd always hated to see Lenora cry, and the circumstances today made it all the more intolerable. "Your mother told you?" he asked, avoiding direct eye contact.

"Yes, but I don't know anything about it. I swear to you."

"You know nothing about the accusations your secretary is leveling at you?"

"What accusations?"

"Ms. Hammon is accusing you of...um...bartering...uh...personal...uh...services with your agent friend to secure his client for your show."

Damn that bitch!

"Dad, surely you must know that Rolanda is lying because I fired her. There was no trading anything—-private or professional—between Jason and me. In fact, I nearly fired Rolanda months ago for making inappropriate offers to Rickie Ross."

"Well, not doing so sounds like another lapse in judgment that is costing you."

"I can't say I disagree with you there. Who told you all of this?"

"Travis came to me."

"Well, of course. He and Ro are working together. They have

been for months. She gave him all the information about my show. And he stole it. And now he's pissed and thinking that I stole his job from him."

"They have emails to prove it. And you yourself said he was just a fun and games relationship."

"That's only because I was trying to protect our privacy. I wasn't ready to tell you that I am in love with Jason and have been practically from the first time we met."

"Well, you didn't protect your privacy well enough. And this nonsense does not stop with the emails. She has a videotape and has already posted it on the Internet. She is threatening to send it not only to all of the PBC executives but the media as well."

"I honestly know nothing about any video. Dad, you have to believe me."

"Well, I will save us both the gory details, but what I saw was obscene and immoral and certainly behavior I cannot....will not condone or tolerate from any employee, let alone the chief executive officer. I am rescinding the offer. I'm sorry, Lenora, but I cannot possibly name you now as my successor at PBC."

"Dad, you can't. I worked too hard to earn that spot. You said it yourself, PBC is my legacy. Please reconsider."

"I thought you had, too, but the lack of judgment you've shown by putting yours, mine, the company's reputation at risk like that is unforgivable. When I saw you, my daughter, doing those things...and now the entire world..." Douglas, unable to find the words, simply stopped speaking.

"Daddy, look at me," Lena pleaded. Douglas turned his teary green eyes her way but was unable to hold her gaze. "I don't know what to say except that they are setting me up."

"Maybe, BUT I SAW THE DAMN VIDEO! And set up or not, I don't care what decade or century it is, having the CEO of your company...*your daughter*," he added, lowering his voice to hide the cracking, "videotaped at a strip club...is too much. How did you let that boy do this to you? I told you those agents were nothing but sleazy bastards."

"Don't blame Jason..."

"I have to blame him because if I don't the alternative is unthinkable. If I don't blame him, and I believe that you are a willing participant in this, then I have no choice to believe that you are not the daughter, the person, or the executive I thought you were."

Lena's breath got snagged in her throat. The tears that ransacked her body fell silently. She was totally embarrassed by the thought that she, by her lustful actions, had gotten her father and his company's good name caught up in a sex scandal. He had every right to be angry at her.

"Daddy, trust me. I did not knowingly make any sex videos."

"And yet, 'TV Exec in the Lap of Lust' exists on YouTube. I don't have a choice. I will not allow my legacy to be dragged through the smut. At the press conference, I will announce that Travis will take over as CEO."

"No! I am so sorry. I don't know how all of this happened, but I am going to find out and fix it. I promise."

"Lenora. What's been broken here, I am afraid may not ever be repairable."

"Don't say that. Don't say that," she repeated in a barely audible voice. Lena stood in the room, staring at her father, willing him to turn to her and tell her she was forgiven. Instead, Douglas covered his face with his hand, refusing to even look at her. "I'm sorry," were her last words as she exited the room, trying to keep her tears from becoming sobs, at least until she could get home.

Lena walked back into the living room and silently beckoned for Jason to follow. Without a word to the others, she departed the apartment, leaving her family, and her future behind.

"Lena, talk to me," Jason demanded as the two of them barreled through her front door. "You cried the entire way home and said nothing. What's wrong? Is it your father? Is he ill?"

"Sick of me, though I can't blame him. Why did you do it, Jason? Why did you have us videotaped at the Riviera Club without asking me?"

"What are you talking about?"

"Your big fantasy, seeing me with another woman. You had it videotaped so you could watch it over and over again. But you knew I'd say no if you asked, so you did it without me knowing. How could you? Everything is ruined now. Everything."

Lena dropped to the floor, unable to contain her emotions any longer. Her sobs were a toxic mix of guilt, anger, humiliation, regret and disbelief. How could any of these people—Rolanda, T.J. and especially Jason—do this to her? Everything was a mess. She really couldn't blame her father for rescinding his appointment.

"It's on YouTube. Rolanda posted it, calling it 'TV Exec in the Lap of Lust.'"

"I swear to you, baby, I had nothing to do with this," Jason said, taking her by the shoulders and forcing her onto her feet. He needed to look in her eyes and let her know he was telling the truth. "I would never, LISTEN TO ME, NEVER do anything like that to you. I love you."

Lena wanted nothing more than to believe him, but right now this entire situation, her life as it stood, was so unbelievable, it was impossible to know what and who was real and in her corner. Besides, had he never taken her there, none of this would have been happening.

"We'll figure this out," Jason promised as he helped her over to the couch. "I'm going to go get the laptop so we can take a look."

"NO! I don't want to see it, *ever*."

Fuck! How did this happen? Jason thought as he held her close. He certainly hadn't arranged for any kind of filming. And then it hit him. The goody bag. Was that what the bouncer at the club was talking about? Was the goody bag code for this party favor that was now fucking up everybody's life? That had to be it, but he hadn't paid for it. Had the guy thrown it in on the house? Lena would be irate if she ever found out.

Lena's phone rang. Neither of them made a move to answer it, letting the service pick up. "Lena, are you there? Pick up!" Aleesa's worried voice requested. "There are a lot of rumors swirling around about you and Jason in a...and this morning there's a blind item in *Gossip Faucet*...."

"What did it say?" Lena said, after getting up and yanking up the receiver. Her heart skipped every other beat, frightened by the thought that this mess was spreading. "Read it to me."

"So it's all true?"

"Just read it!"

"Put it on speaker," Jason whispered. His fear ran deeper than the hurt his girlfriend was experiencing. The potential damage this could do to his partnership chances, as well as the embarrassment to his family, was beginning to dawn on him.

Aleesa's voice filled the room with the distressing news. "What cable broadcast executive was recently caught on tape with her skirt up getting the lap dance of her life? Must be a scorcher if it was too hot for even cable. One must wonder what else is in this exec's secret video vault."

She finished reading and silence crept up and smothered all of the air from the room. Like a new strain of the flu, the ugliness was beginning to spread.

"This is not good. My job. My family. Oh shit, this is not good." Jason's nervous voice broke the quiet.

Lena remained silent, but turned to look at the panic-stricken man sitting across the room from her, furiously texting. It astounded and angered her that Jason was sitting there worrying about his own ass being on the line, when hers was the one the vultures were circling.

"Lena? Are you there?" Aleesa called out. "Are you okay?"

"Yeah, uh, let me call you back. I'm coming over."

"Okay, when?"

"Give me an hour." Lena hung up the phone, walked back over to the couch and sat down. "You okay?" she asked with hint of sarcasm seasoning her tone.

"Fuck no! I am not all right," he answered back. Lena was taken aback by his tone. This was not a side of him she'd seen before. "This is the third text I've had from one of my boys talkin' about my girl being a freak."

"Excuse me? I have crushed my father, who has been humiliated by having to witness his daughter in her first and only bisexual moment so you could get your dick hard, and you're worried about your boys? This has cost me my livelihood and probably my relationship with my father! You made me this freak, remember? This was all your idea."

"I only brought out what was already there. And you always had the option of saying no. I didn't force you to do anything."

"Seems to me this bullshit would make you 'the man' with your boys. You and Tiger now have something in common."

"What we did was a beautiful, *private* thing between the two of us."

"So was Tiger's, until it wasn't. And when Tiger Woods did get caught whoring around with questionable women, you and your boys didn't have shit to say about that except, 'what did she expect marrying a superstar athlete?'"

"You don't get it. The whore's behavior doesn't count. Only

the wife's. Elin came out of this the angel. Bottom line: no man wants the world to see his woman as an insatiable slut."

"So I'm the slut?" The idea that his thinking had turned in such a hurtful direction crushed her. Why was it okay for a woman to be her man's ultimate freak in the dark, but she could not take public ownership of her desires in the light of day? Not one time during any of their saucy encounters had Lena felt anything but a lady, but right now, Jason was making her feel cheap as hell.

"Do you think I want Rickie and the rest of my friends looking at you like you're a piece of ass to pounce on? That would kill me. And what if the agency finds out? Potential clients don't want their kids being repped by someone they're afraid will lead them down some dark, deviant path. I can't be around this kind of bad publicity. And my folks, shit, I've already caused them enough embarrassment. This will kill them. I am so fucked. "

"You're fucked? Your name hasn't even been mentioned. And how did we get taped anyway? You're the one that set everything up."

Jason said nothing, choosing not to share his theory with her, at least not until he checked it out for himself. All he knew was that he had not knowingly been a party to the videotaping. As far as he was concerned, his hands were clean.

"So let's not get this all twisted," Lena continued to blow up at him. "I trusted YOU and I'm the one that got fucked. You're ridiculous, but you're right. You shouldn't be around this bad publicity. I will deal with this myself and protect your fine, up-standing reputation.

"Now, get the fuck out of here, Jason. Take your sorry ass back to Chicago and don't ever contact me again."

"Lena...I'm sorry. It's just...I can't afford..."

"Don't worry, no one will ever know about you. I'll make damn sure that your name never leaves my mouth again."

Chapter Twenty-One

"You're up. Did you sleep at all?" Aleesa inquired as she stepped back into her master bedroom carrying two huge, steaming cups of coffee. Lena was where she'd left her, on Walt's side of the bed, but now sitting up.

"Not really. Too much going through my mind. I don't know what to try and fix first. My relationship with my dad? Lees, he couldn't even look at me. Or my professional reputation? What do I do now?"

"What about your relationship with Jason?" her friend probed. "When you got here last night, you were furious with him. How do you feel this morning?"

"Profoundly disappointed. My dream stud turned out to be a big-ass punk."

"But you love him."

"And? Love got me into this fucking hell hole. I've got to get myself out."

"Well, since you asked me for my sage advice—-"

"I did?" Lena said, cracking her first smile in hours.

"Yes, telepathically. In your sleep. I think today we work on damage control. Hire somebody to keep the media leak from spreading, get your lawyer on the case looking for any legal ramifications against T.J. and Rolanda, and then contact your travel agent."

"Travel agent?"

"Yep. You and I are going to take a little girls' trip. Ten days should be enough. You need to put some space between you and this mess. You'll think more clearly after some time off."

"You have the vacation time?"

"Not a problem. I slept with the boss," she said, sending them both into a bout of giggles.

"Look, just cuz I let one woman, well, you know, don't get any ideas," Lena joked, though the smile did not reach her eyes. "What the fuck was I thinking, Aleesa? I was so curious about what it would feel like, so I did it. And you know the next day, I was really proud of myself for giving into my pleasure like that. Now it feels disgusting."

"Don't beat yourself up. You didn't hurt anybody. You didn't do anything cruel or illegal. Like you said, you were curious and let the man you love take you down an unknown sexual path. We should all be so bold."

"But at what price?"

"Well, this is definitely a conversation to be had over multiple Margaritas in a foreign land."

"Nah, only many, many shots of tequila are going to work here," Lena countered, warming to the idea of running away from this disaster.

"Terrif. How about we head down to Puerto Rico? You can get out of the madness for a bit and when I have you nice and drunk, you can tell me everything that went down."

"Why? So you can add it to Walt's freak book?"

"Absofuckinglutely!"

"What a friend! Using my pain to help you get your nasty on!" Lena said, her humor returning momentarily.

The two took a moment to release some much-needed laughter. "But seriously, thank you for being my rock and having my back," Lena told her.

"That's what girls do. Okay, I'm going to go call the travel agent. You get on the horn with the power people. By Sunday, it's *adios, amigos!*"

LENA AND ALEESA LAY ON THE BEACH AT THE BEAUTIFUL EL SAN Juan Hotel staring at the ocean and drinking away the last few hours of their pity party. They'd been in Puerto Rico for three days, drinking like fish, eating like pigs and whining like two-year-olds, but were coming to the end of their allotted wallowing. Aleesa was worried because she hadn't been able to speak with Walter before leaving the country. She was concerned that he'd not responded to her message telling him that she was in San Juan with Lena. As with every lull in their scheduled communications, she worried that something had happened to her warrior husband, and the life she knew and loved would be over.

Lena, other than staying in touch with her lawyer and PR person, tried to clear her mind from the fiasco and hang on to the fact that her father loved her dearly and her mother was at home being her cheerleader. The tequila was mainly her way of coping with what she'd come to believe as Jason's betrayal.

"According to Lucy, my PR wizard, nothing new has broken," Lena said, scrolling down on her BlackBerry. "I guess with T.J. getting what he wants, there's no need to continue trying to destroy me. And my lawyer says I need to look at the video, which he emailed me because they've taken it down from YouTube, thank God. He says it's important I see it before we file any action."

"That makes perfect sense to me. Do it today. At eight tonight the happy partying begins. Get it all out of your system so you can start paying attention to that yummy Brazilian dude who's dying to pay attention to you. I called the kids. They haven't heard from Walt either," Aleesa said, effortlessly weaving two streams of thought into one seamless conversation.

"He's probably off on a mission and will get in touch with you soon. Don't worry about him. You know he's tough as hell and surrounded by a battalion of Guardian Angels. He asked me to have drinks with him, but I don't think so….Jason hasn't even tried to contact me."

"You didn't want him to, remember? You should have drinks. The boy from Ipanema is fine and will be a good distraction."

"I told him to call the room after eight. We'll see. And yeah, I know what I said, and I really don't want to talk to Jason ever again, but he should at least try. If he was running after me just a little bit, then maybe… "

"Maybe what?"

"Maybe I wouldn't feel like everything between us was such a damn joke."

"You love him."

"Will you stop saying that? And so what if I do. It was never going to work in the long run. Not the way it started. Our whole relationship was built on games, sex and lies. We made bets and then hooked up to have sex at the winner's whim. Hell, he just found out my real name."

"There was a reason for that and you know it. And the real story is that in between hookups, you both fell in love with each other."

Lena picked up a handful of sand and watched it pour through her fingers. "Our relationship was built on sand, and the first time something bad happened it shifted and collapsed. Isn't it time for your massage?" Lena asked, changing the subject.

"Yeah, and I am ashamed to admit that I can't wait to have some manly hands on me. But think about this, maybe Jason didn't have anything to do with the tape and the reason he's running is because he's scared."

"That conversation ended a while ago. Now, I'm going up to the room to take a nap while you're off getting a rubdown. If you're lucky, maybe you'll get a happy ending. God knows it's been a while."

Lena picked up her belongings and headed back up to the suite while Aleesa departed for the spa. She purposely walked into the bright coolness of the white suite accented with bright yellows, oranges and pinks, dropped her beach bag in the marble tile, and made a beeline over to the dining table before she changed her mind. She was going to follow her friend's advice and wrap up her pity party by finally taking a look at the YouTube video. Embarrassed by her now shameful actions at the strip club, but needing to see it for legal reasons, Lena turned on her iPad, logged on to her email and scrolled down to find the email from her lawyer.

She cringed as she clicked on the play button allowing the muffled sounds of human moans and musical lyrics to escape into the air. The lighting was horrible, but Lena's eyes were immediately drawn to the glow of the two golden-skinned women sitting lap to lap, and the man in the chair next to them. She placed her hands over her face as if to hide her shame, and watched the scene through the slits of her open fingers. It wasn't until the music changed to Nelly Furtado's song, "Promiscuous," that she took her hand from her face and looked at the iPad with full focus. That song was never played during her dance.

Like a detective looking for clues, Lena replayed the video, this time studying it with analytical eyes. Mining her memories of that night, it quickly became clear that this was not a recording of her night in the V.I.P. Lounge. First of all, the music was different. They'd danced to Maxwell and Prince and neither were on this soundtrack. And what of the man? Jason had changed chairs during their dance, and the guy in this video didn't move from his spot.

Lena felt the bubbles of excited relief tickle her mood and drive her search for more definitive clues. She paused the frame on the two women. Yes, in form and color, she could see why others assumed it to be her. The woman sitting in the chair favored her, but Lena could tell it definitely was not. Zooming in closer, she could determine that it was Jordyna sitting in the black leather chair. The other woman straddling her had a tattoo running down the length of her side and Lena knew for a fact that Jordy was ink free. It was one of the things she'd admired about her while she'd been on stage.

Energized, she flew over to her handbag and retrieved her cell phone to make two calls. She first spoke to her mother and let her know what she'd learned and begged her to talk with Douglas and help pave the way for her upon her return. She made it clear to her mother that his was not about the job but about repairing their family ties. Tina promised to help and her assurance that Douglas would eventually come around, buoyed Lena's spirits.

She hung up and immediately dialed again. After twenty minutes on the phone with her lawyer, Lena hung up, happy in the knowledge that she now had serious grounds for a defamation of character and libel lawsuit on her hands and the refreshing taste of payback in her mouth.

With much more pep in her step, Lena sauntered over to the balcony and made herself comfortable on the cushy chaise longue. For the first time in a week, she felt the sunshine kiss her face. But in truth, her mood was still only partly sunny. Yes, she now had a way to avenge Rolanda's and T.J.'s libelous accusations and restore her professional reputation, but she and her father's relationship had been irrevocably altered. The actual image he'd witnessed may not have been her, but he'd now pictured her in a light that no father should have to see his darling daughter. Despite her mother's assurances, Lena had no idea if he'd ever forgive, let alone forget her indiscretions.

And what about Jason? She'd placed all of the fault for this fiasco at his feet but in all truth, he had not forced her to do anything she had not wanted to do. He'd always looked out for her safety and physical and emotional well-being in the past, and this night had not been any different. Somehow they'd gotten caught up in an awful mix-up that had caused great damage, but was he to blame?

Lena gazed out into the turquoise blue waters and took a moment to reflect on their nearly six-month relationship. She loved the woman she was when she was with Jason. He had liberated her libido and turned her into a loving freak and made her feel so comfortable in her new sexual skin. Freeing her to explore the limits of her sexual pleasure was the gift he'd given her—a gift that kept on giving and spilled into areas that were totally unrelated to sex. Her sexual liberation had increased her sense of curiosity and adventure; she felt more confident about herself and her visions for the future. She was more spontaneous and less worried about coloring inside the lines of her life. With Jason, life had become a kaleidoscope, twisting, turning and ever changing, but no longer as scary because each experience brought new wisdom with the bad and joy with the good. She'd never felt more alive or in love since knowing him.

Yes, she was in love, but was it with Jason or Mr. Big Johnson? In addition to the list he'd given her, Lena was well familiar with Mr. Big Johnson's favorite things. She knew what to do to turn the heat of his desire on and way up. She knew what and where to touch him to make him come within seconds. She knew how to whip his ass to make him hot, and then cool down the sting with a bevy of kisses. It was dawning on her that she knew all of Mr. Big Johnson's sexual proclivities, but very little real world information about the man he was outside the bedroom.

What she did know was that Jason Armstrong had panicked and bailed when things got rough. His first inclination had been toward self-preservation, even though nothing about this scandal had impacted him directly. He said he loved her, but when the shit got flung, the giving, protective lover ran, revealing himself to be a selfish and "love with conditions" kind of man.

Lena closed her eyes and settled into nap mode. She yawned, breaking loose one last thought: Without Mr. Big Johnson around, would Pocahontas disappear as well? Had she simply been a lusty reaction to one particular man?

Only time will tell, she decided and drifted off to the sound of the Caribbean waves dancing below. In the midst of her nap, Lena was awakened by an incessant tapping on the suite door. She jumped up and headed for the entry, cursing her roommate for not taking her key card.

"You can't be done already; it's a ninety-minute massage," she said, as she opened the door. "Omigod! What the hell are you doing here? And how did you find us?"

Chapter Twenty-Two

Aleesa lay on the treatment table in the Edouard de Paris Spa, pondering why a business housed in a hotel named the El San Juan had a French name. "Yours is not to wonder why," she softly recited to herself.

Her masseur, who had introduced himself as Raul, was in the corner prepping his oils and potions. The room felt warm and cozy, like a caterpillar's cocoon. Aleesa took a deep cleansing breath, inhaling the subtle scent of green tea, and exhaling the stress that had accompanied her here. With the sounds of wind chimes, intermingled with ocean waves tinkling in the background, Aleesa decided that for the next hour and a half, she would relax, let her body and soul be soothed and go on faith that her husband was fine.

"Ready to begin?" Raul asked.

"More than you know," Aleesa replied. One of the things she missed most about Walt was the feel of his hands on her naked skin. Each time she would write a new fantasy in his freak book, it would take her days of self-pleasuring before she could shake the nearly incapacitating need for his touch. Today, her plan was to lay there, close her eyes and let her imagination conjure up her man.

Raul started by folding the sheet down to her derriere, revealing her naked back. He drizzled warm oil between Aleesa's shoulder blades and fanned the silky oil across her shoulders and upper back. Raul's very capable hands worked her shoulders, gently but firmly coaxing out the kinks in her tension-filled muscles. His touch alternated between deep and shallow as he moved down her back, pressing and kneading and helping her to unwind.

In addition to his technique, the best thing about her masseur today was his silence. She hated when the staff ruined her pampering experience by making constant chit-chat. Not getting caught up in conversation allowed Aleesa's mind to go back to their bedroom at home where Raul became Walter caressing her. The lovely thoughts combined with a kiss of cool air on her bare back caused her to wiggle slightly.

Aleesa heard the door open and the low rumble of voices, and then Raul saying, "*Señora, un momento, por favor.*"

"Mmm, hmm," Aleesa replied, not bothering to open her eyes, lost in the delectable daydream of being with her husband. Soon after Raul left, the door opened again. She heard him fumbling around in the corner and then briskly rubbing his hands together.

Warm hands continued her massage. Using the right amount of pressure, they slid up and down her back several times, always coming to rest just at the top of her ass. Aleesa was contently drifting further into the lull of total relaxation when the pressure rub ceased and his touch became more of a soft caress along the length of her torso. As his fingers quickly brushed across the sides of her breasts, a shock of electricity surged through the rest of Aleesa's body. It took with it her calm and replaced it with a different sort of agitation. Shocked back into the moment, Aleesa immediately realized that the hands on her body now were not the same that had touched her before. They were definitely male, but larger and rougher than Raul's.

"Raul?"

"Sorry, Raul had an emergency," a deep voice with an unfamiliar accent replied. "I am Juan. I will finish you."

"Okay," she replied, settling back into her relaxed state.

Aleesa felt air on her behind, as he lifted the bottom of the sheet to meet the top across her derriere. Juan slowly dripped more warm oil onto the back of her thighs. She could feel the slickness begin to drip down her inner leg as Juan's hands kneaded her hamstrings. Without warning, his touch became lighter and more feathery causing Aleesa to release an involuntary moan as his fingers dipped in between and brushed the sensitive inner skin of her thighs.

Oh shit, this was definitely one for the freak book, she though as arousal began to blossom. Aleesa allowed herself to go with the lovely flow for a few seconds before logic and loyalty forced her eyes open. Until now, the contents of Walt's welcome home gift were all based on fantasy. No matter how good Juan was making her feel right now, she would not let the freak book turn into a memoir. Aleesa shook her mind of temptation and looked to the right. Instead of seeing the white cotton drawstring pants and T-shirt worn by all spa employees, she saw the sandy earth tones of desert camouflage.

It couldn't be! Her heart thumped as her eyes traveled north, witnessing no break in the pattern until she got to a face that she recognized and loved. Confusion forced her eyebrows to collapse into each other as Walt's broad smile greeted her.

"Surprise, baby!" he whispered, not wanting to break the serenity of their surroundings.

"How did...when did you get...how long..." Aleesa's ecstatic and jumbled thoughts rushed into her mouth all at once, disallowing any complete sentence to escape. Tears began streaming from her eyes as she jumped up from the table and pressed her naked body against his.

"I got a ten-day leave and was planning to surprise you at home," he explained between kisses. "But when I got your email, I decided to fly straight here instead."

"Baby, how did you know where to find me?"

"I went up to the room and Lena was there. I could not wait another hour for you to get back so she came down and helped arrange my little surprise. The spa manager was real cool about it. Now, let's get your stuff so we can go back to our room and I can do to you what I've been dreaming about for months."

"I'm sorry, sir, but I have at least another forty-five minutes left of massage time," Aleesa informed him with a 'do we dare?' look in her eyes.

"Well, you are already naked..."

"Exactly. Why waste some perfectly good nudity," Aleesa said as she lay back on the treatment table, offering her body for his review. "I am assuming that this is a full-service massage? Complete with happy ending?" She reached over and fondled his crotch through his pants, to make her point clear.

"The happy ending, *Señora*, happens to be my specialty."

Looks like this might be a memoir after all, she thought as her husband's lips came down on hers. The kiss that began as a hello again, quickly turned into an entire conversation about love and happiness. Their lips followed the easy relaxing rhythm of the wind chimes as their tongues became reacquainted. Aleesa periodically pulled away to smooch the rest of Walt's handsome face, each kiss proof that he was really there.

The lure of her breasts tugged at his attention. Walt's mouth began a happy pilgrimage down her neck, across her shoulders and toward the large chocolate nipples he'd gone to bed dreaming about each night. He gave each a warm tongue massage before latching on to the left breast, his favorite because it was the biggest, and sucking hard. Aleesa's hips bucked. Walter's lips smiled. The nipples were still Clitina's wake-up call.

"Hmmm. You remembered," Aleesa said, sitting up so she could unbutton his uniform.

"Sweetheart, every night I go to bed making love to you. So yeah, I didn't forget a fucking thing."

Husband and wife stared into each other's eyes as she undressed him, dropping his fatigues to the floor. Aleesa broke their gaze in order to inspect the body of the man she loved and missed so desperately. For a man in his fifties, the colonel wore the body of a thirty-year-old. Trim, muscled and rock hard, the only clue to his age were the gray hairs sprinkled across his chest and pubic area.

Walt's kiss returned to her hillsides before continuing its journey south. Guided by the delightful moans of his wife, he stopped at her navel, taking a quick plunge with his tongue before moving on to the left and then the right upper thigh. Walt used his left hand to roll and pinch her right nipple, and the other to finish the feather stroke massage he'd begun on her thighs. He ran his hand up to the hairy thatch between her legs and took his index finger to swipe the creamy middle.

"Kit Kat is still my favorite candy," he told her after flavoring her pussy juice.

"You may need a better sampling," Aleesa suggested, as she gently pushed his buzz-cut head between her legs. Walter grabbed both her legs behind the knees and pulled his wife down toward the edge of the massage table.

"Serve me my sweet kit cat, baby," he told her, using his private nickname for her pussy.

Happy to comply, Aleesa reached down and slowly spread her vaginal lips to reveal the glistening pink treasure in between.

Walt dove right in. He laid his tongue flat against her bud and wiggled it quickly to and fro, making Clitina stand tall and sing with joy. Aleesa raised her pelvis to meet his mouth, her pussy deliriously happy to be tasted again. Walter licked, sucked and probed treating her coochie with loving respect for the delicacy he believed it to be.

Aleesa fucked her husband's face with urgency, clenching her muscles and pulling all of her sexual energy to the one spot. Finally getting what she'd been waiting and wanting for so long, the build-up to orgasm was short and very sweet. Aleesa did not fight the release as waves of shakes and shimmies pushed their way to the tip of her clit making it pump and twitch bigger and harder until pussy juice exploded all over his face, and tears on hers.

"Thank you, baby," she sobbed. "Thank you."

Walt lifted his wet face and smiled before quickly exchanging his tongue for his dick. He felt a little prickling of her pubic hair as he entered her, and slid slowly past into a hot, tight, deliciously wet embrace. He moved about slowly, trying to make contact with every nerve ending inside his precious kit cat. Unable to contain himself, Walt began increasing the speed with every stroke. Aleesa could see him beginning to sweat as pleasure took over his usual self-control.

"Oh baby, you feel so good," he told her, as love melted away all of his soldier hardness, replacing it with the gooey softness of a man in love with the woman he was fucking. "I love you, Lees."

"I love you, too. So much," Aleesa replied, punctuating her declaration by clenching her inner muscles to grab his dick on the down stroke.

He grabbed her legs and used them for leverage. He pushed deep inside her. The tip of his big dick teased her spot, sending tremors rippling through her pussy. Aleesa bit down on her lip, not wanting to breech the spa's quiet with the primal noises gathering in her throat. After several minutes of strong fucking,

Walter could hold it no longer and let loose, bucking up against his wife, his balls slapping her ass until his dick exploded inside her.

"Happy enough ending for you, ma'am?" he teased. Surprisingly, his question was met with Aleesa's sobs. "Sweetheart, what's wrong?" he asked as he swooped his wife up in his arms. "I'm here, baby."

"I know, but only for a few days and then you're leaving me again." Aleesa clung to him, knowing she should be grateful for his surprise visit but feeling unable to let him go again.

"My tour is over in a few months and I'll be home for good. So, dry those tears and get dressed. We're going up to my room to make some proper love. I hope you've seen this damn island, cuz I have no intention of leaving you or the room for the next seven days! Don't cry, sweetie. I brought you a gift."

"Walter. You are my gift," Aleesa told him before devouring his mouth in a big, thank-you kiss.

Chapter Twenty-Three

Tina DuPree fumed as she paced the floor of her ex-husband's study. They'd been at this for over an hour and the discussion about their daughter was going nowhere. Despite Tina's pushing, Douglas's pride and pain went too deep. He was a man who valued reputation and discretion and his daughter had violated both.

"Douglas, why are you being such a stubborn idiot about this?" she demanded for the third time. "You are not going through with that press conference next week. Not if you are going to name that slimy Travis Reynolds as your successor."

"Tina, I poured my heart and soul into this company. I sacrificed *everything*—including our marriage—*to* make it what it is. That's water under the bridge, but I'll be damned if I'll let anyone destroy my legacy. Not even my child."

"You jackass! PBC is not your legacy. Lenora is! And the fact of the matter is that it is not her and Jason in that video. She's got the proof and she and her lawyer are using it to pursue legal action against T.J. and that horrid assistant of hers."

"It doesn't matter. I will not have my name sullied by her...her... recreational activities."

"Lena Macy's name might have gotten dirtied up a bit, but *your* name, the Paskin name, has not been tarnished at all. Hell, nobody even knows that Lena Macy is your daughter."

"How could she, Tina? Do such things in a public place? What happened to the lovely girl we raised to love and respect herself?"

Douglas asked, the anger in his voice gone, replaced by a sad help-lessness.

"She grew up, Douglas. Like we all do. She's a woman with desires. And she gets that honestly. Need I remind you, Darling, how you got that scar above your eye?"

"You are an evil woman, Tina Paskin DuPree," Douglas told her, his lips curling upward at the memory.

"And you are a reformed freak who has become totally judg-mental. Everyone else might think you got it on some big adventure, but I was there on that empty playground. You seduced me to have sex with you on the swing. Your pants unzipped. My skirt pulled up to my how do you do. You remember, don't you, Douglas?"

His smiling eyes and matching mouth was her answer. "It was glorious, and the idea that we could get caught any minute made it all the yummier," she continued.

"We never did figure out if the guy walking his dog stopped to watch. We fucked on that swing like nobody's business; that is until you started to cum," Douglas added.

"Yes, and we lost our balance and fell to the ground and you got hit in the face with the swing."

"It was my first and only black-eyed orgasm."

"Yes, and remember the time you ate my pussy in the movie theater?" Tina asked, as Douglas chuckled. Hearing his ex-wife talk dirty again tickled him. It was one of the things—that and her joy and willingness to experiment—that he enjoyed most about their life together.

"Yes. And as I remember, you loved it."

"Of course I did, Darling, because you wanted it and I loved you. We were in love and had an 'anything goes' frame of mind back then. And I don't recall you thinking that I was a slut."

"No, never. Honestly, it made me love you all the more."

"Well, neither is your daughter, Douglas. She's in love and like we did, got carried away."

"I suppose so…"

"Then what are you going to do about our daughter?"

"Tee, I do want her to have it, it's just…"

"It's just nothing, Darling. It appears that this mess has all been contained and there should be no further fall-out. T.J. and Rolanda are getting what they deserve and so should Lenora. Douglas, she deserves that job."

"Do you think that she'd consider resuming her name again? I'd so love a Paskin in that seat."

"I'm sure you could add that to the contract negotiation."

"And she has to get rid of that agent fellow."

"That, my dear, is not your call and a demand like that has no place in the discussion."

"You drive a hard bargain. But, you are, bar none, the best ex-wife a man could ever wish for."

"Of course I am, Darling. That's why I shall remain your one and only."

LENA, WHILE THRILLED FOR HER FRIEND, WAS LEFT WITH NOTHING to do and nobody to do it with. So when the phone rang promptly at eight, she accepted Paolo's invitation for drinks, hoping it would jumpstart her holiday.

She picked through her vacation wardrobe and selected her favorite "go to" dress, a gray multi-tiered cotton jersey that displayed all her good parts and kept hidden the rest. Gunmetal-colored, platform sandals and long dangling earrings completed her ensemble. With her clothing out of the way, Lena showered and then turned to her hair and makeup. Just as her smoky eyes were beginning to emerge, her cell phone rang.

"Lenora?" her father's voice called out.

"Yes." Lena's heart ceased operation as she waited to hear what her father had on his mind.

"Your mother and I had a long talk. She told me about the video. I still don't condone your behavior, but it doesn't have anything to do with the fact that you are the best candidate for the job. It's yours if you still want it. With one condition…"

"Anything."

"It's a family business. I'd like you to use your family name."

"That's it? Done deal," Lena told him through her tears. "I'm proud to do so."

"Very good. Now get back here. The press conference is next week."

"I'll be home soon. Thank you, Daddy. I love you and I will not let you down ever again."

Lena hung up the phone screaming with joy. Everything was working out after all! Her happy dance was interrupted by the buzz of her BlackBerry. She looked on the screen to see she had an instant message. Lena knew exactly who it was as there was only one person who held her pin number. She took a deep breath and clicked on Jason's message.

Lena, I don't know if you've heard already, but the video isn't us. It's actually Rickie's. He had some kind of deal with the bouncer to tape his freak sessions, and the guy put it in my jacket to give to him. I still don't know how Rolanda got hold of it. I am so sorry that all of this happened and that you got hurt in the process. But mostly I'm sorry that I choked like that. I panicked, pure and simple, and I let you down. Please forgive me. I love you, Pocahontas, and we have something so beautiful together. Please, I know we can get past this. Jason

"I love you, too," she whispered into the air. Jason's message tugged at her heart. She wanted to accept his apology and forgive and forget and move on, but she wasn't convinced that she could. She was still so unclear about who she really loved—Johnson or Jason. He'd just told Pocahontas that he loved her. Did he know the difference? Until that was resolved, there was no moving forward. But how could she unwind all that had happened between them already?

Still, Lena agreed with Jason. What they had together in bed was so beautiful. But this incident had revealed a huge gap in their relationship. What was truly driving it—sex or love—had yet to be determined.

Lena picked up her BlackBerry and typed. *Yes, I heard. Things are going to be okay. I appreciate the apology. We'll talk about us when I return.* She sent the message, knowing that while she'd given no definitive answer, she at least hadn't closed the door between them.

"No time to consider that now," she declared, finishing her makeup and pulling on her panties and bra. Lena pulled on her dress and stepped into her shoes. Making an adjustment, she reached into her bra and lifted her breasts so they overflowed the cups and presented her cleavage in a most appealing way. Lena inspected herself in the mirror, smiling at the image staring back at her. She looked beautiful, and felt sexy and confident. Seeing her hard nipples straining against the fabric, she felt the pull of a turned-on clit and broke into laughter.

"Pocahontas lives," she said as she walked out of the door and into the night. Life was good and so was she.

About the Author

Eden Davis is the erotic alter ego of one grown and sexy *Essence* best-selling author. An accomplished writer of both fiction and nonfiction, she created the Eden Davis Series featuring women of a certain age, to be enjoyed by lusty women of all ages. Eden lives in the New York area and is currently working on her next series.

EDEN'S TICKET TO PARADISE:
Pearl Jam

Pocahontas and Mr. Big Johnson had a lot of fun with this trick, and so can you!

What you need:

One 30-inch string of faux pearls. Clean them thoroughly with adult toy cleaner or by washing them in hot, sudsy water.

What you do:

Starting from the tip to the base, wrap his erect penis with the pearls, leaving a tail of pearls hanging below his scrotum. Once he enters you, lift and spread your legs so the tail of the pearls hangs between your butt cheeks.

Eden's advice:

Spontaneity is sexy! The key here is to make this appear as "in the moment" as possible. That way you get points for being inventive and adventurous. I'd suggest that you don't use this yummy treat as an ice-breaker. Save this for when it's time to turn up the heat and add a little umpf to your love life. If you do choose to use this as an initial mind-blower, remember safe is always sexy, so if you aren't in a committed relationship, have him wear a condom under your pearls.

BOOK GROUP DISCUSSION GUIDE FOR
Dare to be Seduced

At forty-two, Lena Macy is standing at major a crossroads in her life. She's been married and divorced, and has a wisdom about sex that didn't exist in her younger years. She's reached a place where her sexual fantasies don't match her passionate realities. Lena finds herself scratching her head and wondering, "Is this all there is?"

Now, while fighting the fiercest professional battle of her career, she also finds herself in the midst of discovering her sexual self. Losing one bet to a sexy stranger has left her happily caught up in a web of lust and love, sex and seduction. Lines drawn in the sand of her good girl upbringing have now been crossed, and Lena must determine how far is too far.

Dare to be Seduced is a true coming-of-age story. It's one woman's sexual awakening deliciously played out on the page for you to enjoy and use as a catalyst to explore the passionate side of your life.

Please use the questions on the following pages to guide your discussion of *Dare to be Seduced*.

Discussion Questions

1. After Lena's hot and heavy one-night stand she tells her friend, Aleesa, "I finally get the joke about stranger sex. In the most basic way it's the greatest sex around. You can really let yourself go and not worry about your partner thinking that you're slutty or easy, and you can just ask—no *demand*—what you want. If you want to scream, talk dirty, bite him, whatever, you can." What feelings do you have about giving in to lust with a stranger? Have you? Could you?

2. Lena's relationship with Jason begins on a very lusty note. Do you think relationships that begin as sex can end in love? Why or why not?

3. Her relationship with Jason becomes Lena's sexual awakening. How important do you think this is in a woman's life? Do you think most women experience such an awakening in their lifetimes? Why or why not?

4. In the book, Lena's assistant, Rolanda, loved sex. Adored it. Couldn't get enough of it. Mainly, she loved the power it provided her. The thing that set her off toward orgasm was that helpless look in some lover's eye that announced that he had crossed to the other side and she now was in pussy control. What do you think about her viewpoint? Do you see her as a woman in control of her sex life or a woman who uses sex to her advantage?

5. Do you find Lena and Rolanda to be more alike or different when it comes to their sexual viewpoints? What role does age and experience play in the way they look at sex?

6. Lena becomes concerned that Jason is more in love with Pocahontas than the real woman. Do you think he loved the fantasy more than the reality?

7. When Jason and Lena argue about the video and Tiger Woods' affairs becoming public he tells her, "Bottom line: no man wants the world to see his woman as an insatiable slut." Lena wonders why it was okay for a woman to be her man's ultimate freak in the dark, but cannot take public ownership of her desires in the light of day. Do you think women are held to a double standard by our men?

8. How have age and experience changed the way you see yourself and act sexually? Did this change of behavior affect your relationship? Positively or negatively?

9. What was your favorite moment in the book? Who is your favorite character? Which storyline do you identify with the most, Lena's personal awakenings or professional struggles?

10. Did certain parts of the book make you uncomfortable? If so, why did you feel that way? Did this lead to a new understanding or awareness of some aspect of your life you might not have thought about before?

IF YOU ENJOYED "DARE TO BE SEDUCED,"
BE SURE TO READ

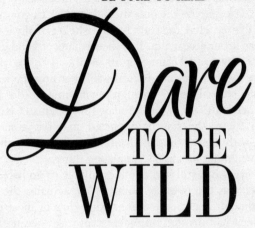

Dare
TO BE
WILD

BY EDEN DAVIS
COMING SOON FROM STREBOR BOOKS

CHAPTER ONE
Havin' Your Cake

"Have you tried giving him a professional?" the radio diva boldly asked her caller.

"They always work for me," chimed in her streetwise, male sidekick.

"A professional what?" Though Livia had not expected a response, sucking sounds, intermingled with soft grunts supplied by the special effects button, was the reply. So this is what relationship advice had come down to in the new millennium? Was oral sex now the modern day Band Aid to whatever ailed him?

"The real question is: Has he tried giving *her* a professional? Why does it always have to be the woman doing the giving? Thank God, I'm old and past the age of dealing with such mess," Livia decided and flipped over to 1010 WIN.

At 49, she wasn't actually ancient but certainly old enough and experienced enough to know that when it came to the game of love, sex was at best a short-term solution to any long-term issues. Particularly when the remedy was, as in most cases, one-sided and service-oriented. Besides, Livia and sex were on the outs these days. Her ex got most of her libido in the divorce. Hell, the truth be told, she'd actually lost that sucker somewhere around year ten. But then whatever smidgen she had left, radiation therapy had claimed as its own.

She didn't have time to concern herself with that now anyway. To stay on task, Livia started going through her mental 'to do' list of every chore she needed to accomplish today. Livia Denise Charles, a list maker. With them, she stayed organized, and felt a sense of accomplishment with every completed job. Without them, she was lost and ineffective. In her life, lists were a good thing.

After this delivery, Livia still had a million things to do before the party tonight. She was the guest of honor. Well, actually, the twins were, and even though her friends were taking care of most of the arrangements, Livia had insisted on making the cake because, well, that's what she did. All it needed was a few finishing touches, but she had to tidy up both the house and herself before the guests arrived. And as with most things these days, both took a lot more time than they used to. No time to dilly dally.

"You have reached your destination," the navigation system interrupted her thoughts to inform her.

"Thanks, Minerva," Liv said, talking to yet another voice coming from speakers in her car. This little baby was well worth the extra dollars it cost her to install. Frankly, anybody who rode with Livia would have pitched in to pay double. Directionally challenged, she could get lost making a U-turn, so anything designed to save her time, frustration and gas money was a worthwhile investment.

Livia pulled her Lexus into the driveway and drove what seemed like another half block around to the back. Her client had left a voice mail, letting her know that nobody would be home and she'd leave the kitchen door unlocked. Since providing the winning cake for the *Today Show Throws a Wedding*, Livia no longer personally delivered her frosted works of art to private homes, but Naomi Maddox was a frequent and valued client. She was a well-connected part of a social circle whose elite members entertained often and had the money (and egos) required to afford couture cakes. When it comes to business, you gotta love the customers who buy into the ridiculous concept of keeping up with the Joneses, no matter what the economy. New clients, via Naomi's very lucrative word-of-mouth, had added over $10,000 to

Livia's bank account in the last six months alone, helping to keep her bakery solidly in the black after only three years.

Havin' Your Cake was fast becoming one of the premier cake suppliers for the nation's cake aficionados. Thanks to the *Today Show* exposure, Livia had become the darling of wedding planners, bridal bloggers and brides-to-be across the country. Most thought that Livia was an overnight success, but her family and friends knew that this had been a long and tedious journey. Livia, who earned her MFA at New York University, had originally set out to be an artist. She quickly learned that talented, starving and poor didn't agree with her upper middle class sensibilities and settled for a job with a large non-profit organization. She spent years raising money for charitable causes before deciding to pursue her second love—baking. After graduating from the Culinary Institute of America with her Bachelors in Baking and Pastry Arts, Livia combined her love of art and baking, and Havin' Your Cake was born. And just in time to fill her days after her twenty-three-year marriage to Dale Charles ended in divorce.

Livia opened the hatchback of her RX450h, slowly pulled the tray with two large, square boxes toward her, got a good grasp on its edges and cautiously carried it to the kitchen door.

"Hello?" she called out gingerly as she twisted the knob and pushed the door open with her foot. "Anybody here?" Greeted with the silence she was expecting, Livia stepped inside and over to the center island that dominated the large kitchen.

You can tell a lot about a woman by her house. And if the kitchen is indeed the heart of the home, judging from this pristine room, Naomi Maddox was a direct descendant of the tin man. Nary a smudge, crumb or smear could be found in this stainless steel and granite space. With a floor clean enough to perform surgery on, Livia detected a sanitizing whiff of lavender and lemon. No lingering scents from last night's spicy beef stew or this morning's cinnamon buns, no unwashed dishes from a mid-morning snack or orphaned coffee cup. This was a show kitchen, a room designed to showcase wealth and good taste, neither of which had anything to do with food or family.

As per Mrs. Maddox's instructions, Livia found the cart designated for her latest creation—a three-dimensional pinup of Naomi's mother looking like she was kneeling on a floor of plump red pillows. The image was recreated from a photo taken when she was 22 with a young husband off fighting the Korean War. Liv found it to be an interesting choice, as the woman was turning 80 years old today. But hey, it was her job to fulfill the client's sugar and spice wishes, not determine them.

Remembering her pressing schedule, Livia quickly assembled the cake and wiped away any excess frosting. She cleaned up the remaining debris and with her ever-ready digital, took one last photo for her portfolio.

"Livia Charles, here's to another job well the hell done." She congratulated herself with her ritual shoulder brush. Livia turned to leave and that's when she heard them—the muffled sounds of low moans and groans, distinctly female, coming from down the hall. Fear turned her blood cold, causing her muscles to freeze as she pushed her face in the direction of the noise, straining to hear.

It sounded like someone was in trouble. God, was the birthday girl here? Had she fallen and couldn't get up? Livia's first impulse was to rush toward the sound and help the poor old lady out. However, the thought that kept her feet in place was the idea that the person who was in trouble might also be in the presence of the troublemaker. She'd already gone through her stint of staring death in the face. Did she really want to go through all that again?

Liv slowly edged her way over to the cordless phone and picked it up from the base. She'd just dialed the 9 and 1, when the thought crossed her mind that the last thing Naomi Maddox would want was a houseful of cops combing over her property when she was expecting an army of caterers.

There it was again, this time co-mingled with a deeper, more masculine timber. Muffled and unintelligible, Livia couldn't make out any words, but the tone sounded demanding. She had to do something. She took a quick look around the place and mapped out a plan. First, she went over and opened the kitchen door in preparation for a swift exit. She then picked a gleaming butcher knife from the block. Like the rest of the appliances, it looked as if it had never been used, so the blade had to be nice and sharp.

Yeah, sharp enough to fillet me if it got into the wrong hands.

She replaced the knife and looked around for another weapon, one that would maim instead of kill. Her eyes immediately were drawn to the set of keys hanging on a hook near the door. She pulled them off the wall and positioned the longest key between her second and third fingers.

Yeah, go for the eyes, she thought.

Armed with the key in one hand and the cordless phone in the other, Livia took a deep breath and went over her quickly concocted plan one more time—ninja down the hall, peek in, access the situation. If it's bad, dial 9-1-1, drop the phone for all to hear and burst into the room, weapon at the ready, sounding buck wild and acting crazy.

Capitalize on the element of surprise and pray that God and some of her self-defense lessons kicked in.

That was the plan. She didn't know how good of a plan, but a plan nonetheless. Livia stepped out of her sandals and as stealthily as possible, tiptoed down the hall in the direction of the whimpers. She didn't have to go far before the noise became louder and more intense. It was coming from a room that, through an open crack in the door, appeared to be an office/den of some kind. Slowly, she pushed the door further into the room, grateful that Naomi kept the hinges in her house well oiled. Liv leaned in slightly and what she witnessed stole her breath and caused her to jerk back into the hallway. She collapsed against the wall and slid down the partition, placing the phone and keys at her side. Weaponry was not going to be necessary.

Somebody was getting worked over all right, but it wasn't Naomi's mother. There was a man in the room watching porn and getting himself off. Livia's torso turned back toward the kitchen but her behind had other ideas. And without her brain's consent, it scooted across the floor, back to the door.

She couldn't see him. He was seated in a high back, yellow leather chair facing the opposite wall. All Livia could see was one golden brown, muscular thigh flexed with sexual tension. His blue jeans were pooled around his ankles and his arm made peek-a-boo appearances as he stroked himself into bliss.

"Yeah, lick her good," a deep, buttery voice requested. "Make that pretty pussy wet. Take those panties in your teeth and pull them. Snap 'em. Yeah, that's it. Now play with your titties. Let her know how hot she's making you."

Livia watched, mesmerized as the women on the flat-screen followed his every instruction. It took a second or two to realize that he'd obviously seen this movie a time or two hundred. She could probably hit the back of the chair with the phone and he wouldn't even notice. Those two women—one chocolate, the other vanilla—had his full attention.

She was embarrassed to admit it, but they had Livia's as well. In fact, in her head, she even gave them names. Coco was lying back on a cream leather couch with her long, shapely legs spread, one over the back and up the wall. All she wore was a tiny g-string and high heels with strings that laced up her legs. She had a great set of breasts, real, Livia determined, with quarter-sized, yummy brown areolas and erect nipples begging to be sucked. Her lips, pouting with pleasure with each stroke of the blonde's tongue, allowed the frequent escape of a grateful whimper. Nilla was on her knees, her apple bottom ass high in the air with her head between Coco's pretty brown legs. Livia watched as Nilla licked her pussy through the whisper sheer panties, getting as hot as the two of them. Well, three, when you count the guy in the yellow leather chair.

She was sitting there, Vikki the voyeur, a peeping Thomasina, getting turned on by watching other people have sex. Livia couldn't tell which version—the real man or the video vixens—was turning her on more. He was a stranger lost in his fantasy, pleasuring himself, and here she was intruding without his knowledge or consent. They were an erotic fantasy, soft and sexy beautiful women turning each other out. All of it made Livia feel freakishly naughty. And she liked it.

"Yeah, touch yourself, baby. Finger your pretty pussy while you eat hers."

The sound of his deep voice, alternately shouting out orders and getting wrapped up in his own physical pleasure added to the heat. Despite his crude language, his directives were forceful but stopped short of being demanding. More like requests that teetered on the line between a beg and bark. The kind that, from the right man, were impossible to deny.

Following his directions, and without conscious consent, Livia's hands joined the party. They slid down her skirt's waistband, separating her 100% cotton panties from her full pubic thatch. With his voice in Liv's ears, her eyes stayed on the screen, watching Nilla suck, lick and tug Coco's clit into crazed ecstasy. She parted the hair with her middle finger, reaching deep inside to find the creamy middle, lubricated her nib with her own juices, and furiously began to finger herself. As her legs began to tense with approaching orgasm, Livia bit her lower lip, forcing the sounds of carnal satisfaction back into her body to join the energy circling around her engorged clitoris. Judging from the sounds emanating from inside the room, the four of them participating in this secret and disjointed orgy were all about to explode. Liv couldn't speak for the others, but it had been so long since she'd been this hot, even longer since she'd actually had sex, that she couldn't have stopped herself if she'd wanted to. She came deliciously hard and silently, and then leaned back against the wall, gratefully gasping for breath, as her body attempted to recover.

A chorus of "YES," singing out in soprano and dominated by a baritone, first made her smile and then forced her out of her afterglow and back into reality. She was sitting in the hall of her best client's home, with her hand down her skirt, masturbating. Livia needed to get the hell out of there and fast. She picked up the phone and keys, got up, quietly power-walked back into the kitchen, and returned everything to its proper place. Quickly, she slipped on her shoes and went out the open door and into the safety of her car.

Livi glanced at the clock before backing out of the driveway. She'd spent nearly forty-five minutes on an errand that should have taken her twenty, tops. She conjured up her task list again and began checking off each completed job starting from number one. Anything to distract herself from dwelling on her most recent and inexplicable behavior.

Order more cake boxes. Check. Confirm the design for the Johnson cake. Check. Deliver Maddox cake. Check. Secretly give myself a mind-blowing orgasm in the company of strangers. Check. Check.

She drove about three blocks before pulling over to the curb and bursting out into crazy, what-the-hell-did-I-just-do laughter. Jasi, Aleesa and Lena were never going to believe this. Shit, she couldn't believe it herself. Then again, they'd never know, because Livia had no intention of telling.